Mayhem and Moonlight

Bedford County Series #3

Jennifer Sienes

CrossRoads Publishing

I'd like to dedicate *Mayhem and Moonlight* to my own little librarian—my daughter Nikki. You were not only the inspiration for Lillian, but you inspire me every day to never give up. I'm one proud mama.

Prologue

Lillian

I'd sat in the same church pew more than a thousand times, but never had its hard wood surface felt like some kind of penance for my poor choices. Until now. Heard it said a good cry soothed the soul some, but I didn't even have the luxury of tears. My eyes were dry as an old woman's skin. What was wrong with me that my grand ideas always turned out to be a fool's errand?

Wrapping my arms around myself, I stared up at the altar. A wood cross hung there with nothing more than a sheaf of cloth draping it. Jesus might not condemn me for my stupidity, but Mama surely would. June bride? More like a June joke! Left at the altar—*how cliche*—so maybe I'd deserve her "I told you so." Oh, she wouldn't say it to my face. She'd say something like, "What did you expect from a grown man goin' by the name of Billy? Not Bill or William, but Billy." If I had myself a backbone, I'd point out that Daddy's name was Donnie, and her own brother went by Charlie.

Oh, Lord, now what am I supposed to do? Thought about Him pulling me in for a hug, and the bite of tears finally came. Could be I wasn't meant for marriage, and that was just fine. But not having babies? That broke my heart more than Billy leaving me. If I was of a mind to think on it long, I'd realize it was the desire for kids that blinded me to the red flags that were surely present.

"Lillian." Sherrie's soft voice broke through my thoughts a split second before she joined me on the pew. What a shame to waste the perfect Maid of Honor dress. The color and style suited her full figure and blond upsweep to a T. She slipped an arm around my shoulders and gave me a little jiggle. "Been looking all over for you. Didn't expect you'd come back to the scene of the crime." From the time we were little, humor had always been Sherrie's go-to whenever tragedy struck.

It worked too. Could feel a smile tugging at the corners of my mouth where a tear pooled. "Another fine mess I've gotten myself into." I dropped my head onto her shoulder and sniffled. "Should've known it was too good to be true."

She let out an unladylike snort. "Girl, you don't really believe that, do you? Billy's mediocre on a good day, and you deserve God's best." Why was it easier to take the truth from her than Mama?

"Should've listened to y'all." I sat up and gave a wayward strand of hair a vicious swipe. "You have any idea how much debt I got hanging over me?"

Eyebrows hitching, she stared at me. "You're talkin' to the queen of debt here. Four years of college and four more of law school didn't come cheap, you know."

"At least your degree got you a good paying job." I tapped my lace-covered chest. "Mine got me little better than minimum wage."

"There are more important things than making money, Lil. You love what you do."

That and five bucks wouldn't get me a fancy coffee at Starbucks, so I ignored her. "And now added to that, I got a wedding to pay for without even bein' married." More hot tears burned at the back of my eyes. I deserved Mama's disappointment.

Sherrie's mouth tightened as she plucked a piece of something from the skirt of her burgundy maid-of-honor dress. Should I offer to cover the cost of the bridesmaids' dresses too? "What d'you mean *you're* paying for the wedding? I thought Billy was footin' the bill for this shindig. Wasn't that the only reason you agreed to the extravagance?"

A headache pounded away like a lunatic bass drummer at my temple. "Used my credit card 'cause I had a six-month, no-interest offer." Even if a miracle came down from heaven, and I was blessed with six years no-interest, I couldn't pay off the bill in time. *Idiot!*

"We'll see about that. He's in breach of contract, and he's not gonna hang all this on you. I'll drag his sorry butt into court so fast—"

"No." It was humiliating enough to be left in such a sorry state without making a *literal* federal case over it. "I truly appreciate you wanting to fight my battles for me, but I gotta handle this on my own." Bless Sherrie's heart. Couldn't remember a time since we first met in kindergarten that she wasn't ready to pounce on anyone who'd take advantage of me. "Once I figure out what to do next."

She blew out a sigh. "Good thing all your stuff's still at our apartment. To be honest, I wasn't looking forward to living on my own."

But I knew she wasn't gonna be on her own for long. It was only a matter of time before she and Josh got married. Just hoped her wedding day was a sight brighter than mine had been.

CHAPTER ONE

Ten Months Later

Luca

Chaos made me twitchy. It wasn't in my DNA to let things get out of hand, but there were so many boxes stacked in each of the rooms, I couldn't pinpoint my priority. Set up my home office? Get the boys' bedrooms organized? Would be good to get the kitchen in order too. All I could focus on was the moving boxes stacked on the countertops labeled *Fragile—Handle with Care.*

"Dad!" Daniel's voice echoed off the bare walls and floors from the family room. "Matty's hogging the T.V."

"Am not!" Matty yelled. "Chase got to watch what he wanted. Now it's my turn."

Eyes closed, I took measured breaths and counted slowly. Should've scheduled the satellite service for after spring break. Once everything was unpacked and the boys were in their new schools. After—

A body slammed into my legs, and I bent to steady Matty only to come in contact with a handful of fur. "Who let Rocket in?" The canine in question looked up at me with his Golden Retriever eyes and whined. Had Daniel fed him? "Daniel?"

"I didn't let him in. Chase did."

"Did not. Matty did."

Enough. I spun around and marched into the obscenely large family room, Rocket literally on my heels. Ignoring the stares of my three boys, I snatched the remote from Daniel's hand and powered off the television.

"You." I pointed at Daniel. "Feed Rocket." With a swivel of my head, I eyed Chase. "You. Make sure his water bowl is full."

"What can I do?" Matty jumped off the L-shaped sectional, his blue eyes widening.

Had to give him a chore or he'd feel unimportant. "How about you make sure the gate is closed and locked. Then walk the perimeter of the backyard to be sure the fence is secure so Rocket can't get out." I knew it was, but Matty didn't need to know that. "And don't forget to check the pool gate too. We don't want Rocket falling in."

"Okay." He rushed off while Daniel and Chase grumbled and rolled off the couch at a snail's pace. You'd think asking a nine and seven-year-old to help out a little was akin to slave labor.

"You boys could use a little of your brother's enthusiasm."

Daniel scowled. "What does he know? He's five."

"Yeah," Chase agreed then shuffled toward the sliding glass door to the patio.

The two of them could have been my mini-clones with their dark hair and eyes—while Matty was the picture of their blond, blue-eyed mother.

"Hold up, Daniel."

He turned with a sigh. "What?" An eye roll would've completed the picture of disrespect, but he was smart enough to know my limits.

I sat on the arm of the couch, so we were eye level as Chase escaped outside. "I could really use your help here, you know."

He scowled. "Wasn't my choice to come to Hicksville." He'd labeled Shelbyville as such from the moment I told them about us moving here. "You made us leave all our friends and Grandma and Grandpa, and everything."

Clenching my jaw, I took a moment to filter my response. How many times had we been through this same conversation? He was a bright nine-year-old, so the logic of the move wasn't lost on him. "It's done, so there's no point in complaining about it. You're the oldest, so by default, you have more responsibility than Chase or Matty. And I really could use your help. This is new to me too, you know."

His mouth twisted. "Yeah, but it was your decision. We didn't get a vote or nothing."

True. "I'm doing what I think is best for all of us." Chicago wasn't the healthiest environment for raising kids. And if we were going to make a fresh start anyway, why not go whole hog? An idiom that wouldn't be lost here in Tennessee.

"Fine." He shrugged. "At least the house is sort of cool."

And huge. How had I not realized just how huge when I made the offer? That's what came of buying real estate sight unseen. "And you always wanted a swimming pool," I reminded him.

"Can't have much fun swimming without any friends." The boy was determined to hold onto a glass-half-empty mentality.

"You'll make new friends. How could you not with that positive attitude?" I gave him a light punch on the arm.

"At least I have Rocket."

"If he doesn't starve to death."

Daniel wrinkled his nose. "Can we at least go do something for a while before we gotta work?"

Struck me then that the top priority for the day was giving the boys something to connect to their new hometown. "I'll see what I can find."

Thirty minutes later, we piled into the CRV.

"Where're we going?" Matty piped up from the back.

"Surprise." I backed the car out of the long driveway at the sound of a raucous bird.

"What's that?" Matty said.

"Mockingbird." My eyes met his for a moment. "You can tell because they don't stick to one kind of song. They supposedly mimic other birds."

As I looked out the windshield, a cardinal swooped from the cottonwood tree that sat at the front of the house and disappeared in the copse of trees bordering the property. The sounds and sights of spring weren't so easily available in Chicago—or more accurately, Wheaton—unless we were hanging out at one of the parks. Of course, I'd miss Lake Michigan and the culture, but there was plenty here to keep the boys occupied, and hopefully, out of trouble. Maybe get them some cowboy boots and introduce them to country-music culture. Once I figured out just what that was.

I had already put our destination into my phone, and the map was on the display screen of the car. I followed it, one ear tuned into the boys' conversation as they debated the high points of their new bedrooms. That was a start. Positivity. The hallmark of success.

I had just turned into the parking lot when Daniel's positivity went out the window. "The *library*? This is our special outing?"

"Thought you liked to read."

He snorted. "Thought we could go get an ice cream or something. We could've stayed home and gone swimming."

I put the car in park and raised my eyebrows at him. "Swimming? Don't you think it's a little cold for that?" It was hovering in the high 60's, which was some warmer than Chicago, but still not pool weather.

"It's so *boring* here." He crossed his arms and pouted like a two-year-old.

"We've been here all of five minutes, kiddo. You need to relax."

"I like books," Matty said. At least there was someone on my side, even if he had the littlest voice. How long would it be before he abandoned me for Team Daniel? A year, maybe two?

As we stepped into the front door, Chase tugged on my arm. "What time is it, Dad?"

Once I'd extricated myself from his grasp, I checked my watch. "2:50. Why?"

"Story Hour." He pointed to a chalkboard easel announcing *Story Hour with Miss Lillian from 3:00-4:00 Tuesday thru Friday*. "Today's Wednesday, right?"

I had to think about it for a full five seconds. How easy it was to lose track of the days when we didn't have anything to anchor us to them. "It's Thursday, but that still works."

"Thursday?" Daniel huffed out a breath. "That means we only got three more days before we gotta start school. In Hicksville, Tennessee."

There were moments I could throttle the boy. Needed to rethink church as a priority. Maybe he could muster a little joy for Jesus.

"What am *I* gonna do about school?" Matty slipped his hand into mine and tugged on it. "Is there a preschool here or do I get to start kindergarten?"

I ruffled his hair. "Don't you worry, kiddo. I already found you a great preschool. Treasured Tykes." There must've been a God in heaven to provide that little miracle. Was able to appeal to the owner's heart since Matty was only going to need to attend until August when he'd start kindergarten. Still, I didn't want to discount even the smallest wins.

"Hey, Dad." Chase pointed across the library. "Kids are sitting down over there. I wanna hear the story."

"Let's go." I ignored Daniel's eye roll and herded the boys to sit on the floor with the other kids then I stepped out of the picture. No doubt Daniel's attitude would improve without me as an audience. He was probably acting out his rebellion for my benefit.

I took a few moments to peruse the library. It wasn't large—not by Wheaton standards—but it appeared well stocked. Homey. Colorful. Warm. It wasn't three floors of every conceivable book available, but the boys wouldn't know the difference.

An upbeat voice pulled me from assessing the library back to where maybe a dozen kids were now gathered in front of a young woman. Miss Lillian, I presumed. Didn't look like any librarian I'd ever seen. Wasn't in the market for a wife (been there, done that) but it didn't mean I didn't wonder if Miss Lillian was truly a miss, or if that was just the vernacular. Long dark hair, wide smile, and if I wasn't mistaken, eyes so blue, they glowed. Yeah, maybe hanging out at the library wasn't a bad way to pass the time.

It just couldn't be my priority.

Lillian

Sunlight poured through the library windows like a beacon of hope. Or maybe it was the little bodies sitting in a semi-circle in front of me that lightened my mood. Story Hour was the absolute best part of my job, and I took a moment to toss a quick prayer heavenward. Life was far from perfect, but this here moment was about as close as it got, and I was gonna bask in it while I could.

"Good afternoon, children." I hugged the picture book to my chest and leaned forward to capture their attention. "Are y'all ready for today's story?"

The kids responded with an off-kilter chorus of, "Yes, Miss Lillian."

I recognized most of them. Little Karly with the perpetual runny nose; Jason, his hair sticking up every which way; Susie, hugging her look-a-like dolly to her chest...but there were new faces too—three little boys separated some from the others like they weren't sure they belonged. Brothers? The two older ones, with their dark hair and brown eyes, for sure.

"I've got one of my favorite picture books for you, and I bet most of you are familiar with it." I propped it on my lap so they could get a look at the cover. "*Alexander and the Terrible, Horrible, No Good, Very Bad Day* by Judith Viorst. Illustrated by Ray Cruz. Can y'all tell me what 'illustrated' means?"

Immediate answers boomed across the room. Last week's lesson on library voices hadn't stuck, but their enthusiasm tugs a grin from me.

"You're right. An illustrator is the person who makes pictures for books." I laid it back on my lap. "Now, I'm gonna ask you a question, and I wanna only see a show of hands. No talking, okay? There are lots of people here trying to read their own books or studying for school, so we don't want to disrupt them, do we?" A few heads shook. I lowered my voice to near whisper-level. "How many of you have either had this book read to you or read it for yourselves?"

Nearly every hand shot into the air.

"That's good. I like to read books over and over again, because each time I do, I can learn something new." The Bible was a perfect example but saying so might could stir up a few of the parents. Instead, I opened the book and positioned it to the side so they could see the pictures while I read the text.

I cleared my throat and waited a beat to be sure they were with me. "'I went to sleep with gum in my mouth and now there's gum in my hair and when I got out of bed this morning I tripped on the skateboard and by mistake I dropped my sweater in the sink while the water was running and I could tell it was going to be a terrible, horrible, no good, very bad day.'" I blew out a breath with a chuckle. "That's quite a mouthful, isn't it? Y'all ever go to sleep with gum in your mouths?"

The story continued to list the trials and tribulations of poor Alexander, and how his attitude contributed to the awful day making it grow like a seed of bitterness. Might not be the Bible, but the lesson Judith Viorst intended wasn't lost on me. I'd had an awful case of the grumbles for nearly a year, so I had to believe the Lord was the One who picked out this particular book for me to read. Again.

Once I finished the story, I spent some time asking questions that might cement it into their young, impressionable minds. Took me a few glances at the new boys and couldn't help but notice the biggest—maybe nine or ten years old—seemed particularly attentive. Could be Alexander's misfortune hit a chord with him?

After I wrapped it up, some of the kids came up to give me a hug. I had a tissue ready for Karly—poor thing suffered from allergies something fierce—and was sure to greet Susie's baby, Susie Q. Learned weeks ago that Susie's mimi helped name the doll. As the last of them wandered off, the smallest of the new boys stood to the side as if waiting a turn.

"Hey, there. I don't believe I've ever seen you before. What's your name?"

His blue eyes went wide, and as he grinned, dimples popped out on both cheeks. *Precious.* "I'm Matty." He wandered closer, swiping at a blond strand from his forehead.

"Well, Matty, I'm pleased to meet you. I'm Miss Lillian. Is this your first time at Story Hour, or did I somehow miss you before?"

"Nope. First time."

"Matty." The biggest of the three boys stood at the threshold of the children's section and waved Matty over. "Dad's waiting. Let's go."

Matty wrinkled his nose. "That's Daniel. He's my brother."

I itched to pat the cutie on the head but folded my arms across my chest instead. "Well, you best do what he says. You don't wanna keep your daddy waiting."

"Okay. Bye."

I couldn't help but smile as he scooted off with his brother, but the joy wavered some when he passed Sherrie heading my way. Between our schedules and her wedding plans, we hadn't had more than a few minutes to catch up over the last few weeks, which was just fine by me. I'd been like the proverbial ostrich—head stuck clear down into the sand, so I didn't have to face the inevitable. Kept hoping a miracle would provide me a way out, but God had other ideas. Just wished I knew what they were.

"Hey, Lil." Sherrie was the poster girl for an up-and-coming career woman. Feminine suit, killer heels, every blond hair in place, while I was the exact opposite. If my boss would let me wear sweatpants and slippers to work, I'd probably muster up the energy to dance a jig.

Until then, giving my bestie a hug would have to do. "Decided to go slumming, huh?"

"Had me a little free time and thought I'd take you to supper tonight. You're off at five, right?"

I knew what she wanted and softening the blow with comfort food wasn't gonna ease the pain. "Sorry to disappoint, but I'm on till seven. Thursday, remember?" Her mouth tightened, but it was the cloud of worry crossing her eyes that had me caving. "Got a fifteen-minute break right now, though, if you wanna talk." She deserved better than a delusional friend and roommate.

She slipped her arm through mine with a sigh. "How about we go outside? It warmed up some, and there's hardly a breeze." It wasn't sunshine on her face she was wanting but a little privacy, so I wouldn't humiliate myself in front of my co-workers. But I'd play along.

She wasn't lying about how nice it was, and if a fist of fear wasn't burning a hole in my belly, I would've appreciated it more. "Look, Sherrie, I know what you're gonna say, so let me save you the trouble." I led her to a seating area on the back patio of the library. Thankfully, there was no one around, so we had the privacy she was wanting.

"That's fine, Lil. But what're you gonna do? Our lease is up the end of May, and if you're gonna stay, they need thirty days' notice. You have any luck finding yourself another roommate?"

Didn't have the heart to tell her I hadn't even tried. Couldn't imagine sharing an apartment with a stranger. What if she turned out to be a complete psycho, like Amy Elliot Dunne in *Gone Girl*? Why did Sherrie have to get herself engaged? Why couldn't being an old spinster-cat-lady alongside of me until we died be enough for her? Not that I cared much for cats, but that was beside the point.

"Don't you worry about me. I'll figure something out." From my lips to God's ears. *Are You listening, Lord? I've gotten myself into quite a pickle, and I don't have any idea which way to turn.*

Sherrie cleared her throat and ran a thumb along the crease of her black slacks. "Have you considered asking your folks for help?"

She ought to know I'd rather live in a cardboard box than grovel at Mama's feet. "Even if I didn't owe what feels like the National Debt, I couldn't afford the rent on our place alone." Which was why she'd been after me to find a roommate.

"I was thinking more along the lines of moving in with them." The grimace on her face was proof she knew the can of worms she was opening with that suggestion. That'd be the only thing worse than asking them for financial help.

"You think I should move down to Florida?" It was a betrayal of our friendship. "Even if Mama and me didn't get on like oil and water, I'd have to leave everything I know here. You, my job..." Was that it? Was that all I had?

"You're right, Lil." She took hold of my hand and squeezed. "I'd hate for you to be so far away, but I don't know how to help. You refuse to take money from me, and you won't go after Billy for what he owes you. What else is there?"

I closed my eyes and turned my face up to the sun. *His mercies are new every morning. Great is Your faithfulness.* The sudden warmth of peace unfurled the fist in my belly. Stubborn pride had gotten me here; maybe it was time for a little humility.

CHAPTER TWO

Lillian

It took me a couple days to muster up enough humility to call Mama and Daddy. Well, Mama, anyway. Daddy was like a Moon Pie—gooey soft on the inside surrounded by a whole lot of sweetness. There'd been times I would've appreciated a little tough love to go alongside his unconditional support. Maybe a reminder now and again that doing the opposite of whatever Mama thought best wasn't the wisest approach to making decisions. But calling him wouldn't do me any good—he'd just go through Mama anyway. Best to eliminate the middleman if I wanted an answer anytime soon.

Instead, I ran a load of laundry, scrubbed the toilet, and flicked a dust rag here and there while my stomach flip-flopped like a fish out of water. *Call her already. It's not gonna get any easier.* I dropped onto the couch and reached for my phone sitting on the coffee table. Heart racing, breath short, I said myself a little prayer before tapping Mama's number. Then I waited. One ring. Two rings. Three rings...should I leave a message or disconnect?

"Lillian?" She didn't have to sound so shocked. It's not like I never called.

"Hey, Mama."

"What's wrong? You doin' okay?" The words were rushed, like she was expecting the worst and wanted to get to it right quick.

"Doing just fine." I clenched the dust rag. Wasn't the best opening to ask for a favor. "How's Daddy doin'?"

A cluck of her tongue came through loud and clear. "You could've phoned him if that's what you were wanting to know. What's goin' on, Lillian?"

I tossed the rag onto the table. Why did Mama always have to make things so hard? And how could I even think about moving in with her and Daddy when it took every bit of nerve to just call? If only I could find a way to heat that ol' cardboard box that was looking some better.

"I'm kinda in a spot, Mama." There. I said it.

A sigh poured over the line. "This on account of Sherrie getting married and moving out pretty soon?" There wasn't much lost on her.

"Yes, ma'am."

"How much do you need?" Disappointment slithered through her words like the serpent in the Garden of Eden. Had I expected anything different?

"It's not money I'm calling about." Unless she was willing to pay my rent for the next decade or two. "Was hoping you could see your way to me moving in for a bit." The thumping in my chest was loud enough to hear into the next county.

Silence. Did we get disconnected?

"Mama? You there?"

"Just looking around for my jaw. Dropped clear to the floor." Hilarious. She picked a fine time to develop a sense of humor. "We both know you don't wanna live in Florida. Didn't you say something snarky about cockroaches and hurricanes bein' the only season when your daddy and me said we were moving here?"

Snarky? Me?

"And if money isn't an issue, why would you need to move in with us in the first place? You think you're gonna find a job here that'll make getting yourself that expensive degree worthwhile?"

That tune was getting old. Hadn't I beaten myself up enough over it already? "That's not fair, Mama. I've told you a dozen times I had no way of knowing there'd be a lack of jobs available. It's just a matter of waitin' before I land something that pays better."

"Cashier at McDonald's pays better than you get, Lillian. No shame in taking something outside a library, you know. Not if it's gonna allow you to live on your own. No self-respecting daughter at your age will be happy living at home."

My throat tightened and tears bit at the back of my eyes. What had I been thinking asking for her help? I knew it'd just get me a whole lot of judgment and heartache. What had I done to earn her disdain, apart from being born?

"Let's set aside your school loans for the time being," Mama continued as if she hadn't a clue how hurtful her words were. "You still paying off that farce of a wedding, or were you able to get Billy to take on his fair share? After all, it was his idea to cater the thing. All that wasted food, not to mention the venue—"

"Never mind, Mama," I managed to choke out. "I'm sorry I bothered you. Hope you and Daddy have a nice weekend." I thumbed the disconnect button and tossed my phone aside as tears pooled in my eyes. *Oh, Lord, why does Mama dislike me so?* When was the last time I'd heard a kind word from her?

Wasn't at all like that for Mark. She never had anything but praise for my older brother. As a college professor, he chose the perfect career. Chose himself the perfect wife, too, and they had themselves two perfect kids—a boy and a girl. Who could compete with that? After all, she and Daddy followed them to Florida rather than stay right here in Tennessee with me. It could be going after a degree in library and information science was a way to show her I was smart, too. Just wasn't a romantic dreamer with my head in the clouds. And maybe, accepting Billy's proposal played into it some, too. Look where that landed me.

Feeling sorry for myself wasn't going to get me anywhere. I pushed off the couch to collect my laptop. Had to be a dozen sites out there to help with a roommate search. And if I ended up with a crazy person, I had only myself to blame. Mama might be lacking in subtlety, but she wasn't wrong.

Only thing was, I really did love my job. There was something about being around books that made my heart sing a little. All those creative people able to put down in words stories and emotions that captured a reader's imagination. Made me wanna write a book of my own. Course, it would be a children's book. Maybe about how much God loved every one of them, even if their own mamas didn't seem to. I could see the pictures in my head that'd go along with it. I was pretty good at drawing. Might be able to illustrate it myself.

By the time I was back on the couch, laptop open and a cup of Pink Lady tea at my side, the ache in my heart had eased up a bit. God loved me, even when I did the opposite of what He'd have me do more often than not. And Daddy loved me, too. Course, the both of them loved everyone, so that wasn't a whole lot of consolation.

After a search, I came across several rental sites, but Craigslist was the only one that wouldn't cost me anything. I was pinching pennies like an old miser. Why the others advertised as free but required a fee to actually communicate with a potential roommate, was a puzzle. Then again, Daddy often said, "You get what y'all pay for." He learned that one when he bought the bargain gas barbecue at Home Depot instead of one with a good reputation. Not a year later, he ended up dumping it and buying the more expensive one, anyway. That lesson didn't play out well for me, though, since I went for a college degree and paid for an expensive wedding and ended up with nothing to show for it but a lower credit score.

Maybe if I'd heeded Proverbs 22:7, I wouldn't have gotten myself into this mess. *The rich rules over the poor, and the borrower is the slave of the lender.* Ain't that the truth! Sometimes I needed to learn the hard way. Never would trust in some guy again just because he had nice eyes and dimples. What was that quote by Abraham Lincoln? *Character is like a tree and reputation its shadow. The shadow is what we think it is and the tree is the real thing.* I'd be sure to check out the tree instead of being taken in by the shadows. Another hard lesson learned.

Posting an ad for a roommate was more challenging than I'd expected. What I wanted was a quiet, saintly woman with high morals and little drama. Bor*ing*. Wasn't it the quiet ones that had the deepest issues? It'd be like seeing only the shadows Abraham Lincoln referred to, and not knowing what was real and what was for show.

I wrestled with it for so long, I forgot to eat supper. Texting a few times with Sherrie, it didn't appear she'd be home anytime soon. She and Josh were working on wedding details—like whether we'd all end up with chicken or finger food. They were a whole lot smarter about planning within their budget than I'd been. Or I should say Billy had been, because I would've been just as happy with everyone bringing picnic baskets and hanging out at Tims Ford Lake for the reception.

It was near midnight before I finally dragged myself to bed. Once my ads were placed, I'd played around with a children's book idea—even had me a few pictures sketched out. It wouldn't go anywhere, but it was fun to dream a little. I laid awake for a while writing out the story in my head. Next thing I knew, someone was shaking me.

"Hey, girl. It's almost nine. Didn't realize you were still sleeping." Sherrie planted herself on the edge of my bed. "You feeling all right? Never knew you to sleep in."

My head was fuzzy. "What time did you say it is?"

"Five to nine. I'm fixing to head out to meet Josh for church unless you need me to stay. You sick or something?"

Closing my eyes, I shook my head. Only way I'd make it on time now was if I had some superpower that'd have me showered and dressed in ten minutes. My heart raced for the few moments it took for me to remember it wasn't my day to teach Sunday School. Just had to hope God was gracious enough to give me a pass.

Luca

There must've been a church on every street corner in Bedford County. More than half of them listed on the church finder website were Baptist. And the closest one to the house was Mount Hermon Baptist. It made the choice easy, which was a good thing, because nothing else about getting the boys out the door came close.

Daniel sat at the breakfast table, chin in hand, scowling at the eggs I'd spent a good ten minutes making. Would've been easier to give him cereal since he wasn't eating anyway.

"Why do we gotta go to church, anyway? Is it like a requirement for living in Hicksville?"

"I wanna go." Matty had already devoured his eggs, two pieces of bacon, and cinnamon raisin toast. Getting him dressed would be the challenge. I'd made the mistake of making the boys unpack their own things, and somewhere along the way, half of Matty's clothes had gone missing. How that was possible was anyone's guess.

"Suck up," Daniel muttered.

I flicked him with a dishtowel hard enough to get his attention but not so hard he'd call CPS on me. "Watch the attitude, kiddo. That right there is reason enough to drag you into church. Might do you some good to be accountable to someone besides me."

"You mean God?" Chase snatched the last piece of bacon from the plate I'd set in the center of the round table.

"Yes. God." Of course, that meant I would be held accountable, too. I hadn't stepped into church since the boys' mother was gone, and it didn't escape me that doing so now was hypocritical. It was as if I couldn't cut it as a parent, so I was going to pass the baton over to God. Maybe if I'd started with God, my dad-skills would've been acceptable.

It took a few threats and lowering my standards of appropriate church wear for Matty to get us out the door on time. I ignored Daniel's constant grumbling and turned up the music until it drowned him out. Satellite radio tuned to The Message should get us all into the right frame of mind. Hadn't I heard somewhere that worship music was a vehicle to getting the heart right with God before listening to the sermon?

Sermon. That was a daunting word. Sounded like a divine hand slap—or head slap—depending on how far I'd fallen from grace.

I hustled the boys from the car and led them up the stairs to the wide front doors of the church. It was an historic one—lots of wood and brick—with hardware that appeared to be as old as Tennessee. Spring was in the air, and for the briefest moment, I contemplated ditching the whole thing and taking the boys to the Lake. Tims Ford wasn't on par with Lake Michigan, but being around the water might be the ticket to getting Daniel out of his state of discontent.

But then half the battle had been getting them fed and dressed. It would be a foolish waste of time to do all that only to back down now. Might not be a huge fan of church myself, but finding my way back to God after Bridget was gone? That would be a good thing, even if it was a battle. Learned the hard way that things worth fighting for weren't easy to come by. I just hoped it would prove to be true in this case.

"Welcome to Mount Hermon Baptist. I'm Phillip Winton." A man around my dad's age greeted me with one hand out to shake and the other offering a bulletin. "New here?"

"Yes." I shook his hand, took the flyer, and gathered the boys around, ignoring Daniel's scowl. "Luca Giordano, and these are my sons—Daniel, Chase, and Matthew." There was no one else in the foyer, although a glance through the tall, wooden doors showed the church to be bustling with activity. "Are we late?"

"No, sir. Most everyone comes in through the back door." He grinned. "Just like family. We're pleased as can be that you've joined us this morning. Hold on a sec, won't you?" He stepped halfway into the sanctuary and waved another man over—this one nearer my own age. "Josh, this here is Luca and his boys." He grimaced. "Can't remember their names. Some days it's like my brain up and left me clear behind."

"Hey, Luca." Josh shook my hand. "Y'all don't listen to Phil. He's a good ol' boy who's forgotten more than I've learned in a lifetime. Come on in, and I'll introduce you around."

We stepped inside the sanctuary with wooden pews leading up to a large altar. A pulpit was set up behind that backed by what appeared to be a choir section filling up with both men and women. A wide overhead screen advertised events in vibrant colors.

"I'd like you to meet my fiancé, Sherrie Jenkins." Josh put his arm around a pretty, blond woman. "Sherrie, this here is Luca—" He turned to me. "I'm sorry, I didn't catch your last name."

"Giordano." I tipped my head at Sherrie. There was something about her eyes that told me she didn't miss much. "And these are my boys—Daniel, Chase, and Matthew—Matty."

"It's nice to meet y'all." Sherrie took the time to shake the boys' hands. "Is this your first visit with us?"

"Yes, it is." I rubbed my chin. Would those sharp eyes go wide if I confessed this was the first any of us had stepped into a church in five years? "We just moved here from Wheaton."

"Near Chicago?"

"That's the one."

"Well, we're glad to have you." Sherrie touched Josh's arm. "Sunday school classes meet after the service, if you're interested."

Josh nodded. "Love to have you join us." He looked to the boys. "How old are y'all?"

"I'm five." Matty raised his hand, all five fingers spread wide in case there was any doubt.

Chase piped up. "He's still in preschool. I'm seven, and I'm in the first grade."

I held my breath when all eyes turned to Daniel. There was no telling what would come out of his mouth, and it struck me that if anyone was to blame, it was me. A kid's behavior was reflected by their parenting—a sobering thought.

"Nine," he mumbled. "I'm gonna be in fourth grade."

"Not until next school year," Chase corrected as if Daniel was trying to pull a fast one.

I placed a hand on his shoulder. "Once you finish up this year. Only a couple months from now." Last thing I needed was to referee a verbal sparring between the two of them right here in the church sanctuary.

Daniel glanced up at me. If I didn't know better, I'd say his eyes were pleading with mine. "Do we have to go to Sunday school?"

I smiled at Josh and Sherrie. "Promised the boys we'd start off slow. Appreciate the offer, but maybe next time." If they embarrassed me, there might not be a next time. I could see us hopping from church to church to stave off the humiliation of their behavior.

"No worries," Josh said. He reached behind him and retrieved his wallet. "If there's anything you need while you're getting settled in, don't hesitate to give me a call." He withdrew a business card. "My cell number's on there as well as my work number. Know how hard it can be in a new place. I moved up here a few years ago from Louisiana." He wrapped an arm around Sherrie's shoulders. "Best move I ever made." His brows went up slightly, and I could see the question in his eyes. Where was the boys' mother? And if we were together, why wasn't she at church with me? Or maybe it was paranoia playing a trick on my mind.

"Appreciate the offer of help, and I just might take you up on it."

Slipping his wallet back in place, he shrugged. "Call me either way. We can maybe get together for lunch. You play golf?"

Not since Matty was born. Who had time? "Used to. You?"

Sherrie chuckled. "Only every chance he gets."

Before I could say more, the intro music started. As I guided the boys to a half-empty pew, I glanced at Josh's business card. Joshua Cummings, Attorney at Law. There were the phone numbers he promised and an address. No company name. A lawyer joke flitted through my mind, but I tamped it down. Josh seemed like a decent guy—and there might come a day when I could use a good attorney. I slipped his card into my pocket as I took a seat beside Daniel.

Had a strange sense I was at the right place at the right time. Where had that come from? And more importantly, why? Crazy. I shrugged my shoulders as if it would dislodge the notion as the choir director stepped up. He asked the congregation to stand while we sang the opening hymn, "Come to the Table, Sinner and Saint." The first lines felt like a reminder straight from the Lord that I needed something from Him, and uneasiness churned in my gut.

Come to the table, sinner and saint,
strong-hearted, mighty, weary and faint,
empty, repentant, seeking a place.
Christ welcomes you with joy and with grace.

CHAPTER THREE

Luca

I f I survived the boys' first day in a new school, I'd thank Mom for all she'd done for me over the last five years. Had I been so immersed in my own world that I was unaware of the challenges of single parenting? Mom (and Dad to some extent) had my back while in Wheaton. She took the boys to and from school almost every day, stayed with them when I was out of town, and kept the freezer stocked with homemade meals. What had I been thinking, hauling my sons five hundred miles from their grandma, from the only support I'd known since Bridget was gone? And if I was going to be brutally honest, even before she was gone. She never was mother material.

But now I was on my own. And after finagling two spots in Thomas Magnet School, and another in Treasured Tykes Preschool, we were going to make a bad impression on the first day. To make matters worse, it would take a miracle for me to be back home in time for my Zoom appointment. If it hadn't been abundantly clear before, it was now. I needed help.

Thought I had it all planned out down to the last detail. Set everything up the night before—lunches made, clothes laid out, backpacks filled. Didn't take into consideration Daniel's attitude, Matty's pokiness, or Chase's penchant for getting distracted. Now I knew to schedule in time for the unexpected. Not doing so made for a chaotic morning with me ready to pull out my hair. To top it off, Rocket somehow got out, and had to be found before we could leave.

Finally got the boys piled into the car when Daniel, riding shotgun, decided to be the voice of reason. "Why don't we just skip today since we're gonna be, like, an hour late, and go tomorrow?"

"I'll give you points for effort, but no." I backed the car out of the driveway. Would've saved a good twenty seconds if I'd done it last night. "And you're not going to be an hour late. Twenty minutes, maybe."

"Everyone's gonna be staring at us if we walk in now." There was a layer of fear running through his words and clouding his eyes. He could bluster all he wanted, but he was just a scared kid, and I needed to cut him some slack.

"Hate to break it to you, bud, but they're going to stare regardless because you're new. In a perfect world, I could've planned it so you started on day one, but this isn't a perfect world. And although you might find it hard to believe, I'm far from being a perfect dad. Doing the best I can here."

Chase chimed in. "I miss Grandma." *Amen, kid.*

"Am I gonna be late, too?" Matty wouldn't have given it a thought if Daniel hadn't made an issue of it.

"You're in daycare, dummy," Daniel growled. "You can't be late."

I swallowed a sharp retort. "There's no need—"

"I'm not in *daycare*!" Matty's screech arrowed into my temple and set off a headache. "I'm in preschool."

"Whatever," Daniel mumbled.

"That's enough." I pulled up to a stoplight and looked at him. "I get you're not happy about the move, and the new school, and just about everything in your life right now. But don't take it out on your brother." Or me, I wanted to add. But what was the point? He'd only use it to his advantage.

We arrived at Thomas only fifteen minutes late. Not my finest moment, but I chose to look on the bright side—it wasn't Daniel's predicted hour. Might not be worthy of celebration, but I'd take my wins wherever I could get them.

Despite Daniel's assurance they'd be fine on their own, I walked the boys into the office to be sure they had their class assignments.

As I drove Matty across town to Treasured Tykes, I prayed like I hadn't done in years. That the boys would make friends and come to appreciate how fortunate they were to get into a magnet school. If I'd been wise, I would've limited my housing choices to its vicinity, thereby cutting down the school commute. But focusing on the mistakes I'd made wasn't productive. No looking back.

"Is my teacher gonna be nice?" Matty's voice interrupted my thoughts, and I glanced at him in the rearview mirror.

"I spoke with her personally when I registered you for the school, and I'd say she is very nice. Her name is Miss Annalee." Sounded strange to refer to a person as such—but in a good way. A quaint tradition that would most likely get watered down with the influx of transferees from other states. That would be a shame.

I'd driven past both schools after church the day before to get the lay of the land—not that it had helped in the long run. Treasured Tykes was just outside of town on Wartrace Pike. Its front entrance had—what I'd learned from a landscape-friend of mine—was called curb appeal. Planters filled with spring blooms lined the walkway leading to the glass entrance. Didn't know one flower from another, but it was welcoming, which I suspected was the idea.

I took Matty's hand and led him up the pathway. Generally, he'd be the one leading me, excitement making his steps quick. Had Daniel's grumbling gotten to him? "You okay, bud?"

"What if no one likes me?" His voice pitched.

I stopped and squatted down, so we were eye level. There was a little wrinkle between his brows and a slight tremble to his lips. Of the three of them, I figured he'd be the least challenging. It wasn't fair to him that I'd made such an assumption because it meant I didn't pay him the attention he deserved.

Chucking his chin with a finger, I smiled at him. "I don't think that's even a possibility. You're the most likable person I know." And I wasn't just saying it, either. It was the God's honest truth.

"Really?" His blue eyes widened, and the wrinkle smoothed out.

"Really." I planted a kiss on his forehead. "Now why don't we go in and see what Miss Annalee has for you today?"

"Okay." He took hold of my hand and tugged me toward the door. If only every fear was so easily assuaged.

I waited until Matty got settled in before leaving the preschool. Starting the car, I noted the time—8:15—and groaned. What kind of a productivity expert misses a consultation with a new client?

I returned home, placated the client, and slumped back in my office chair with a sigh. I'd bitten off more than I could chew. If only I knew someone who could help—but I did. It took a good five minutes to find Josh's business card still in the pocket of the slacks I'd thrown in the laundry hamper after church. He must know people or at least know people who knew people.

Sitting at my desk again, I pulled out a pad of paper and a pen before punching in his number. Chances were, he wouldn't answer, but I could leave a message, and—

"Joshua Cummings." His voice was abrupt—lawyerly.

"Yes, Josh. This is Luca Giordano. I met you yesterday at church."

"Yes, of course." His tone warmed up several notches. I could relate. No telling who was on the other end of an unknown number. "What can I do for you?"

I chuckled, even though there was nothing funny about my predicament. "Truth is, I got myself in over my head with this move. My parents were a huge help with the boys when we were in Illinois, and now that it's just me...well, I was hoping you'd know of an agency I could call."

"Hmm." At least he didn't dismiss me out of hand. "What're you looking for? Full-time, part-time, live in?"

"Part-time could work. Maybe someone willing to live here. I'd offer free room and board" —*God knew we had the space*—"along with a paycheck." Here I was rambling like I was desperate or something. Which I was. "My mom used to cart the boys to and from school, cook up some meals, that sort of thing."

"I might have an idea. Why don't you leave me your number, and I'll get back to you as soon as I check it out?"

"I'd appreciate anything you can do, Josh. Truly."

"Don't you worry about it. We'll get something figured out for you. You're in the South now. We like to do what we can for each other."

A fifty-pound boulder rolled off my shoulders. It wasn't a promise, but it was a start. More than I had when I stumbled out of bed this morning.

Lillian

Common sense (and a blog post I'd read) suggested that I not interview a potential roommate at my apartment. It'd be like handing the keys of my life to a complete stranger who may turn out to be just one more mistake in a line of pitiful choices. Yes, Ginny Glover would want to see the place before she could make a decision, but I'd only agree to that *if* it turned out she wasn't certifiable, and we took a liking to each other. She sounded normal on the phone, but you never truly knew a body until you lived with him or her. A face-to-face meeting was a start. I was taking baby steps from here on out. No more jumping in with both feet only to find myself drowning.

We decided to meet at The Coffee Break on the Square at ten Monday morning. I spent a whole hour reading my Bible and praying after Sherrie left for work, hoping for divine guidance. It was just so hard to imagine living with anyone other than her, even if she wasn't home much. I'm ashamed to admit I whined some to her about having to spend part of my precious day off to meet up with this Ginny girl as if it was her fault for abandoning me. And I suppose it was, but that didn't give me license to act like a child.

Climbing from my car, I lifted my face to the sun and breathed in the spring air. It was fixin' to be a beautiful day. Lots of sunshine with just a few puffy clouds, and just the slightest breeze. Never could tell here in Tennessee. Might be in the seventies one day and clear down to the forties the next. There was for sure a biblical lesson in there somewhere—a theme—I could use for a children's book. The fickleness of the weather and people compared to our God who never changed. I tucked the idea away at the back of my mind to ruminate on another time.

I wove through the few round tables out front of the coffee house, where chatting women took advantage of the sunshine, before stepping inside where every one of the small tables was occupied. I could just make out an old 70's tune accompanying the din. Might be it was such a popular place because there wasn't anything else quite like it in town. They served coffee, obviously, but they also had scrumptious pastries along with a full breakfast and lunch menu.

Glancing around, I didn't spot anyone sitting alone. Could be Ginny wasn't here yet or maybe she'd gone up to the loft seating. First things first. I needed me a strong cup of coffee, and I was fixin' to splurge on a pastry even though Mama's *tsk, tsk, tsk* was more audible in my mind than the Lord's grace. She always was more apt to judge me than He was. Yes, I was dirt poor, but if I couldn't even afford a muffin, what was the point?

I slid my plate to the edge of the sideboard and was filling my cup from the coffee carafe when someone sidled up to me. "You Lillian Murphy?"

Flicking a glance her way, I nodded. Not at all what I was expecting. You know how some people perfectly match their voices while others not so much? Ginny fell into the not-so-much camp. She somehow sounded taller over the phone and blond—illogical, I know. Or maybe I just wanted her to be Sherrie's clone. "Hey, Ginny." She barely came to my chin, and her dark hair was super short. Maybe she'd cut it off and donated it to Locks of Love, which was admirable. At least she wouldn't be borrowing my hair products.

"You're an on-time person." She nodded. "That's good. Says a lot about a person's consideration for others when they show up when promised."

Couldn't disagree with her, but the way she said it gave me the sense there was a mental checklist she'd run through before deciding. I was more the intuitive type, although that hadn't done me any favors considering I was still single and seeking a roommate. "Do you wanna go up to the loft?" I tilted my head toward the steps.

"That's fine." She wiggled the metal number holder at me. "Just let me tell the staff so they know where to bring my order. I'll meet you up there."

After she turned away, I collected my muffin from the sideboard and headed upstairs. Loft seating sounded quainter than it really was. Just bigger tables to accommodate larger parties. When Ginny appeared, I was still holding my coffee and muffin, glancing around at the limited seating options.

"You wanna see if there's an outside table available?"

She wrinkled her nose. "Rather not. I don't like sunlight."

A shiver skittered up my spine. "Are you allergic to it?" I'd heard of people with photosensitivity—like in the movie *The Others*.

"No." She slid into one of eight chairs that surrounded a picnic-size table covered in dark blue plastic. "Just don't care for it."

What was she, a vampire? Come to think of it, her skin *was* awfully pale. If I had me a mental checklist running through my head, she'd have just earned her first demerit. I set my things on the table and sat across from her.

She stared at my plate and frowned. Hungry? Didn't she say she had an order coming? Head tilting, she sighed. "Do you have any idea how much sugar, not to mention preservatives, are in that muffin?"

Great. A health nut. "It's all good." I nipped off a piece and popped it into my mouth. "It's full of blueberries, so I'm sure their antioxidants will counter the negative effects of all those nasty byproducts." We needed to cut to the chase, because I was wasting precious time for this—hours I'd never get back.

"Tell me, Ginny, aside from your dislike of sunlight, sugar, and preservatives, what are your top three pet peeves?"

Before she could answer, one of the staff came up the stairs carrying a salad. "Here you go." She plopped it down on the table, snatched the metal number holder, and left while Ginny rummaged around in her bag.

"My, that looks tasty." It was a bald-face lie, but I was at a loss for words, which wasn't a normal occurrence. Don't get me wrong, I like me a good salad.

But this one was a plateful of dry greens—not even dressing to make it go down a tad easier.

Ginny pulled a packet from her purse and held it up. "It will be once I get a little avocado oil and vinegar on it." Yum. Maybe I ought to trade in my muffin for a pile of leaves. "What was it you were asking?"

I picked off another bite of my muffin. "Pet peeves. You have any?"

She tilted her head. "I don't think so. I'm an easygoing person—oh." She held up a finger. "There is one thing. I don't care for clutter. I mean, there's a place for everything, right? So why leave stuff laying around? Why not just put it away to start with?"

Just like her comment about being on time, this wasn't something I could disagree with. I liked things to be tidy, too. It was the gleam in her eye that tipped me off, though, like she might go plumb crazy if she found something out of sorts. That reminded me of the husband in the book *Sleeping with the Enemy*.

"What else?" I was looking for something concrete. If Sherrie asked me why I didn't choose Ginny as a roommate, I could hardly tell her it was because punctuality and neatness were important to her. She'd think I was just looking for excuses. Which I sort of was.

Ginny tapped her lips with a finger. Guess germs on her hands didn't offend her as much as sugar and preservatives. "This isn't a pet peeve, but it's important you know. I'm gluten-free and a vegan, so countertops need to be sterilized if any meat or dairy touches them. Also, my cutting boards are off limits. And unless you use the dishwasher daily, we should keep our plates and utensils separate, too." She stabbed a forkful of leaves and smiled. "But other than that, I'm easy peasy."

Even Sherrie'd give me a pass once I shared Ginny's oddities with her. My mother was downright pleasant in comparison. I could take some comfort in that little revelation if it changed my circumstances any. How many applicants would I have to waste precious time on before I found me an acceptable room-mate—if one even existed?

If this was a sign of things to come, I'd be begging Mama to let me come live with her before the week was out.

CHAPTER FOUR

Lillian

Meeting up with Ginny Glover opened my eyes to a whole lot of crazy, which I supposed was a good thing. I'd had three phone calls the day before with potential roommates, and I was a lot more discerning about the questions I'd ask. Wouldn't surprise me any if a rumor went around town that I worked for the FBI or the CIA or whatever governmental outfit grilled people within an inch of their lives. Not a one of them passed my litmus test, which left me in a quandary, as well as tossing and turning all night.

I finally gave up on sleep at oh-dark-thirty and stumbled out of bed. I'd heard Sherrie come in late, so I tiptoed to the kitchen on stockinged feet to be sure not to disturb her. Aside from our brief conversation when she woke me on Sunday morning, we hadn't talked once since Thursday. It was like we were more like pen pals communicating through notes left on the kitchen counter. Wasn't a whole lot different than living on my own. Maybe that's why the idea of a new roommate was so hard to swallow.

Coffee in hand, I clicked on the heat and snuck back into my bedroom. If the Lord woke me this early, He probably had a thing or two to share. Maybe He'd be gracious enough to provide me a miracle. After all, if He parted the Red Sea for the Israelites and shut the mouths of lions for Daniel, surely, He could help dig me out of the hole I'd found myself in. *Found myself.* Now that wasn't quite true, was it? I mean, it wasn't like I'd been sucker-punched. Yes, Billy left me at the altar, but in hindsight, he'd done me a favor—one I probably could've seen coming had I looked. Would've been a whole lot more appreciated if he hadn't stuck me with the bill, but still...a man who had the backbone of a snake couldn't be counted on for the long haul. He hadn't even made it for the short haul.

Taking up my Bible and journal, I snuggled back onto the bed, pillow at my back and blankets tucked beneath my arms. Flipping to Exodus, I did a read-through of the Red-Sea-miracle, amazed once again at God's faithfulness. I jotted down a few scripture references then moved into Daniel. Between him surviving the lion's den and his three friends coming out untouched from the fiery furnace, it was clear the Lord was a God of the last minute. When had I ever stepped out in faith and let Him be *my* last-minute Hero?

A light tap on my door drew me from my musings. "Lil? Are you up?"

"Come in." I closed the Bible and hugged it to my chest.

Sherrie poked her head in. "Goodness. It's not even four. Can't sleep?"

"That was gonna be my question for you. It was after midnight when you came in. What're you doin' up already?"

She crossed the room, cinching the belt of her robe, and sat on the end of my bed. "Should've given serious thought to eloping. On top of the wedding nonsense, my boss handed me a big case yesterday, and—" She widened her eyes and patted my leg. "I plumb forgot. How'd the meeting go? Got yourself a new roomie?"

I wrinkled my nose. "You remember that show *Monk*?"

She frowned. "The OCD guy who was a crack detective?"

"Ramp up the OCD a few notches, take away the detective skills, and add disdain for sunlight, and you get the general picture."

"What?" She laughed. "You're kiddin', right?"

"Afraid not." I slid the Bible onto my nightstand. "Taught me something, though."

"Yeah? What's that?"

"Know what questions to ask. So, when I talked with three more potentials later in the day, I was way more prepared. Not a one of them is gonna work. I don't think any of them even read the ad. Two were smokers, like to party, and probably hadn't read a book since high school, and the third says she's a witch."

"She's a—what?" Her shoulders sagged. "Oh, sweetie, I'm so sorry. But you just started the search, so—"

"No." I swept her optimism away. "I'm done looking." I pushed back the blankets and crossed my legs. "Figure I have two choices here." Quirking a brow, I waited for her to bite.

"Which are...?"

"I could either convert to Catholicism and become a nun. Figure living in a convent would take care of the housing issue, and it might do me good to take a vow of poverty."

She burst out laughing. "And choice number two?"

I pointed to the ceiling. "Leave it up to God. Been going to church ever since I can remember, but I'm beginning to think nothing's stuck."

Her mouth turned down. "I don't think that's true. Known you my whole life, Lil, and you're about the sweetest person—"

"That's not what I'm talking about." Resting my elbows on my knees, I leaned forward. "You can be sweet as pecan pie and still like to control things. I didn't pray about what the Lord wanted me to do for a career, instead I got being a librarian into my head and went full speed—right into debt."

She waved both hands like she was erasing my words. "You love your job. Isn't that a sign right there it's what you should be doing?" A bit of panic clouded her eyes. Could it be I touched a nerve?

"Yes, I love parts of my job, like picking out the children's books and reading to the kids. But I didn't need to get a master's degree for that. It's an entry-level position; you know that. Anybody with a high-school diploma qualifies." And that was the bitterest pill to swallow. Not even that the pay wasn't good.

"Maybe it's not your lifelong dream, but you gotta start somewhere. It's like me starting as a law clerk."

I reached out and touched her hand. "Hey, don't think what I'm saying about my life has anything to do with you. You're a planner. You didn't jump willy-nilly into your career like I did. You've been working toward being a lawyer ever since debate club in middle school."

She swept a strand of hair off her face. Were those tears?

Taking hold of her hand, I dipped my head to look her into watery eyes. "What's goin' on? Did I upset you?"

"It's not you." She shrugged. "Josh and I started talking about what we're gonna do when we start having babies, and things got a little heated."

"Why? Does he want you to quit work to raise a family?" Who even thought that way anymore?

"Not exactly." She squeezed my hand and pulled away. "Let's talk about it another time, okay? I'm still processing." She blew out a breath. "So, any decisions about the lease?"

The abrupt change of subject threw me off some. Maybe it was that lawyer brain of hers, but I didn't shift gears so fast. She was only a month or so away from getting married and things weren't appearing all that rosy. If I'd paid attention to the red flags popping up every which way before my own wedding day, I could've saved myself a whole lot of grief. And if Sherrie was having second thoughts—

"Earth to Lil." Sherrie's sing-song voice reminded me she was waiting on an answer. "The lease? What d'you wanna do about it?"

Okay, Lord, I'm stepping out in faith here. "Let's give notice." I had a whole month before He needed to bless me with that last-minute miracle. Thirty days. Seven hundred and twenty hours. Didn't even need to start packing for a few weeks yet. Just in case.

"Then I got something to tell you." She curled her hair behind her ears. "Sunday at church, Josh and I met a man and his three little boys. Just moved here from Illinois—right outside Chicago." She screwed up her face. "Can't remember his name—something Italian, I think—and I don't recall the boys' names, either, but—"

"If this is a setup, forget it. I'm not interested."

She rolled her eyes. "It's not a setup. For all I know, he's married. But he called Josh yesterday needing to find help with the boys. Someone maybe part-time who could run them to school, do some cooking and such. Of course, with your culinary skills, you might could get creative with the take-out orders."

I'd take the high road and ignore her crack. "So, he's wantin' a nanny?"

"Kind of, I guess. But the thing is, he told Josh that he's got plenty of space for a live-in, and he's willing to offer room and board along with a salary."

I did love kids, but... "What d'you know about him? I mean, if he *is* married, why ever would he need a nanny?" Unless they both had challenging careers. That was always possible.

She shrugged. "I already told you, I don't know what his marital status is, although I'm guessing he's single. I mean, it was just him and the boys at church. He's definitely tall, dark, and handsome." She grinned as if that would make a difference one way or another. Which it wouldn't, because I wasn't going to hitch myself to someone for a good long time—if ever. Especially if I joined that convent.

"Handsome doesn't mean a thing. For all you know, he could be another Ted Bundy or maybe the Casanova Killer."

She scowled. "You need to stop reading true crime stories."

"You're missing the point. It wouldn't be any different than me taking on a roommate here. Instead of being stuck in a lease, I'd get myself all attached to the kids, which is even worse. Who needs the heartache?" Certainly not me.

Luca

With the necessary adjustments to my schedule, I managed to get the boys to school on time. Felt like I'd summited Mount Everest Base Camp. A far sight from the top, but at least I'd made progress. Points for me. I'd hoped Josh would come through with the help I needed—he'd sounded optimistic on the phone the day before. Then again, I had to be practical—good help wasn't easy to come by, and when it came to the boys, I had to be choosy. They were too important to trust with just anyone. So, though I was disappointed with Josh's news, I wasn't surprised.

"Says she's not interested, but Sherrie and I both think it's still worth pursuing," he'd informed me on the phone as I was driving to Thomas Magnet to pick up Daniel and Chase.

"Why is that?" I almost blurted, *What makes her so special?* but even in my head, it reeked of derision. "Does she have a lot of experience with this sort of thing?" I didn't even know what to call it. Nanny? Babysitter? Errand girl?

"Well, not like you'd expect. She's great with kids, though. Runs the Story Hour at the library."

Miss Lillian? "You mean the librarian?"

"That's the one."

"Then she's already got a job. How would that work?"

"You said part-time was a possibility."

"That's true. Doesn't matter, though, if she's not interested." I pulled up to a red light behind a pickup that made my CRV look like a Tonka Toy in comparison. Wouldn't want to pay for the gas to fill that tank.

"She's a little gun-shy, I'll give you that. But I'm sure if she got to know you, she'd be open to the idea."

I laughed. "*You* don't even know me. I could be a mobster or an art thief."

His chuckle filled the car. "Nah. I'm better at discerning character than that. And if I wasn't, Sherrie certainly is. Nothing much gets past that quick brain of hers."

"Good to know."

"If I were you, I'd take your boys over to Story Hour one afternoon. Hang around and introduce yourself. Tell her you're attending Mount Hermon Baptist."

But was I really? One visit was a stretch. "Why would she care?"

"It's her church. She wasn't there last week, but that's unusual. She's one of the Sunday school teachers."

I was still mulling over our conversation as I queued up behind what seemed to be a thousand other cars in the pick-up line a half hour early. *If* Lillian could even be convinced to take the job, and *if*—this was a big one—I felt confident she was right for it, what would it look like? Could she leave the library to pick up the boys? And then what? Summer break was less than six weeks away, and I'd still need someone to be with them during the day. And what about business trips?

Retrieving my laptop from the passenger seat, I muttered, "It can't work" to thin air. Unless God was listening. But why would He? I'd all but turned my back on him recently, aside from those quick prayers tossed up whenever I was in a panic. Wasn't exactly a devoted follower. More of a fan when it suited me.

Tapping the laptop cover, I peered out the windshield toward the sky. *I imagine I've been quite a disappointment lately, Lord. It appears unless I have You on my schedule, You don't get much of my attention. I'm sorry for that. I'll try and do better. The thing is, I could really use a little guidance here. Maybe I shouldn't have made this move to Tennessee without consulting You. Wouldn't be the first time, as You already know. You have no reason to help me out here, given everything. But I'd really appreciate it if You would.*

Could have used a text message or email confirming He'd heard my prayer, but I'd have to make do with the slight sense of peace that came over me as I opened my computer. Was able to set everything else aside as I knocked out a good portion of the proposal due the next day.

Might be a fool's errand, but once I'd collected all three boys, I headed for the library. Tried to convince myself that it was for their benefit—they'd enjoy Story Hour—but maybe there was more to it.

"Where're we going?" Chase peered out the passenger window as we passed our turnoff. "Our house is that way." The kid always did have an uncanny sense of direction.

"Figured you'd like to go to the library—you know, Story Hour."

Chase and Matty enthusiastically shared their opinions in stereo, but they were easily pleased. Daniel was the wildcard. I glanced in the rearview mirror to catch his slight smile and head bob. Probably just happy to put off his homework for an hour, but I'd take it. Dad liked to say, "Beggars can't be choosers." Never quite appreciated that quote until I had children.

Matty led the charge into the library with Chase close behind. Daniel, hands tucked into the front pockets of his jeans, hung back with me, too cool for school. *Where'd that old saying come from?* I could only hope it was a phase, this attitude of his. Otherwise, we were going to find ourselves butting heads often.

I stopped just inside the doors and watched as Matty and Chase claimed a spot on the floor among the growing crowd of kids. "You going to join your brothers?"

He shrugged. "I guess so. It's not like there's anything else to do here."

"You could start on your homework." I pointed out the tables set up in the corner. "Or maybe pick out a couple books to take home." Needed to get library cards before we left.

Without another word, he ambled over to the semi-circle and plopped down next to Chase. He put on a good act, but I knew better. Probably missed his grandma reading to him. Always was the first on the couch when she pulled out whatever book they were going through. Now that job was left to me, and I wasn't excelling. Fact was, if someone cared to grade me, a D would've been generous.

Wasn't a minute later that Lillian took her place in front of the young audience while I leaned against a post from a distance and listened. She read with enthusiasm, but I hadn't caught the name of the book. The fact I didn't recognize it was more proof I hadn't read aloud to the boys much. Came across an article once that claimed reading aloud to kids had many long-term benefits—improved language and literacy skills, gave them a love of words, and even built better connections with them. Maybe if I'd been better at it, Daniel and I wouldn't be at odds so often. Never too late, I supposed.

Lillian's lilting voice was pleasant. There was nothing flashy about her, except maybe her smile. She was pretty, in an understated, natural way. Bridget would slather on about ten pounds of makeup before she'd go out the door. Literally had to paint her face on. It took me too long to realize it was a mask that hid a dark side.

I wandered up and down the aisles of books, along with other parents, keeping an ear tuned into Story Hour. Lillian was adept at changing her voice for the characters, which drew a smile from me on more than one occasion. I didn't have the first clue what to say to her once I introduced myself. Hadn't had much practice with women—not since Bridget. It's not like I had time to date—or an inclination, for that matter. The boys and work were all I could handle, and it was obvious I hadn't been excelling at the latter.

I found a C.J. Box novel and settled into a corner table, although nothing I read stuck. When it was clear Lillian was wrapping things up, I returned the book to the shelf and made my way over to the children's section.

As the kids dispersed, I slogged through them like a salmon swimming against the current. The boys joined me as I approached Lillian stacking the books she'd just read. My hands were clammy, but only because this meeting was important. If she didn't like me, I wouldn't stand a chance.

I leaned toward her. "Hello." Brilliant repartee. That ought to wow her.

She hugged the books to her chest and flashed a smile. "Hey, there. Do you belong to these handsome, young men?" Her smile grew as her gaze moved across the boys.

"I do." I started to offer my hand but thought better of it. Instead, I swiped it down the leg of my jeans. "I'm Luca Giordano. And you've met the boys."

"Not officially." Her eyes lit on Matty. "Except for this one here. Matty, right?"

He nodded, a grin stretched from ear to ear. "Yes, Miss Lillian." *Miss Lillian?* Two days in preschool, and he was already turning into a polite Southerner. Nothing wrong with that.

I patted Daniel's shoulder. "This is my oldest, Daniel. And the middle one there is Chase." Now what? "We're new to the area."

"Dad made us move here." Daniel said. But somehow, the attitude was missing from his words. Maybe Miss Lillian had mad skills after all.

"He's right." I forced a chuckle. "Thought this might be a better environment to raise them."

"Welcome. Have y'all found yourselves a church yet?" It was like she was channeling God. What else could explain her offering the opening I needed? She must've taken my silence for offense, because before I could answer, her mouth twisted into a grimace. "Don't mind me. You'll find right quick that most people from these parts like to ask two things when they meet you—where're you from and where do y'all go to church?"

I nodded. "Not offended at all. We've only been here a week, but we did visit Mount Hermon Baptist this last Sunday."

Now why in the world would that shift her smile to a frown and cause her eyes to narrow?

Chapter Five

Lillian

Sleepless nights throughout the week finally caught up with me. I slapped the snooze button so many times Sunday morning, my alarm clock gave up on me. Figured if I got up at five, I'd have plenty of time to put together the Sunday School craft and create something edible for the church gathering afterwards. Although "edible" was subjective. It was six before I dragged myself out of bed. Lucky me—I had a lasagna I'd picked up at Costco some time back. And it'd only been sitting in the freezer six months.

By the time Sherrie got herself up, the casserole was thawed enough for me to squeeze it into a nine-by-thirteen glass baking dish, and I had about a hundred pink tissue blossoms scattered along the breakfast bar. I turned the oven on to preheat just as she sauntered into the kitchen, eyes still puffy from sleep, and plopped down on a stool in front of my mess.

I detoured to the coffee maker. After filling up a mug and doctoring it just the way she liked, I handed it to her. Flicked a few blossoms clear so she'd have somewhere to put it, too.

"Thank you." Her voice was gravelly. Maybe I should've made the coffee a tad stronger. After she took a sip, her eyes widened like she was seeing things for the first time. "What in the world are you doing?"

"Today's Sunday School lesson is called *April Showers Bring May Flowers*." I swept a hand Vanna-White-style to encompass the pieces of twisted tissue. "These here are flower buds. I was gonna get—"

She waved a hand to hush me then pointed to the lasagna. "I was talkin' about that."

An untrained eye might think it was a blobby mess, but once everything warmed up and the ice crystals had melted, it wouldn't appear any different than the casseroles Miss Amy or Miss Carol brought. "Did you forget the luncheon after Sunday School?"

"No, ma'am. Fixed a batch of cookies and another of brownies last week. They're in the freezer to keep 'em fresh." She took a slurp of the coffee. "So, what's that supposed to be?"

I tossed her a scowl. "It isn't *supposed* to be anything. It *is* a lasagna."

She straightened her spine and peered over the bar until her glance fell on the packaging. "Frozen?"

"Yeah? So? Your baked goods are frozen. What's the difference?"

Digging a finger and thumb into her eyes, she spoke around a yawn. "Made mine fresh is all. Why are you putting it into a baking dish? What's wrong with the foil pan it came in?"

I planted a hand on my hip and huffed out a breath. Talk about the third degree. "You know, Sherrie, I don't appreciate it when you treat me like one of your clients."

She tried to hide a grin behind her hand, but she wasn't fooling me. "Are you gonna try and pass that off as homemade, Little Miss Honesty? Everyone knows you can't hardly boil water without burning the pot."

"Well, don't you worry yourself over it. If anyone asks if I made it from scratch, I'll be sure to tell them the truth." The oven beeped, and I slid the dish inside as my thoughts landed on Luca Giordano (if he wasn't pure Italian, I was a five-star chef) and his three adorable boys.

The reminder had me turning on her. "And speaking of deceitful." I slapped the oven mitt onto the counter. "You have a little explaining of your own to do." I'd had a good mad going Tuesday night, but it had fizzled to mere annoyance over the last several days. If we hardly saw each other now, we'd be complete strangers after she got married.

She sat up straight, eyes going wide. "What'd *I* do?"

"Had me a visit the other day from your good-looking Luca." Had to give her that much—he was definitely easy on the eyes, which had me putting up a wall right quick. Had no intention of tripping all over myself to impress a man again. Besides which, he was stiff as a broom handle. Not that it made a whit of difference to me.

What did I care if he resembled a young James Garner? Mama always did have a thing for his movies and that show *Maverick*, so I was very familiar with his black hair, liquid brown eyes, and olive complexion. Except, he also had a killer smile. That's where the resemblance took a nosedive. Luca's looked more like a grimace.

Her eyes cleared, and she frowned. "I told Josh you weren't interested, so my hands are clean." She held them up for my inspection. Then her lips twitched. "Told you he was a sight, didn't I?"

"Whether he is or isn't doesn't matter, 'cause I'm not about to jump from the fryin' pan into the fire, no matter how hot that fire is." Just talking about it had my cheeks going warm. The whole thing reeked of a set up, and I wanted no part of it.

Shaking her head back and forth slow as the pendulum on Mama's Grandfather clock, she huffed out a laugh. "How many church luncheons have we had the last year or so?" Talk about coming out of right field.

"Why?"

"'Cause your go-to contribution's always been a green salad with bottled ranch dressing. Could your uncharacteristic need to make a culinary impression have anything to do with our newest member?"

I snorted. "Hardly. He probably won't even be there." Didn't care much for the subtle accusation she was making, but I couldn't discount it either. Was I trying to impress Luca Giordano? If so, I was a pathetic mess.

"You're deflecting."

Scooping my blossoms into a gallon-size Ziplock bag, I threw her a glare. "And you're interrogating. Just thought I should make more of an effort is all. Has nothing to do with this guy Luca or any other man. I learned my lesson with Billy." Instead, I was fixin' to be a cat lady, even if I had to do it solo. And I wouldn't succumb to the charms of any man no matter what he had to offer.

Sherrie slid off the stool and carried her empty mug to the sink. "You know, Lil, you should at least *consider* the idea. While you're waiting on a better job offer, you'd have your rent paid for and a little extra money on the side. Sounds like a sweet deal to me."

Squeezing the air from the bag, I sighed. "Thought Ginny Glover sounded like a sweet deal, too. The thing is, we know nothing about this guy. I mean, do you even know what he does for a living?"

She shrugged.

"And what about the boys' mama? Are they divorced? Did she die?" I zipped the bag closed. "Or maybe he's still married, and she just doesn't care for church."

"What difference does it make? You're not gonna marry the guy; you're just gonna work for him."

An uneasy knot formed in my belly. "You're talkin' like it's no big deal to move into his house. He could be a serial killer or a rapist. I'd have to be outta my mind to step into that." No one knew that better than me. "A person's history matters. It plays into their character, and their character plays into the choices they make. And if he's looking to hire someone to watch over his boys, it should matter to him, too. Would you want some stranger takin' care of your children?"

She turned away, but not before I saw her eyes go cloudy. "No, I suppose not."

I tossed the bag of tissue blossoms aside and took hold of Sherrie's arm before she could escape. "You wanna talk about what's going on between you and

Josh? You having second thoughts?" Because if she was, it would be foolish to go forward with the wedding.

"It's nothing, Lil. We're both working hard, tired from the long hours." She gave me a weak smile. "You know how it is."

"Yeah, I know exactly how it is, which is why I think you should talk about it. If not to me then to someone you trust."

"Aside from Josh, there isn't anyone I trust more than you. And it's really not about the wedding or even about Josh and me, so don't worry yourself over it. I'm praying on a few things, and when we have time to sit down without a schedule breathing down our necks, I'll be sure and share it with you, okay?" She offered up a smile, and I was relieved to see it reached her eyes.

Nodding, I pulled her in for a hug. It could be I was transferring all my own baggage onto her. Sherrie wasn't me, and Josh certainly wasn't Billy. They'd be just fine.

Wish I could say the same for me. Still waiting on that last-minute miracle, and I was sure hoping God didn't actually wait for the last minute to provide it, because that would surely test my faith.

Luca

The boys and I piled into a pew just as the intro music (or whatever it's called at church) began playing. We weren't officially late, but in my world, that didn't hold water. My dad told me after I got my first job at a local hardware store that if you're on time, you're late and it stuck. Couldn't abide tardiness. It was inconsiderate and unprofessional. And it was all too common with me these days.

While the choir belted out a rousing rendition of "Blessed Assurance," I split my attention between settling the boys when they squirmed (which was a lot) and glancing around the church for Josh and Sherrie. Well, maybe Lillian, too. Didn't appear I made much of an impression on her the other day. Felt like I was interviewing for a job with which I had no experience, when it should've been the other way around.

Finally, I spotted Josh and Sherrie sitting two pews from the front, but Lillian wasn't with them. The worship music was coming to a close when I caught a figure skulking down the side aisle. *Lillian.* She squeezed in next to Sherrie just as we all sat. Couldn't help myself—I glanced at my watch. Ten minutes late. Just as well I made a poor impression on her, because if she was this late for church without having three boys to corral, no telling how inept she'd be otherwise.

Tucked that piece of information away when the pastor stepped up to the podium. Brother Paul, if I remembered correctly. I opened one of the church Bibles to Ephesians 1, placed it on Daniel's lap—since he sat between Matty and Chase—and indicated that the boys should follow along. Opened a second Bible for myself and did my level best to pay attention. No point sitting in a pew if the time wasn't well spent.

When the service ended with a prayer, I tucked the Bibles away. Had a few people come up and greet us before Josh and Sherrie made their way back.

Josh ruffled Matty's blond head. "You staying for Sunday School this morning, young man?"

Three pairs of eyes turned to me in panic. The boys were so well-behaved during the service, it seemed like they should be rewarded with a hard pass. "I don't know—"

"Give it a try," Sherrie cut in. "They'll meet a lot of nice kids, and the teachers always make it fun for them. Besides, there's a gathering afterwards with lots of great food. Y'all won't go away hungry."

"Cookies, too?" Matty's bar was rather low.

Sherrie laughed. "Cookies, pies, brownies. Probably mac 'n' cheese, barbecue chicken, baked beans." She wriggled her eyebrows. "Anything your little heart desires."

Daniel shrugged. "Okay. We can try it out." Could've blown me over with a feather.

"Great." Sherrie flashed a brilliant smile then looked up at me. "I think Chase and Daniel are probably in the same class. Why don't I take them while you get Matty settled into his? I'm sure their teachers will bring them to the fellowship hall after, so you don't need to worry yourself about collecting them."

Before I could answer, Josh offered to show me to Matty's room, and we were off. "After we drop Matty, I'll take you to our Sunday School class."

Outside the sanctuary, the church was a maze of floors and classrooms. We all walked downstairs together. Sherrie took Chase and Daniel in one direction while Josh led me in another. We stopped at the end of the hall.

"Pre-K and kindergarteners meet in here." Josh stepped aside so I could enter with Matty. "I'll wait for you."

With a hand on Matty's shoulder, I stepped into another world. Bright blue walls with a huge tree painted in one corner covered in pink tissue blossoms greeted us. On either side of the tree were scripture verses: *I am fearfully and wonderfully made; In the beginning, God made the heavens and the earth; You are the God who sees me.* There was even a colorful mural of Bible characters—Jonah and the big fish, Moses and the ten commandments, Joseph in a multi-colored robe. The most impressive was David facing Goliath with nothing more than a slingshot. The wood floor had a large red, blue, and green carpet in the middle beneath a round table surrounded with little bodies in miniature chairs.

So enthralled was I by the vibrancy of the classroom, it took me a beat to notice the two ladies gathering materials in the corner.

Matty tugged on my hand. "It's Miss Lillian."

Sure enough, it was Lillian. The smile she planted on Matty disappeared when her gaze met mine. A cloud of what appeared to be annoyance came into her eyes as she crossed the room to greet us. Or more aptly, to greet Matty.

"I'm so glad you came." She reached for his hand as the other woman joined us. "This is Matty. Matty, I'd like you to meet Miss Hannah."

"Hey, Matty. We're so happy to have you with us this morning." She glanced up at me. "And you must be Matty's daddy."

"Luca Giordano." I shook her hand as Lillian led Matty to the table with the other children. I might not have impressed her, but the way she was dismissing me...had I done something to insult her?

"Are you planning to attend our little get-together afterward?"

I smiled. "It was what I used to bribe him into staying for Sunday School." I glanced past her to where Matty was already making friends with the little girl who sat next to him. "But it appears this'll be the highlight of his day."

"Well, if you'd like, we can bring him to the fellowship hall after we're done here."

"Sounds good."

As I sat in the Sunday School class with Josh, Sherrie, and about thirty other adults, I mulled over the meeting at the library with Lillian. What had I said or done to put her off? It didn't matter in the scheme of things—especially since she'd already decided she didn't want the job I was offering—but it had gotten under my skin. I didn't need everyone to like me, but it would've been nice to know why she had an issue. Maybe she didn't like the influx of out-of-state people moving in, and I was a convenient target. Although that was a stretch.

Josh nudged me with an elbow. "Let's go get us something to eat."

Wasn't until then I realized class was over. Forty-five minutes gone, and I'd spent the entirety of it immersed in fruitless contemplation over things I couldn't control or change.

One wall of the fellowship hall was lined with tables laden with enough food to feed a third-world country. Large round tables, surrounded by fold-up chairs, spilled through open double doors to a large patio with more of the same. Even in the crowd, it didn't take long to find the boys—they started at the end of the line where the desserts sat.

I weaved through the throng and stepped up behind them. Sure enough, their plates were filled with various cookies—not a nutritious serving between them. "Let's find you boys something healthy to soak up all that sugar." I ignored their "Aw, Dad"s and herded them to the other end of the line. Upon close inspection, it didn't appear the fried foods and cheesy casseroles were a better choice.

Sherrie stepped up to us, a skimpy amount of food on her plate. "There's some lasagna down a ways. Lillian made it. Might wanna give it a try. Josh and I are sitting outside, if y'all would like to join us."

That was all the boys needed to hear. As if Lillian had some magic sway over them, they moved as one down the table and squeezed between the pastor and a rather large man filling their own plates to get themselves a generous portion of lasagna. I led them to the outside patio where Josh and Sherrie were holding seats for us.

Josh took inventory of the boys' loaded plates. "What've you got there?"

"A coronary just waiting to happen." I sat between Josh and Matty with my own questionable choices. No doubt it all tasted great, but how anyone ate this way every day and survived to talk about it was a mystery.

"Try this, Daddy." Matty stuck his fork in my face.

I had little choice. Either eat it or wear it. I chose the former and allowed him to scoop it into my mouth. *Not bad.* "Is that Miss Lillian's lasagna?"

Matty nodded. "It's good, huh?"

"Hey," Chase yelled. "There she is. Miss Lillian!" He hopped up and waved his arm to get her attention.

She was exiting the fellowship hall, plate in one hand and a Solo cup of something in the other, when she turned toward us. Could tell the moment she caught sight of me because her smile disappeared. Didn't deter her from coming toward our table. No doubt she'd cut off her right arm before disappointing a child. Admirable.

"Hey, Lil." Sherrie jumped up to pull out the empty chair beside her. "Come join us. The boys were just *raving* over your lasagna." That was a stretch, but I was willing to sacrifice a little integrity to get on her good side.

"It's very good." I speared a piece of broccoli salad swimming in a mayo dressing. "You teach Sunday School, run a library, and cook. Is there anything you can't do?"

Cheeks going pink, her gaze darted to Sherrie before landing on me. "I don't run the library. Not even close."

"She will one day, though." Sherrie grinned at her. "Won't you, Lil? Maybe not our little community library, but no doubt she'll put her degree to good use."

"Degree? In what?" I shot the question across the table.

She didn't bother to glance up from her plate of food. "MLIS."

"What's MS...MLS?" Chase said.

Lillian smiled at him. "M.L.I.S. It's short for Master of Library and Information Science? It's a college degree you need to advance as a librarian."

"Wow." Was there a touch of hero worship in Daniel's gaze? "You gotta be really smart, huh?"

Sherrie chuckled. "She is, Daniel." Then she looked at me. "And she can cook, too."

A Jill-of-all-trades, it would appear. It didn't matter how she felt about me. It was clear the boys adored her, and if I wasn't off my game, the feeling was mutual. That was more than they'd gotten from their own mother. Too bad she'd taken a dislike of me. I'd need to find an alternative.

CHAPTER SIX

Luca

I'd made it my mission to find someone for the boys before the end of the week. I could schedule from here to kingdom come, but there was only so much of me to go around. We were still living out of boxes, and the house seemed to be growing more cluttered by the day. Wouldn't be helpful to hire a housekeeper until things were at least unpacked.

I had two interviews set up for Monday, Tuesday, and Wednesday. Six applicants. At least one of them would be acceptable. After all, the agency I'd contacted assured me all these women were experienced, professional, and available. They'd been wrong.

Three were under the age of twenty and juggling college courses. Their schedules were non-negotiable—nights and weekends off—which meant they could work while the boys were in school. Two of the women were old as Grandma Moses, short of breath, and the distinct aroma of cigarette smoke clung to them. Couldn't stand the smell of cigarettes, and having the boys exposed to second-hand smoke was unacceptable.

Wednesday afternoon was my last chance with this crop of applicants. *I could really use Your help here, Lord. If not for me then for the boys.* I'd just ended the prayer when the doorbell rang. *Here we go.* Took a deep breath before opening the door. No telling what would greet me on the other side.

"Hello. I'm Maggie Spencer. Are you Luca Giordano?" Her drawl was as warm and smooth as her smile.

"I am." We shook hands then I stepped back. "Please come in." So far, so good. Had to be in her mid-fifties, so she'd be settled. Pleasant demeanor with just a bit of spunk in her step. She'd need to be energetic to keep up with the boys. "We're still in the process of unpacking, so you'll have to forgive the clutter."

"Don't you give it another thought." She adjusted her purse on her shoulder, her gaze taking in the foyer and family room. "The house is just fine. Big, isn't it?"

"It is. Bigger than we really need. Why don't we go into the family room and talk before I show you around?"

She paused at the built-in shelves where I'd managed to put a few photos. "Are these here your boys?"

"Yes. This photo is a couple years old. Daniel's nine, Chase's seven, and Matty's five."

"They're adorable." She tapped Matty's likeness. "The little one must favor his mama. Is she here? Your wife?"

"No, ma'am. It's just the boys and me, which is why I need the help." I waved a hand toward the couch. "Can I get you something to drink? Don't have any sweet tea, but we have water and some La Croix in the refrigerator." Didn't realize until the last applicant that not having sweet tea on hand was on par to being unpatriotic.

She flashed a smile and sat. "Thanks anyway, but I don't need a thing. I—" Her face contorted, and she let out a huge sneeze. "Goodness, I apologize." She took hold of her bag and pulled a tissue from inside. Before she could get it to her nose, she let out another sneeze then blew her nose as Rocket meandered from the kitchen, his bushy tail wagging at the sight of company.

Maggie's eyes widened, and she waved the tissue at Rocket like a flag of surrender. "You've got yourselves a dog?" You'd think he was a bear the way she was staring at him. "I'm afraid that won't do. I'm highly allergic to dogs."

"Oh." I jumped up and latched onto Rocket's collar. "Let me just put him outside."

"Won't do a—" *sneeze* "—bit of good. It'll be in your rugs and furniture." Her face was turning an unbecoming shade of splotchy red. "You're gonna have to get rid of him and have everything cleaned top to bottom. That's the only way I'd consider working here."

Get rid of Rocket? "That's not possible, Maggie. Rocket's been with us seven years. The boys would sooner cut off an arm than give up their dog." And I'd be right there with them.

"Well, I'm—" *sneeze* "—afraid it won't—"*sneeze* "—work out." She plucked more tissues from her purse and raced to the door like the hounds of hell were on her heels.

Rocket sat at my side and stared up at me with his liquid brown eyes.

"Now what?" I scuffed his ears. "Might be time to swallow my pride and beg Lillian. You're good at that, boy. Maybe you could give me a lesson or two." Had to do something. For a productivity consultant, I'd been highly unproductive since we'd landed in Tennessee. Barring a move back to Wheaton—which in effect would be the adult version of running home to Mommy—I'd be willing to do just about anything within legal limits. If that meant crawling on my hands and knees, so be it.

It wasn't hard to get the boys on board with Story Hour that afternoon. They'd been singing Lillian's praises since Sunday. Especially Matty. It was, "Miss Lillian" this and "Miss Lillian" that. He'd be hard-pressed to choose between her as his Sunday School teacher or Santa Clause as his grandfather.

I hung back while Lillian worked her storybook magic. Obviously, she'd know I was here since the boys were front and center, but irritating her with my presence wasn't the best strategy to win her over. Instead, I finally got around to getting a library card and picked out a couple John Grisham books—not that I had time to read. What kind of books would impress someone like Lillian? Leo Tolstoy's *War and Peace* or Henry David Thoreau's *Walden*?

Once Lillian wrapped things up, I intercepted Daniel and handed him my books. "Hold onto these for me, okay? You and your brothers should pick out a couple of books to read at home."

He scowled. "We gotta read in school, Dad. Do we gotta read at home, too?"

"Yeah," Chase chimed in.

Couldn't blame them since I hadn't done my part to instill a love of books. "Then pick out something I can read to you all at night." Lillian was moving toward an employees' entrance door. "I need to talk to Miss Lillian for a minute. Find something. Anything." I patted Daniel on the shoulder and hustled to reach Lillian before she disappeared.

"Lillian."

She turned, one eyebrow arched. "Hey, Luca." Hugging the books to her chest, she stepped back and frowned as I drew closer. Wariness clouded her eyes. What had I done to put her off?

"Do you have a minute? I really need to talk to you about something."

Her gaze darted across the library. "If this is about working for you, I'm not interested. I have me a job here, and I'm not about to quit—"

"I wouldn't want you to." I tucked my hands into the front pockets of my jeans. "I'd just like a chance to talk to you about it. See if we can't work something out."

She shrugged. "I don't see how we can, but I suppose it won't hurt to hear you out." She tilted her head toward a table in the corner. "I have a break coming."

Seated across from each other, I folded my hands on the table and picked through my brain to find the right approach. If she didn't care much for me, appealing to my needs would be baseless. But the boys? That was most likely her weakness.

I cleared my throat. "My boys really like you."

Her features softened. "I like them, too. They're sweet."

"They have their moments." If she accepted the position, she'd learn soon enough. "The thing is, this move has been harder on them than I expected.

Harder on me, too, if I'm going to be truthful." Her mouth tightened, and I rushed ahead to get back on track. "I know you working with them would make it a lot easier." *On all of us.*

She glanced at me for a beat. "I appreciate what y'all are goin' through, Luca. But even if I was open to the notion, I don't see how I can help." It wasn't an outright no. That was progress.

"But I think you can. If we divided some of the load between us, like working parents do, then it would be enough."

Her eyes went wide. "Working *parents*?"

That struck the wrong chord. "Wait." I held up a hand. "That's not what I meant. I mean, not like parents..." What then? Partners? That wouldn't sound any better.

Rubbing my forehead, I sighed. "This is coming out all wrong. I just thought you could drop the boys at school before you clock in here, and I could pick them up. Help out with dinner at night, get them organized for the next day, and into bed while I finish up with my West Coast clients." And she'd be a lot more effective getting them into books than I'd been. Probably a better communicator, too.

She sighed. "Neither of us knows a thing about the other. I don't even know what you do for a living that you'd have clients on the West Coast."

"Nothing glamourous." I shifted in my chair. "I'm a productivity specialist."

"A what?" Her reaction was what I'd expected. No one seemed to know what it was—not even me until I needed to make a career change.

"In a nutshell, I help companies increase productivity in the workplace or individuals in their jobs, homes, or even retirement."

"That's a real thing?" She grinned for the first time, a glint of humor in her eyes. "You're an expert at getting stuff done, and you need *my* help? Must not be very good at your job."

I chuckled. She had me there. "You have a clear grasp of the situation I find myself in."

"So, whatever made you choose that particular line of work? I mean, don't most little boys dream about bein' a fireman or an astronaut?" Maybe her interest in me was a good sign. *It's a step, Lord.* "Professional baseball player," I corrected her with a chuckle. "I was going to be the next Roger Clemens."

A grin flirted around the edges of her mouth. "What happened?"

"Turns out, I can't pitch worth a darn. So, I got my MBA instead of playing for the MLB. Took what I knew and turned it into a valuable commodity so I could work from home."

She quirked a brow and nodded. "That's very resourceful of you."

I glanced at her. "So, will you at least come to the house, take a tour, and see if there is something we can work out? Free room and board, plus a paycheck." I held my breath while awaiting her answer.

Lillian

Even though I had the gist of what Luca's profession was, the minute he and the boys left the library, I googled it. Sounded daunting—and boring. No wonder he came across stiff as a broomstick. He was probably one of those anal-retentive types. A perfectionist who liked things to be just so. I didn't see how me taking on the job could work, and that would be the easy part. Living with him? It wouldn't even be a consideration if I could afford my own place. Still, I promised to stop by on my way home, and I always kept my promises. Unlike some people.

Luca had given me their address, and I followed the map app on my phone to find it. It was almost five-thirty when I parked in the driveway, and the sun was warm on my face as I locked the car. There was a bit of a breeze, though, reminding me the weather was fixin' to cool off tomorrow.

The house was a brick and vinyl two-story with a wrap-around porch and a whole bunch of windows. It was on a lot big enough so the neighbors on either side had breathing room, and the boys had plenty of space to run. A large tulip poplar tree stood in the center of the yard, its pink blooms peeking out from the dark green leaves, a mockingbird raising quite a ruckus from its branches.

Before I could ring the bell, the door flew open. Matty and Chase each grabbed a hand and tugged me into a generous entry hall where a set of stairs led to the second floor. "Were y'all watching for me?"

"Dad said you were coming." Matty was prancing on his tiptoes. "You wanna see my room?"

I placed a hand on his head to see if it'd settle him any. "I sure do. But maybe after your daddy and I talk, okay?" If I went down that rabbit hole, there was no telling if we'd ever get our scheduled chat done with. Even if I didn't have the least little intention of taking this job.

Luca showed up. "You're here." He slapped a hand on his chest and blew out a breath. Didn't he think I'd come? "Before we go any further, there is something I should've asked—" A large golden-red ball of fluff bounded into the entry hall, its scrambling legs flailing on the tile floor as it slid into Luca, cutting his words off with an *oomph*.

The dog quickly regained its balance, sat at my feet, and looked up at me expectantly.

Matty grabbed hold of its collar. "This is Rocket." Appropriately named, I'd say.

"Rocket, huh?" Its tail thumped a welcome. Was it possible for a dog to smile? If so, this one did. "Does that mean it's a boy?"

"Yeah." Luca cleared his throat. "Sorry about that. I was going to ask if you're allergic to dogs."

"Allergic?" That would be an easy out—and a lie. "Not that I'm aware of. I wouldn't say I'm a fan, though. More of a cat person." I patted his soft head just the same.

Was Luca's grimace caused by a distaste for cats or because he was afraid my issue with dogs could put a wrench in the job offer?

"Everybody loves Rocket." Matty wrapped his arms around the hairy beast and hugged him as if to prove it. "He's our friend."

"I can see that. I bet he's really good at protecting you, too." I supposed every boy needed a dog.

"Let me show you around." Luca waved me to follow him. "Boys, why don't you take Rocket out back?"

One more pat, and I sidestepped Rocket while Matty and Chase did as their dad asked. The family room was huge with fifteen-foot ceilings and an entire wall of built-in cabinets made of cherrywood. All those shelves wasted with only a few photos of Luca and the boys. Their frames appeared lost in all that emptiness, miniature nothings in contrast to the massive flat-screen television. What Luca needed was books, books, and more books. What I wouldn't give to have space for my collection that now sat in boxes in Mama and Daddy's basement.

A U-shaped sectional with a square coffee table sat in the center and there were boxes stacked along the perimeter that also appeared a little lost in all that uncluttered space. No artwork on the walls, no other pieces of furniture tucked into the corners, not even toys littered the floor. It looked as lived-in and warm as a prison cell.

"As you can see, we still have a lot of unpacking to do." Luca, hands planted on his denim-clad hips, glanced around as if trying to see it through my eyes.

A double set of French doors led to an in-ground pool surrounded by a black, wrought-iron fence. Beyond that was lots of lawn, where all three boys were running around with Rocket, their laughter and deep doggie barks tugging a smile from me. Just like the house, the yard was huge, and other than the beautiful pool, stark. A landscaper's blank canvas.

"Let me show you the kitchen."

There wasn't a doubt in my mind it would be the sort of kitchen Sherrie would kill for, and I was right. The farmhouse sink was probably big enough to bathe Rocket. The same cherrywood in the family room built-ins were used for the cabinets, which appeared near empty through the leaded glass doors. Didn't the man own a proper set of dishes? Granite countertops, stainless steel appliances (right down to the double oven), and a commercial-size refrigerator at least took up some space. Even though I was a hot mess when it came to anything culinary, I could appreciate the luxury of this room. Only thing marring its perfection was a big ol' whiteboard stuck on the wall above the kitchen table that was tucked into a sweet nook.

"What's that?" I blurted out the question before filtering it through common sense as I moved toward the board.

"Our task list and calendar." Was there the least little bit of defensiveness to Luca's tone? "Not much on it yet, since we haven't gotten settled."

Not much on it? Seemed Luca had every bit of their time all mapped out—when to eat breakfast and supper, what time to leave in the morning, what time they'd get home in the afternoon. Even had my Story Hour times listed under a "Library" heading. If he wasn't a type-A personality, I was Julia Child.

I stared at the grids, no doubt created with the precise measurements of a ruler and colorful dry-erase markers. "Doesn't leave a whole lot of room for spontaneity, does it?" Again, the words came out before I had a chance to think better of them. What difference did it make to me how Luca managed their time since I wasn't taking the job?

"Considering I get them out the door late more often than not, we seem to err on the side of spontaneous these days. Which is where I'm hoping you'll come in."

Drawing in a deep breath, I turned to face him. "About that."

He held up a hand to stop me. "Let me at least finish the tour before you turn me down." His eyes pleaded with mine. "Then if you still think there isn't anyway it'll work, I won't ever bring it up again."

What else could he show me that might change my mind? I tagged along behind him while he went back into the family room, through the entry, and down a well-lit hallway I hadn't even noticed when I came in. Could be the big, furry dog distracted me.

Luca stopped at the closed door at the end of the hall. "I think this is supposed to be a master suite. There is another upstairs, and I prefer to be there where I can be closer to the boys." He opened the door and stepped aside to let me go first.

It wasn't a master suite—it was a master mansion. "I could fit my entire apartment in here." It put my place to shame, and that was the truth. More built-ins, French doors going out back, and a seating area bigger than my living room. I didn't have furniture to fill it, and what I had was pathetic. How could I even think of tarnishing this space with my sorry, childhood bed set?

"You have your own bathroom through there," Luca pointed to a set of arched doors, "with a walk-in closet."

It was an invitation, and I wasn't about to pass it up. Of course, the bathroom was every bit as lavish as the bedroom. Large glass-and-tile shower, claw-foot tub, custom cabinets (again with the cherrywood), double sinks, and the promised walk-in closet—bigger than my apartment bedroom. Was it a blot on my character that such a fancy room had me drooling?

"Total privacy." Luca stood in the doorway, arms crossed. "What do you think? Are you willing to try it out?"

Weak and broke were powerful motivators—not to mention three adorable boys. "Let's talk about logistics, and then we'll see."

CHAPTER SEVEN

Lillian

There'd been a knot in my belly since the moment I'd agreed to give Luca and his boys a chance. I'd prayed all through church this morning that the Holy Spirit would blanket me in peace over this decision. Kind of hard to know the difference between the Lord's still small voice and my own wayward thoughts. I always expected God would choose for me the opposite of whatever was easiest, which was why I tended not to follow Him. Comfort and easy had been my leaning. Nothing about this decision was either.

Now here I was surrounded by my own collection of moving boxes—even if it was a fraction of those lining the walls of Luca's family room—fixing to move in with a man I didn't know. If that didn't take courage, I don't know what did. Of course, I wasn't *really* moving in with Luca. I was moving in with his boys. Someone had to take care of them. If their daddy had his way, they'd be scheduled to within an inch of their lives.

"It's only temporary." Sherrie's voice cut into my musings.

I lifted my gaze from the sea of cardboard and looked at her standing in the doorway of my bedroom. Or rather, my former bedroom. After today, I'd never set foot in this apartment again. I'd never live with my best friend, again, either, unless the world went completely topsy-turvy and we both found ourselves lost and alone.

"Temporary?"

"You living in Luca's house. It's a stopgap, Lil." She crossed her arms and leaned against the door jamb. "Soon, you'll have yourself that librarian position you've been drooling over at MTSU and be able to afford a nice place of your own. No more roommates. No more compromises."

I smoothed out the packing tape on one of the boxes. No more compromises? Couldn't hardly get through a day without making one of those. "I liked having you for a roommate these past ten years. Can't imagine what it's gonna be like apart." I offered a weak smile. "But I suppose life doesn't stand still for long, does it?"

"Not unless you're dead." She blew out a breath. "It'll be okay, Lil. You'll see. Did you ever find out what happened to the boys' mama?"

"Nope. Luca didn't offer an explanation, and I didn't ask." I hooked a strand of hair behind my ear. "He's a touch odd, don't you think?"

She arched a brow. "Not so I noticed. Maybe you're just used to Southern men."

I snorted. "Not likely. Take yourself a look at the schedule he put above the kitchen table then we'll talk."

Shaking her head, she hefted one of the boxes. "Josh and Luca should be here any minute. You about ready?"

Thankfully, Josh had been able to borrow a friend's truck to move my stuff. Luca's neighbor (I suppose my neighbor now, too) offered to watch the boys for a while. "I should be asking you that question." I grabbed my own box and followed her to the living room. "You're getting married in six days. Guess we're both stepping into the unknown. Are *you* ready?" The two of us still had a list a mile long to finish up.

"Be more so after having to stay at my mama's place for the rest of the week. I love her to pieces, but living with her for more than twenty-four hours would try the patience of Job."

I laughed. "Yours doesn't have anything on mine." My smile wavered as I thought back to what Mama had said when I told her I was moving in with Luca. Or rather, his *boys*. You'd have thought I was throwing myself into the pit of hades. Took me almost ten minutes to convince her it was a bona-fide job offer with room and board. And I wasn't compromising my Christian morals by living with a man without benefit of marriage.

The men showed up, and it didn't take more than an hour to get the boxes loaded into the truck along with my bed and dresser. A sad collection of stuff that wouldn't come close to filling that huge ol' suite.

Once we were loaded up, Josh and Luca drove the truck while Sherrie and I followed in my car.

"Can't wait to see this place," Sherrie said. "Must be some kind of something if you were willing to change your mind."

The knot in my belly fisted a bit more. Was I making a mistake being swayed by a fancy house and my need to mother those three little boys? "I truly don't know how this is gonna work out. It's not like I can give two-week's notice and move on easy as you please if it doesn't." What had I been thinking? "You know, he's gonna expect me to do some cooking. Even you said I can't hardly boil water."

She grinned. "I got a recipe book from one of Mama's friends as a wedding gift. It's too elementary for me, but it'd be perfect for you. You just need to follow the directions."

I'd need a whole lot more than a cookbook to pull this off. I'd need my own personal chef. "And did I tell you they have a dog? A big, furry, messy dog. If it was a little thing, I might could handle it, but it's huge. Reminds me of Clifford."

"Clifford?" She looked at me like I'd lost my last marbles.

"*The Big Red Dog*. You remember those books from when we were little?"

She barked out a laugh. "You do tend to exaggerate. It'll be fine, Lil. Besides which, if memory serves, Clifford was a gentle giant. I'm sure Luca wouldn't have himself a dangerous dog with those three little boys. And as for the rest of it, didn't you say he'd start you off slow? Y'all will figure it out as you go. Take yourself a deep breath and relax."

Easy for her to say. She was fixing to start a whole new life with the man of her dreams while I was stepping off a cliff with no idea where or how I'd land.

I'd no sooner parked the car behind Josh's truck in the drive when the boys came tearing from the neighbor's front yard. They were all gangly arms and legs in their shorts and t-shirts, and it appeared Matty had grass stains on his knees. Better than his pants. It struck me I'd probably be in charge of washing their clothes, too. Just call me Cinderella.

"Can I help?" Daniel was reaching for a box bigger than him the minute Josh had the tailgate down. Was that a smile on his face? The only one I'd seen so far was in the photos in Luca's family room. I was beginning to think he didn't know how anymore.

"Hold up." Luca stepped in and eased the boys away from the truck. "I think it would be best if you leave it to us. There could be breakables in here. Unless you can afford to replace Miss Lillian's things." He quirked an eyebrow at them as if waiting for an answer.

And just like that, Daniel's enthusiasm melted into a scowl. Couldn't Luca see how he'd just deflated the child? It was a pure shame. Maybe God put me here for reasons other than chief cook and chauffeur. It was pretty clear Luca could use a few parenting lessons, even if I wasn't the most qualified for that particular task.

I waited until Josh and Sherrie had each collected a box and headed inside before stepping in. "If it's alright with you, Luca, maybe Daniel can give me a hand with my load. In fact, all three of the boys would be a huge help." Four pairs of eyes landed on me. "But these boxes are kinda heavy, so you'll have to carry them together."

Luca shrugged. "Sure, if you're okay with it."

Daniel crossed his arms in front of his narrow chest. "But if we drop them, won't the stuff inside break?"

"Nah. They're books. Although, they're important to me, so you still need to be a little careful, okay?" I led them to the back of the car and popped the trunk. I handed one to Chase and Matty, and bit back a smile while they walked sideways up the driveway, each holding an end.

"I can take one by myself," Daniel said. There was a hint of pride in his eyes I wasn't about to squash.

"You got it." Made sure I picked out one he actually could carry on his own and put it in his skinny arms. Then I got one for myself and followed him inside.

The boys passed an empty-handed Sherrie in the ridiculously large entry hall. Her eyes widened as she grinned at me. "Amazing. You have your own suite, and a bathroom I could absolutely live in."

"You haven't even seen the kitchen yet," I reminded her. "Go sneak a look before you come back out for another load. And be sure to check out that color-coded schedule I was telling you about." I rolled my eyes with a smirk. Yep, there could be a thing or two I had to teach Luca.

Luca

From my experience, women were pack rats. They collected clothing like squirrels gathering acorns for winter and had a pair of shoes or two for every conceivable occasion. Don't even get me started on beauty and hair products. Bridget couldn't contain all hers in a full-sized suitcase. She'd have creams and lotions spread from one end of the bathroom counter to the other, while the shower was bursting with shampoos, conditioners, and containers of body wash. That was just the personal stuff.

The kitchen was a whole other ballgame—specialty pots, pans, and gadgets she'd acquired at Pampered Chef parties that stretched my credit card limit. Several sets of dishes—three every day, two special China—glasses coming out of our ears. Most of which I donated when we moved. And then there was the furniture and dust collectors that cluttered every empty shelf space in the family room.

So, I was prepared for whatever literal baggage Lillian came with. Color me shocked when everything she owned fit into the back of a pickup truck, including her bedroom furniture. A minimalistic female? I had no idea God had ever created such a being.

"This is it?" I'd asked Josh as he shut the tailgate on the last load we brought from the apartment. "What'd she do with the rest of her stuff?" Surely, she had a storage unit somewhere in town.

"This is all there is." He shook his head and grinned. "Boggles the mind, doesn't it? Only thing she's attached to are her books and the box of art supplies I stashed on the back seat. Course, it could be Sherrie had enough for both of them when they moved in together, so you never know. Might find her bringing things home to fill up whatever space you've given her."

Wasn't used to having strangers in my home. It'd been the boys and me, Mom and Dad on occasion, and a friend or two when time permitted. But Josh and Sherrie didn't appear to be in a hurry to get on with their Sunday afternoon once we'd unloaded everything, so what could I do but invite them to stay?

The boys were in the pool, Lillian and Sherrie off unpacking boxes, while Josh and I sat on the patio with a beer. A warm breeze and squeals of the boys' laughter filled the air. Could close my eyes and take a nap right where I sat. Too many sleepless nights and chaotic days.

"What's with that chart in the kitchen?" Josh's question jarred the peaceful moment. He quirked an eyebrow at me and tilted his head toward the house.

"I like to be organized." His bark of laughter should've hit a nerve but instead pulled a grin from me.

"I can see that. Never did hear what you do for a living." He took a pull from his beer, eyes on me.

"I'm a consultant." I scraped the label of my bottle with a thumbnail. "Productivity specialist."

His eyes widened as he lowered the bottle. "Come again?"

Heat climbed my neck. "I help create production plans and workflow solutions."

"Huh. Didn't know that was a thing. So, you consult with big companies?"

I shrugged. "Yes, and small companies, and even individuals. A lot of people working from home these days struggle with prioritizing. Part of that is scheduling, another part is learning to use the optimal time for the most important tasks. How to use what time we have wisely."

He chuckled.

My own lips twitched in response. "Boring, I know." For some reason, my work didn't earn the same respect here that it did in Chicago. Could be a difference in philosophy, or maybe it just came across as pretentious. It would probably appear odd to me if I didn't have the inside track.

"It's not that." Josh couldn't seem to get his grin under control. "I can see you're the serious type. After all, it's your business. Lillian...well, she's more of a free spirit. It'll be interesting to see how this plays out."

Free spirit? What'd he mean by that? Before I could ask, Rocket interrupted for a round of attention before bounding back to the side of the pool to keep watch on the boys.

"And just so you know," Josh continued as if we hadn't been interrupted, "she's not a fan of dogs. More the cat type."

I nodded. "Caught that. Don't think she's a fan of mine, either. Feels like she's holding back a reprimand whenever she's around. Reminds me of my grandmother."

He threw his head back and laughed. "If you have half a brain, you won't tell her that." He swiped moisture from his eyes. "I'm sure once she gets to know you...she's been hurt. Probably not my place to share this since I hardly know you. But just understand it's been hard on her. Didn't get a whole lot of emotional support from her mama, either."

Interesting. Seemed wrong to push, but I couldn't help but wonder what exactly happened to her. "What about her father? Is he in the picture?"

Josh grimaced. "Yes and no. Sweet guy, from what I understand, but it's her mama that wears the pants, if you know what I mean." He sat back with a sigh.

"Anyway, I'm just givin' you a peek inside the mind of Lillian Murphy. Use the information wisely." There was a warning beneath his casual words. "She's easy to like, great with kids, and dependable, so y'all should be just fine."

"Any tips on how I can get into her good graces?"

"I do." Sherrie stepped through the French doors from the family room.

Josh scowled. "You eavesdropping, counselor? That's fruit of the poisonous tree, you know."

"Good thing we're not in a court of law," she quipped back, reaching for his beer and taking a swig.

Did I miss something? "What are you two talking about?"

She licked her lips and returned the bottle. "Don't mind us, it's just a bit of lawyer humor. You want my advice or not?"

Josh peered around her. "Where's Lil?"

"Got a call from her mama, so she'll be a few minutes. Here's the thing, Luca." She sat across from me and leaned her elbows on the patio table. "That beautiful space you have for her is beyond luxurious, but it needs more furniture. I've offered some of mine, but she's being stubborn and independent. Instead of letting me give her a bookcase, she's stacking her books on the floor like some kind of pauper."

Furniture? "I'm afraid that's not in my wheelhouse. Got rid of everything I could before I moved here."

She wrinkled her nose. "I can see that. The whole place looks barren."

Josh shook his head. "Way to be subtle there, babe." He glanced at me. "You'll have to forgive her; she tends to say it like it is."

I grinned. "It's refreshing. Truth is, I bought this place sight unseen and didn't know what I was getting myself into. I could use someone with skills to help."

"I'll give you the name of a couple furniture showrooms in Murfreesboro. You take some snapshots of your house, and their sales staff won't have trouble setting you up."

Matty, dripping water, padded across the pool deck, Rocket at his side. "I'm hungry, Daddy. Are we gonna get something to eat?"

My own stomach rumbled in response. "How about I order us some pizzas?" I glanced at Sherrie and Josh. "What do you say, guys? Up for an early dinner?"

Sherrie grinned. "Just so you get the lingo down, we call it supper here. I'm game if Josh is?" She nudged him with an elbow. "You good with that?"

Lillian stepped outside, a bottle of water in hand. She didn't have Sherrie's confident stride. In fact, she seemed timid and a little hesitant. Couldn't imagine it was easy moving into someone else's house—especially if it was a choice made of necessity, which this appeared to be. It was up to me to make her feel at home. That wasn't exactly in my wheelhouse, either.

Chapter Eight

Lillian

Gray hues shadowed the walls, and my heart hitched before my world righted itself once again. Or at least as right as possible given I was in a strange room, in a strange house, with people I didn't know. Shoving the covers aside, I sat up in my bed—at least *that* was familiar—and fumbled the lamp until my fingers caught hold of the switch. The weak 60-watt bulb didn't even reach to the corners of the cavernous room.

I raked the hair from my face as I checked the time on my phone. A quarter to five. What would I do if I was back in my apartment? Use the bathroom and get myself a strong cup of coffee. Everything looked a sight better after a dose of caffeine. I snatched up my robe, which I'd left on the end of my bed, and slipped into it. I couldn't go traipsing through the house in my nightie like usual. Had me a feeling there would be a whole lot of changes I'd need to make now that I was living under the same roof as four males.

I couldn't help but grin as I stepped into the gargantuan bathroom. Felt like my own personal spa. I'd better not get myself used to such luxury, 'cause there was no way I'd find myself living in such a way in the future. Either Luca made himself a boatload of money running other people's lives, or he'd inherited it. I padded across the cool tile floor and made use of the facilities. While washing up at the sink, I dared to squint into the mirror. My hair was a rat's nest of tangles, there were circles under my eyes, and a few wrinkles around them that appeared to be new. Or maybe it was the runway lighting that wouldn't allow a woman to hide even the tiniest flaw. I was gonna go with that one.

When I stepped back into the bedroom, a golden hue of light was pouring through the sheers that covered the double French doors leading out to the back patio and the pool beyond. Never had me a pool before. Swimming was supposed to be great exercise, and I wouldn't have to hightail it to the gym, either. I crossed the room and fingered the sheers aside to catch a glimpse of the sun rising over the shimmering water. It pulled a sigh from me. This might not be such a bad gig after all.

The house was quiet as death as I made my way down the long hall, past the stairs in the entry hall, and across the family room to reach the kitchen. It was enough to wind a girl. I was greeted by the scent of coffee and low wattage lights illuminating the counter from beneath the upper cabinets. The invitation couldn't have been clearer if it was engraved in gold. Now I just needed to find a coffee cup. And sugar. And a spoon. It was too early to be faced with such challenges.

"Morning." Luca's deep voice took a good five years off my life, and I spun in a circle to see him seated at the kitchen table, coffee cup in hand, laptop open. The glow of its monitor spotlighted his chiseled features. How'd I miss him?

"My word, you scared me spit-less. You oughta warn a girl."

"Sorry." He grimaced. "Not used to anyone being up this early." He closed the laptop and pushed from the table. Unlike me, he was fully dressed in jeans and a t-shirt—which had me feeling a tad exposed. "Let me get you a mug. Need sugar? Milk?"

"Please." I gathered the edges of my robe together and took a deep breath. From now on, I'd get myself showered and dressed before leaving the bedroom. "I suppose it's gonna take a little time to get used to each other."

He moved from cabinet to pantry to fridge and set everything in front of the coffee maker. "Well, now you know I'm an early riser. Only way anything gets done before the boys are up."

"And what time would that be?" I filled the mug, added a spoonful of sugar and a drop of milk.

"Six is my preference, but it's usually a battle. Need to leave here by 7:15 to get Daniel and Chase to school on time."

I glanced at his silly chart before sitting across from him at the table. There it was in blue—C & D, TMS; L, TTP. "TMS must be Thomas Magnet School." I'd remembered that much from talking to him before. "But what's TTP?"

"Treasured Tykes Preschool. It's—"

"Oh, yay. I know Annalee Pritchard." Finally, something familiar. "Soon to be Annalee Daniels." Seemed everyone was getting married except me. "Matty will love it there. She's a wonderful teacher."

His lips twitched as if he was trying to hold back a grin. "I'm glad to hear it. Starting to wonder if I'm doing anything right." The self-deprecating comment tugged at my heart and had my face heating. Was he aware that I'd been judging him as if I had a right? Maybe I wasn't the only one feeling like a misfit.

"Can't imagine it's easy raising three boys on your own."

He grunted. "Had a lot of help before we came here. Guess I wasn't aware how much my mom did. Last time I take her for granted."

"You're lucky to have such a supportive mama." After fearing he was aware of me being judgy, I hesitated to ask about his wife. But who wouldn't be curious? Maybe it'd come across as odd that I *didn't* ask. "So, you've been a single daddy for how long?"

As he opened his mouth to answer, a clatter came from the family room before Rocket skidded into the kitchen. All two hundred pounds of him. Okay, maybe Sherrie was right, and I tended toward exaggeration, but when the dog was in motion, he was the example of Einstein's $E=MC^2$.

"Rocket slept in Daniel's room, so he must be up already." He stood. "Guess miracles really do happen. Let's go outside, Rocket."

And quick as that, my chance to ask about Luca's wife went out the window. I'd take it as a sign from God the timing wasn't right. Could be He saved me from some embarrassment, although He'd surely allowed me to make a fool of myself in the past.

From the moment the boys tumbled out of bed until I had them buckled into my car, I was watching the clock. Things simple as eating breakfast, teeth brushing, and getting dressed turned into a battle of wills between the boys and their daddy. Never one to have myself anything more than a piece of toast (which I excelled in making, by the way) and a cup of coffee in the morning, I was struck dumb by the choices Luca offered his sons. One wanted eggs, another hot cereal, and another insisted on waffles. And not the kind you stuck in a toaster, either. No wonder he was always fighting to get them to school on time.

I might've stood on the sidelines being no more help than a bump on a log, but if I was gonna do this job right, there needed to be some changes. Had me a feeling Luca was operating from a place of guilt over taking the kids from their nana, but I didn't have the same compulsion.

Once we were in the car, I laid down Miss Lillian's Law. "Y'all are blessed to have a daddy who wants to make you happy. My own daddy was like that. Always bending over backwards to keep a smile on my face."

"Yeah," Matty piped up from the back seat. "Daddy's nice."

"But as you know, he's hired me to take care of some of those time-consuming chores, like gettin' y'all ready for school in the morning. The thing is, I have me a job of my own, too. Except for Sundays and Mondays, which are my days off, I have to be at the library by 8:30."

Daniel eyed me from the passenger seat. "You got lots of time. We start at 7:45."

I nodded. "That's true, but I also need to get Matty to his school after dropping you and Chase off. So, here's what I'm proposing."

"What's posing?" Matty asked.

"Not *posing*, dweeb. She said *proposing*."

"Proposing?" Chase's voice squeaked from behind me. "You mean like getting married?"

Daniel sighed and covered his face with a hand.

"Proposing is the same as suggesting." I'd need to be more careful about choosing my words. "So, what I'm *suggesting* is this. We fix only one kind of breakfast whether it's hot cereal or eggs." I wasn't about to offer up waffles since I didn't have the first clue how to make them. And I surely didn't want to clean up afterwards, either.

"But Daddy says we can have whatever we want." I didn't have to see Chase to know he'd jutted out his bottom lip.

"Well, your daddy put me in charge, and I don't have time on school days to fix three different breakfasts, so we'll compromise. You can have what you want on the weekends."

The boys fussed all the way to Thomas Magnet School, but I ignored them. If they wanted to complain to their daddy, and he chose to fire me, so be it. I wasn't gonna become a slave to three prepubescent little boys or Luca no matter how desperate I was. A girl had to have boundaries.

As Chase and Daniel climbed from the car, I collected their backpacks from the trunk. A van pulled up behind me, and I gave the driver a casual wave. It wasn't until three little girls piled out the back door that I realized it was Meghan Marshall—one of Shelbyville's most loyal library patrons and fellow church member. It couldn't be a coincidence that her daughters attended the same school as Chase and Daniel. Inspiration struck, and I knew it was from the Lord.

Now if only Luca could see the divine design behind it.

Luca

Silence. It was the first morning since we'd landed in Tennessee that I was able to jump into work before 7:30. How far I'd fallen to feel like two extra hours was on par with Jesus healing the blind. But I could finally breathe a little easier knowing I wasn't doing this parental gig on my own—even if I'd had to hire the help.

I'd just signed off a Zoom meeting when noises from downstairs alerted me Lillian was back from dropping the boys at school. How odd it was to have a woman I hardly knew in my home. Stranger still that she'd come stumbling from her bedroom this morning in a robe and barefooted, looking oddly sexy. A memory of Bridget dressed the same flashed through my mind. The difference was, Bridget's hair was never out of place, and she wouldn't be caught dead with smudged mascara beneath her eyes. And her bathrobe was always the silken variety—not a cotton number faded from age and too many washings as Lillian's appeared to be. If Lillian was broke it wasn't because she spent an inordinate amount of money on herself.

I typed up my notes from the meeting and took care of a few loose ends before heading downstairs for a second cup of coffee, leaving Rocket asleep beneath my desk. I'd considered putting a Keurig and small fridge in my office for convenience, but not doing so forced me to get up and move around periodically.

As I descended the stairs, I noted scuffling noises coming from the family room. Entering, I spotted several cardboard boxes opened. Some empty and on their sides, others with their flaps jutting up, exposing their contents. Lillian was kneeling on the floor, arranging DVDs on the shelves beneath the television.

"What're you doing?" Stupid question.

Lillian whipped her head around, a tinge of pink staining her cheeks. Her fingers fumbled the DVDs she held, and they spilled onto the hardwood floor.

"Oh, sorry. Was I disturbing you?" She snatched them up and stuck them in line with the others.

Should I be irritated at her for taking liberties with my things or thankful she felt compelled to help? A dichotomy. I didn't like them. Didn't care to weigh my emotions, either. But taking out my lack of social niceties on her wouldn't do either of us any good.

"You're fine." I blew out a breath. "Isn't there something you'd rather be doing than this?" I swept a hand across the chaos in the room. Except it wasn't all chaos. Books lined the upper shelves, and she'd rested the so-called artwork against the walls where they were out of the way—and ready to be hung. Seemed she'd gotten more done in a couple hours than I had in a week, and without benefit of a well-honed calendar.

She pushed up from the floor and fingered a strand of dark hair off her face. The rest of it was twisted up in a clip that should've looked messy and unappealing but didn't. Instead, she appeared fresh and unassuming. "I unpacked all my things yesterday. Thought I'd start on the boys' laundry, but I'm not sure how to run your washer and dryer. I always take my clothes to the laundromat. Can't hardly break those machines—they're bomb-proof."

I hadn't even given her a tour of the upstairs, so she couldn't know where they stashed their dirty clothes—when they didn't leave them on the floor. "Let me show you their rooms." I turned back toward the foyer, expecting she'd follow. And she did. At the top of the stairs, I turned right. There were three large bedrooms and two bathrooms on the east side of the upper floor. My bedroom and office were on the west. I entered the first bedroom and waited for Lillian.

"This is Chase and Matty's." We'd set up the two full-size beds on either side of the room along with a dresser and nightstand. The blankets were rumpled on Chase's and spilling onto the floor of Matty's. It was a bright room with two large windows overlooking the backyard and open shelves to house their books and containers of toys. As expected, there were pieces of clothing cluttering the floor along with toy trucks and a myriad of Legos, K'nex, and ZipLinx.

"This is nice." Lillian hung back at the entrance and eyed the room. "Do they have a laundry basket?"

"You'd think not since they have half their wardrobe on the floor." I crossed to the walk-in closet and threw open the door. "The basket's in here, but as you might guess, it's almost empty. I assume anything on the floor is dirty."

She nodded but didn't say anything. I swore there were wheels turning in her head. She was obviously intelligent but tended toward the quiet side. My dad always said it was the quiet ones you had to watch out for. Of course, Bridget was anything but quiet, and she was a handful, so it didn't hold true.

"The bathroom is here and connected to Daniel's room on the other side." I stepped past her and led the way. His room was every bit as messy as Matty and Chase's, which had me gritting my teeth. Mom had catered to them for so long, they hadn't learned the concept of picking up after themselves. And truth be told, I didn't have the energy to fight it.

"If you could just show me how to work your washer, I'll take care of this."

"I don't want you cleaning up after them, Lillian."

She grinned. "Don't you worry yourself about that."

We went downstairs and through the kitchen to the laundry room on the other side. I grew up with the washer and dryer in the garage. This was just one more ridiculous salute to extravagance with its ceiling-high cabinets, a large folding table, and an ironing board that retracted into the wall. Had to be a woman who designed this space.

I gave Lillian a quick intro to the workings of the washer. "Any questions?"

"It's awfully complicated for what seems like a simple little chore, but I'll figure it out in no time. Don't you worry at all." A wrinkle formed between her eyebrows, and she frowned, which didn't do much to instill confidence. But like she said, it was a simple enough chore.

"I did wanna talk to you about a couple things though, if you have a few minutes." She led the way back into the kitchen and leaned against the sink.

I glanced at my watch. Had twenty minutes before my next meeting. "Okay. What's up?"

She sighed. "First off, I told the boys I wasn't gonna fix them anything they wanted for breakfast, 'cause I could clearly see that's where things go all cattywampus in the mornings. They can all have either eggs or hot cereal, and we're gonna save the waffles and such for the weekends. Are you okay with that?"

Sounded like she was asking for forgiveness rather than permission. "And you didn't get a lot of pushback?"

"None that I can't handle." She folded her arms and started to speak, then clamped her lips like she was holding back.

"What were you going to say?" This would only work if we could communicate.

Blowing out a breath, she looked at me. "The thing of it is, I get the feeling you might could be accommodating them 'cause you feel some guilty about taking them away from their old home and their grandma."

She had me there. It was exactly what I'd been doing. "Very astute."

"I don't have anything to feel a bit guilty over, so they can't hardly use it to get their way."

I chuckled. "Are you sure you don't have some kind of kid-raising degree?"

A smile flirted at the corners of her mouth. "Let's just say my mama never was one to coddle, and maybe that's not a bad thing."

The woman was a puzzle for sure. What had her upbringing been like? I'd made the assumption that everyone in the South had a Mayberry-type experience. But I knew from experience assuming could get a person in trouble. "You said there were a couple things." Couldn't wait to hear what other brainiac idea she'd come up with.

"When we talked last night about taking the boys to and from school, you said something about possibly hiring someone to collect them and watch over them Tuesday through Fridays, since I'm not available and you need the time to work."

I nodded. Where was she going with this?

"When I dropped the boys off this morning, I ran into a real nice lady who lives right close to the library. She brings her girls in all the time. And I got to thinking what if she picked up the boys and brought them to the library after school? They could do their homework right there, and I'd bring them home with me at the end of the day."

"I don't know, Lillian. Seems like there could be some glitches in your plan. First off, how well do you know this woman? And is it even possible for you to have the boys with you while you're working? Wouldn't your boss have something to say about it?"

"I know Meghan real well. Like I said, she's been bringing her girls into the library for a long time. She and her husband, Pete, actually attend our church. I'll be happy to introduce you on Sunday. And as for my boss, she won't care. The more kids that use the library, the better our funding."

"And what about Matty?"

"That's not a problem, Luca. She'll collect him, too. She's happy to do it."

I shook my head. "I don't know. Why would she do this when she doesn't even know them or me?"

Her eyebrows drew together. "It's the Southern way, that's why. We do for others here. I'm not sure what it's like where you came from, but we take pride in our community." She huffed out a breath of air. "Only thing is, I don't think it'll work on Thursdays. I mean the boys can be dropped off, but I don't get off till seven. So, I was thinking that could be your special evening with them. Maybe pick them up at five or so and take them out to pizza or something like that." She smiled like she'd just solved all the world's problems.

"You have it all figured out, don't you?" I wasn't proud of the sarcasm dripping from my mouth, but I'd been duped by a strong-willed woman before. And I wasn't about to be taken in again.

A wrinkle formed between her brows, and her eyes resembled Rocket's when I'd reprimanded him too harshly. "I'm just trying to help, Luca. Isn't that why you hired me?" Made me feel like a heel. "You're gonna have to trust somebody, and since I'm here doing my best, it may as well be me."

I might've underestimated Lillian Murphy. Just didn't know if that was good or bad.

Chapter Nine

Lillian

Looking after three little boys kept me busier than a moth in a mitten, but it didn't take more than a day or two before I began to see nuggets of blessings in the midst of it all. Matty was especially quick with the hugs and sweet talk. He'd be a heartbreaker for sure. Chase bein' the pickle in the middle, needed a little extra attention to know he was seen and heard, and he lapped it up like a kitten to a bowl of cream. Daniel...he was gonna be a challenge, no doubt about it. He carried attitude around like it was his right. But there were glimpses I'd spotted that told me he was softening. Even if I had to peer through a microscope to see them.

Didn't take into account that caring for the three of them would spark some new inspiration for my job. One of my tasks was to create fun and educational activities for the kids in our community. Watching the boys, and what drew their excitement, gave me ideas I wouldn't have thought of otherwise. And although I would've cut out my tongue before telling Luca, his way of charting every little detail was beginning to make sense. It was a whole lot easier to plan out activities if I could foresee the pitfalls and be prepared for them ahead of time.

It was while I was working through such an activity in the back room of the library on Thursday night that Sherrie blew in, face flush and eyes a little wild. It was a mere forty-one hours and counting before she became Mrs. Joshua Cummings. Of course, knowing Sherrie, she might balk at taking Josh's name. And I'd surely cringe if anyone dared to label her by his first. She'd wanna be plain ol' Sherrie Jenkins-Cummings. Boy, was that a mouthful!

She'd told me on the phone earlier there were still a hundred little details that needed tending to, and she was fixing to come apart. Appeared she wasn't kidding, either. "You might wanna breathe, Sherrie."

Hand to her chest, she plopped into a chair and huffed out an exaggerated sigh. "Should've just eloped, Lil. I don't know how you did it, but I'm plumb wore out. Josh has all these activities planned for our honeymoon, but the only thing that sounds good right now is sleeping in till noon every day and ordering room service."

Took me a moment to respond as I waited for the pang of emotion to hit me like it always did when she talked of her wedding. And a honeymoon like the one I was paying for with nothing to show for it but heartache. But it didn't come. No green-eyed monster lurking in the background. No sudden lump rising up in my throat. Nothing.

"What's wrong?" Sherrie reached across and grabbed ahold of my hand. "You okay?"

Now tears bit at the back of my eyes, but they were the joyful variety. "More than okay." I flashed her my biggest smile to prove it. "Was waiting on the pain of regret or disappointment or something. But all I have is a whole lot of happiness for you." *Thank You, Jesus!*

A few tears of her own shimmered in Sherrie's eyes, but whether it was empathy for me or exhaustion, I couldn't say. And this meeting wasn't about me—it was about assuring her she had nothing to panic over.

"Now," I squeezed her hand and straightened my spine, "what's left to get done?"

She dug into her bag and pulled out her phone. "Got me a list right here. You put the favors together?"

"Yes, ma'am, all but the last few." Chocolate chip cookie mix in mason jars was a whole lot more time-consuming than I'd expected. All that measuring and such. But it'd go well with her rustic barn wedding venue, and I thought it was sweet—on two levels.

"You have enough ingredients, or do I need to pick up more of anything?" Wrinkles appeared between her eyebrows, and she tapped a fingernail on the Formica-topped table.

"Hey." I waited until her eyes met mine. "Everything is gonna be just fine." Or was it? Maybe her panic had more to do with *after* the wedding than the event itself. "You ready to share what had you fretting a few weeks ago?"

She slumped back in her chair with a sigh. "It's got nothing to do with marrying Josh. I love him, and I know he's the man God planned for me all along."

I couldn't argue with that, especially since I hadn't even bothered to check in with God before jumping into my own fiasco of a wedding. But that didn't account for the worry in her eyes or the slump of her shoulders.

"Then what has you looking like you just lost your best friend?" Which was never gonna happen.

She kept her gaze focused on her folded hands, like she couldn't look me in the eye. "Ever since I can remember, I wanted to be a lawyer. You know that better than anyone."

Sure did. She shared her big life plan with me before we hit the fifth grade. I thought she was nuttier than a pecan pie. What nine-year-old announces she's gonna be a lawyer so she could defend the underdog? If someone was trying to take that from her, it would be enough to cause the dejection that was etched now in her features.

"You said before that Josh wasn't saying different. He's not trying to guilt you into quitting to start a family?"

"No. If he was, he wouldn't be the man God had for me." She wasn't making a whole lot of sense. Maybe now wasn't the best time to talk about it, but if her marrying Josh was causing such anguish, wouldn't it be better to know before she made vows?

"The thing is, Lil," she lifted her gaze, "I poured a lot of money into getting my degree, not to mention the time and energy it's taken to get this far."

"I know it. I've been right beside you. Studying hard, going after clerking jobs, and doing all the menial tasks needed to be taken seriously." Maybe it hadn't been enough. "Those big mucky mucks you work for aren't trying to ease you out, are they?" How unfair would that be? I surely didn't know what all Sherrie did, but I knew she put everything she had into it. They were blessed to have such a dedicated—

"I wanna quit." The words burst from her on a puff of air, and the minute they were out, she covered her face with her hands and groaned. "Oh, Lil, I have a mountain of school loans, and I've worked so hard to get where I am, and there's no telling how far I could go if I stuck it out."

Quit? "I don't understand. Is someone harassing you? I mean, we see it all the time, and even though things have slowly changed, you're still in a boys' club."

"No. It's not like that. And it's not like I want to quit right now, but when Josh and I start having kids, I don't want to leave it up to someone else to take care of them." She barked out a laugh. "Who would've thought I'd turn out to be the maternal type?"

The pang of envy that was absent when she talked of her wedding and honeymoon came back in full force. Being a mama—now that would be something. "So, what's the problem? Josh doesn't support you staying home with the babies? Is he worried about your school loans?"

"That's not it. The thing is, his mama gave up on her career to raise him and his sister. Then she spent most of their lives blaming them for failing to reach her full potential, as if it was their fault. Can you imagine?"

"So, he's worried you might feel the same?"

She shrugged. "I suppose. It's a kind of PTSD for him. He knows in his heart I'm nothing like her, but his head's having a hard time with it." With a flick of her hand, she dismissed the conversation. "Enough about me. How's it going with Luca and his boys? You gonna bring him to the wedding as your plus-one?"

A laugh burst from me, and I clapped a hand over my mouth—like shutting the barn door before all the horses got out. "You're kidding, right?"

"Well, why not?"

"I'd like to keep as much distance between us as possible, thank you very much. The boys and I are doing just fine, but Luca's a whole other story."

"Why? What happened? You cook for him?"

I snorted. "Not yet. But I did flood the laundry room with a whole bunch of suds. I looked like an idiot." Felt like one, too. "And get this. I came up with what I thought was a brilliant idea to save some of his precious time in the afternoons, and it practically took an act of God to get him to agree. I tell you, there's something off about him."

Sherrie fought back a grin, but it finally took hold. "Don't take this the wrong way, Lil, but you're not the best judge of character. You went into this with some preconceived notions about Luca. Give him a chance." She raised a hand. "And a night out. I'm sure you can find someone to watch the boys. Consider it research into his character. You can learn a lot about a person by the way he dances."

Luca

Could've bowled me over with a feather when Lillian asked if I wanted to attend Josh and Sherrie's wedding with her. Never saw it coming. Of course, she was quick to point out it wasn't a date. She needed a plus-one, and it would give me a chance to meet a lot of people in the community. She thought I should network with lawyers, doctors, and other professionals who might need my services. Consider it no different than attending the Rotary Club or BNI—just better dressed, with a lot of food, and fun music.

I planned to decline—Saturdays were reserved for the boys. Even had the words on the tip of my tongue, but what came out instead was, "Who will watch the kids?" Of course, she had that figured out, too. Already talked to Mrs.

Hutchinson next door just in case I said yes. Lillian was a strange mixture of timidity and boldness.

When she told me, as maid of honor, she'd need to be at the church early and would take her own car, I breathed a little easier. It truly wasn't a date. I had no time or inclination to get caught up in an emotional entanglement, especially with a woman who I now depended on to care for the boys. Business and pleasure didn't mix. First rule of a successful endeavor.

Even as I walked into the church, I was asking myself why I agreed to attend the wedding. I could pretend it was because Josh and Sherrie were becoming friends. Weak. I could agree with Lillian that networking had merit, but I'd never stooped to using a wedding to that end. If I was going to be brutally honest, I'd have to admit I was curious about Lillian. The woman lived in my house, coaxed the boys to behave in ways I never had, but wasn't competent to do laundry without step-by-step instructions—which I made sure she had *after* the debacle of the other day.

One glance around the attendees had me wanting to slink right back out. Here I was dressed in a suit—tie and all—when almost everyone else appeared as if they were going to a hoedown. Most of the men wore jeans and boots, while the women's attire ran the full gamut between casual and formal. It could be I was out of touch with reality since the last wedding I'd attended was my own.

Nodding politely, I practiced a smile on the couple that sat on the other end of the pew as I slipped into it. I should just go. Would rather be horsing around with the boys in the swimming pool, maybe grill some hot dogs for dinner—or rather supper. A root canal would be more comfortable than being here.

I finally decided to make my escape when piano music started. I turned to see a little girl dressed in satin walking down the aisle, a basket of rose petals in one hand. Could hardly plow past her, so I swallowed a groan and stayed put. I'd suffer through the vows and head for home while everyone else went to the reception. Having a plan made breathing easier as the bridal party followed the flower girl.

Until I spotted Lillian. To say she cleaned up nice would be an understatement. If it wasn't for her deep blue eyes and the massive amount of dark hair framing her face, I might not have recognized her. The mid-length teal dress fit her like a glove, and if I wasn't mistaken, she'd grown three inches since she left the house that morning in a rush. A quick glance at her feet proved my assessment to be true. It'd be easier to walk on stilts than the heels she was wearing. Of course, stilts wouldn't show off her legs nearly as well.

I spent the entire ceremony giving myself a talking to. Had no business checking out Lillian's legs, or any other part of her. She was an employee. That was it. It was all she could ever be, so even entertaining anything else was foolish and doomed to end badly.

It was with this thought running through my mind that I headed for the side door the moment the wedding party left the church. The heat of the sun felt more like summer than spring, which made my escape even more appealing. Should pick up some ice cream on the way home, and maybe—

"Luca!"

I didn't have to look to know it was Lillian. *Pretend you don't hear her. Keep moving.* Instead, I stopped and turned to face her. Like she was a magnet, and my brain was made of metal.

Staring toward the sun, she tented her eyes with one hand and teetered her way toward me. "I was hopin' you'd give me a ride to the reception." She wrinkled her nose and glanced down for a brief moment. "Don't think I can drive in these silly shoes." Shocker.

I grappled for any excuse besides the truth. Slinking away like an anti-social clod reminded me too much of high school. There was a reason I'd been voted Class Nerd. "What about your car?"

She shrugged. "We come back this way to get to your house. I'll pick it up after the reception. One of the helpers took all our things from the back room and hauled them to the reception venue, so I'm kind of stuck with these."

A little honesty was called for under the circumstances. "The thing is, I wasn't planning on staying to the end, and I know you've got bridesmaids' duties"—I sliced a hand toward her—"or whatever you call them."

She flashed a grin and shrugged. "That's fine. I'm sure I can find someone to get me back here at the end of the night." She hitched a thumb behind her.

"They're all heading that way now, so if I can just get a ride over, I'd really appreciate it."

It didn't appear I had a choice unless I wanted to tell her the whole truth—which I wasn't about to do. "No problem. I'm parked on this side of the lot." I had to slow my steps to match her unstable ones, and after walking ten feet or so, I took ahold of her elbow. "You're going to break your neck on those things."

A chuckle filled the air along with a mockingbird's song. "Don't I know it. I told Sherrie flats were in, but she had her heart set on a certain look."

"Flats?"

"Shoes. As in no heels."

Didn't know a thing about fashion, and I was all about comfort, but had to admit there was something sexy about a woman in heels. Or at the very least, Lillian in heels. Which was why I'd have been a lot smarter running the other way.

Had no idea where the reception was being held, but I didn't need to with Lillian as my passenger. First couple of minutes, I had to focus on her directions since it seemed we needed to weave through town before reaching the main road out toward Grace Family Farms. I switched on the air conditioner, although I would've preferred fresh air. Even I was aware a woman dressed like Lillian wouldn't want her hair to be messed up by the wind.

"Thanks for going outta your way to give me a ride." Lillian picked at something on her dress before smoothing it out.

"I was going there anyway, so it's not out of my way at all." The lie slid a little too easily off my tongue. Never was comfortable with subterfuge, even when it was necessary. Ironic, considering the half-lie I was living.

She huffed out a laugh. "Truly? 'Cause it looked to me you were ditching the whole thing." Humor trickled through her words.

I shot a brief glance her way. "What makes you say that?"

A sigh. "If I wasn't obligated by friendship and duty, it's what I'd be doing right now." Could be she was a kindred spirit. Hadn't had a lot of that in my life.

"You and Sherrie go back a long way?" Safer topic.

"Kindergarten." A soft laugh filled the car. "I'll never forget the day she marched up to me and said, 'I'm Sherrie Jenkins, and you're Lillian Murphy. We're gonna be best friends, okay?' And we have been ever since. Like Mutt 'n' Jeff. She's all class and self-assuredness, and I'm...well, I suppose I'm not." She said it matter-of-factly, not like she was angling for a compliment.

"The world would be a dull place if we were all the same, don't you think?"

She brushed something off the skirt of her dress. "I suppose. And there's nothing wrong with settling into a life of humdrum when stacked up against foolish choices. And I've made more than my fair share."

Her and me both.

It was with relief I parked my car in the lot of Grace Family Farms and put some distance between the two of us. Being enclosed in such an intimate space with Lillian for much longer would've had me pouring out my own sad story—one I'd left Illinois to get away from. Why take a chance on resurrecting it here in Tennessee? Nothing good could come of it.

CHAPTER TEN

Lillian

Of all the tasks expected of me as Sherrie's maid-of-honor, the most trying was standing up in front of everyone to give a toast. I didn't care much for being the center of attention, unless it was a passel of kids I was reading to. As I rose from my chair with a glass of champagne in hand, palms sweaty and heart racing, I glanced at Luca who was sitting at a table with a couple of Josh's single friends. There was something both intimate and calming in his dark eyes, and it settled my heart some.

Then I turned to Sherrie who sat at my left with her new husband. "You've been my best friend from the time we were knee-high to a grasshopper, as my granddaddy would say. We grew up sharing our greatest dreams and our biggest disappointments." I couldn't help but think of last summer when she was fixing to toast my soon-to-be-aborted wedding, and I had to swallow down a lump of emotion. "You're the sister I never had, and for that I'll always be grateful." I took hold of the hand she reached out to me and shifted so my focus included Josh. "There was no doubt from the first date y'all had, you were meant to be together. And I'm sure everyone here would agree. May the Lord abundantly bless your marriage; may you grow to love each other more every day; may you have wisdom, health, and the children of your dreams." I raised my glass. "To the bride and groom."

A shout of agreement nearly lifted the timber off the barn walls.

The catering staff made short work of cleaning up the dishes and clearing the dance floor. Sherrie and Josh had hired a D.J. to play music, and he switched from classic instrumental to Ed Sheeran's "Perfect" and called the newlywed couple to their first dance. It'd been Sherrie's favorite song since it came out, and I'd known she chose it for this reason. Still, the sweetness of the lyrics drew up from me a kernel of loneliness.

Couldn't help but notice a few of Josh's friends (mostly from the singles' table) eyeing me like they'd never seen me before. It was enough to go to a girl's head, except I had me a feeling it had more to do with the dress and less to do with me. These were the same boys I grew up with, and they hadn't given me the time of day before today. Could be the reason right there women spent a small fortune on flattering clothing and a boatload of makeup. Problem was, a person could only hide behind the facade for so long. Come morning, Cinderella's dress would once again turn to rags, and the magical coach and steed nothing more than a pumpkin and mice.

"That was a beautiful toast." Luca's deep voice from behind sent a shiver of awareness up my spine.

Shifting, I offered a smile. "I'm just happy I didn't swoon like some kind of Victorian maiden."

A short laugh erupted from him. "You don't strike me as the swooning type." What he saw as strength was a whole lot of bravado.

But when I glanced up to tell him so, the nearness of him snatched the breath clear from my lungs. Caught the dark stubble on his chin, the deep cleft of his dimples, and of all things to notice, the whiff of laundry soap that would forever remind me of the suds spewing from his fancy washing machine only a couple days before. Swooning was exactly what I was doing right then. A combination of attraction and the music playing on my senses.

I put some distance between us and drew in a deep breath. I needed to clear my head. He was my employer. That was it. If falling for Billy was foolish, then thinking there could ever be anything between Luca and me was downright looney. And it wasn't only my heart I needed to think of—it was those of his three little boys.

"Are you okay?" Luca reached out as if to take hold of my arm.

Hands raised, I backed away even more. "Just remembered I have…" What? *Think girl.* "I have to be sure the caterer was paid." The lie landed like a wet cow pie, but I walked away like I owned it. If he thought I was attracted to him, it would ruin everything. I'd just gotten my budget figured out. As long as this job worked out, I'd have that blasted wedding paid off by this time next year. Then I'd start working on my school loans. I couldn't forever let debt call the shots.

"Your boyfriend is finer than frog hairs." Chloe latched onto my arm and walked alongside me. The girl might've been Sherrie's cousin—which was the only reason she was a bridesmaid—but they were nothing alike.

"He's not my boyfriend." The words were no sooner outta my mouth, I wanted to shove them right back in. Had nothing to do with me wishing otherwise because I didn't. Had a whole lot to do with knowing I'd just unleashed a man-hungry predator onto a weaker prey. Luca didn't stand a chance against Chloe's prowess. The girl could make a living teaching gals how to reel a man in. It was the holding onto him she needed to work on.

"You're kiddin' me." She spun me around so we were facing—and nearly had me toppling over. "Sherrie says you're living in the man's house. It don't get any easier than that, Lil. You got the inside track here."

A slight twist of my arm, and I was free of her claws. Had she no shame? "I'm workin' for him, Chloe." A warning to keep clear of him danced on the end of my tongue, but I wasn't Luca's keeper. He was a big boy, although I hadn't known a man yet who could resist her when she turned on the charm.

"So?" Her penciled eyebrows arched high enough to disappear behind her blond, lacquered bangs. With those baby blue eyes, high cheekbones, and model-thin frame, she didn't need to resort to trickery to get herself a man.

"So, I need this job."

Her mouth tilted. "Guess that means the path is clear for the takin' then." As if it would've made a whit of difference to her if I'd said different.

A dull thud hit my belly. "Guess it does." Turning away, I headed for the ladies' room where I wouldn't have to watch The Chloe Show. Never was a fan of reality TV.

"Lillian?"

I spun back around. Nathan Wells slid to a stop in front of me, a cocky grin on his bearded face. His eyes seemed to dance, or maybe he'd been drinking, a fact that revealed itself as he leaned closer like he was fixing to share a secret. Hand against his chest, I pushed him far enough away to escape beer fumes.

"Thought you might wanna dance." He wriggled his eyebrows as if the word dance was a euphemism for something else entirely. "Don't recall you ever looked this good in high school."

This is what came of dressing up. "Appreciate the invite, Nathan, but—"

"No buts." He clamped onto my wrist with the speed of a striking snake and grinned like the devil himself. "You ain't lived until you've been spun around the dance floor by me. Ask anyone."

Cloaked in a tight dress and stilettos might've put me at a disadvantage, but I had a few moves of my own—the self-defense variety. Was fixing to use one on Nathan's overgrown ego when I spotted Chloe leading Luca to the dance floor like a lamb to the slaughter. Although it didn't appear he was struggling to break free, so maybe she was his type. Made a whole lot more sense than him going for someone like me.

"You comin', Lil?" He raised his free hand above his head and swiveled his hips. "Let's get our groove on."

It was enough to make a girl vomit. But why let the hours spent looking like I did go to waste? Might as well have a little fun. Let Luca see I was more than a librarian and glorified nanny.

Luca

Couldn't help but watch Lillian's less-than-graceful escape through the hoard of rowdy guests. What was that all about? One minute she was laughing and the next...never could figure out women, not that I had a lot of experience. And what I did have proved I was no match for the fairer sex. They were the definition of a conundrum.

Best thing to do was head home. Lillian said she could get a ride, and from the way the men in this group were ogling her, they'd be fighting for the honor. Still, I felt responsible. What if her escort was drunk? It didn't appear she could take on a hissing kitten let alone a drunken lech.

Lillian had my mind so wrapped up, a stunning blond was crowding my personal space before I had a chance to make an escape.

"Hey, there. I'm Sherrie's cousin, Chloe. As one of the bridesmaids, it's my job to be sure every guest is havin' a good time."

Didn't know if it was the confident way she approached me, the too-perfect appearance, or the smell of her perfume, but something about her reminded me of Bridget. Heard the people in Tennessee were friendly, but she had an agenda. "Nice to meet you, Chloe. I'm Luca."

"Saw you standing here all by your lonesome and thought I'd come over and introduce myself. You here alone?" Her blue eyes were framed by lashes so thick they couldn't be real.

Despite the towering ceilings, the room was stuffy—too many bodies and not enough air. Tugging my tie loose, I slid my gaze across the dance floor past couples whooping it up and caught sight of Lillian. Even from this distance, I could see the scowl she threw at the guy holding onto her arm.

"Or did I see you come in with Lillian?" She did a half-turn, her hip brushing up against mine. "I believe that's her over there with Nathan. Best dancer in all of Middle Tennessee. You like to dance?"

"Not especially." Wasn't a fan of flirting, either.

"Maybe you haven't had the right partner." She slipped her hand into mine and flashed a smile so white, it was enough to blind a person. "Give me a whirl, and I promise you'll enjoy it." Inexperienced or not, I knew a double entendre when I heard it. Couldn't miss the suggestive wriggle of her eyebrows, either. "One dance. Promise I don't bite."

I was immune to whatever power this woman thought she had over me. I'd been burned by the best. I also knew the quickest way out of this situation was through it. "You got it, Chloe. One dance." And then I was heading home. Might even get there before the boys fell asleep.

She tugged me toward the crowded dance floor, her hips suggestively moving to the beat of "Let's Dance" as David Bowie's voice boomed from the sound system. I glanced to where I'd last seen Lillian—and now she was heading my way. That Nathan character was as persistent as Chloe or I'd misread the situation.

The moment Chloe faced me, David Bowie faded away. In his place, a slow drum beat and guitar queued up Thomas Rhett's "Blessed" as if she'd planned it. Stood awkward as a kid at his first dance while Chloe's eyes glowed like she'd just won the first round. Nothing to do but concede and allow her to melt into my embrace. Couldn't help but think of the last time I'd held Bridget—the same cloying perfume and artful moves. What was it about me that drew manipulative women? Did I have a stamp on my forehead that said, "Easy Target"?

As my dance partner nuzzled my shoulder, I glanced above her head. Only reason I was looking for Lillian was so when the dance was over, I could let her know I was leaving. No doubt it was too early for her, but I wanted to be sure she had a ride home.

I spotted her at the edge of the dance floor, struggling to get loose of Nathan's embrace. Elbows raised to his chest, she pushed back, but he held tight. Her lips were pressed together like she was holding in a scream, but it was anger that flashed in her eyes—not fear. Maybe she could wrestle a kitten after all, but it made me sick to think anyone would take advantage. Not a woman using the art of manipulation and certainly not a man forcing himself on someone.

"Excuse me," I mumbled, letting loose of Chloe. Had to weave through several couples, and by the time I'd reached Lillian, she'd freed herself from Nathan's grasp, but he didn't appear to be giving up. He was grabbing at her and she was slapping him down.

"You okay, Lillian?" I maneuvered myself between them, Nathan at my back and Lillian almost as close as Chloe had been only seconds before.

"Who d'you think you are?" Nathan's slurred words behind me had me gritting my teeth. He was just lucky I didn't take a punch at him.

It appeared passivity didn't work, and I was shoved from behind, knocking into Lillian, who stumbled. Couldn't get a hold of her flailing arms, and she landed flat on her back. Ignoring the drunken tirade from behind, I dropped onto my knees next to her, both to be sure she wasn't hurt and protect her from the guests who were crowding in.

Grimacing, Lillian struggled to sit up.

"You shouldn't move."

"I'm fine." One of her shoes had slipped off, and her face was beet red as she yanked off the other. "Please, just help me up." Her eyes pleaded with mine. "This is embarrassing."

"Lillian!" Sherrie shoved through the crowd. "Oh, my word, girl." She dropped down next to me, her wedding gown billowing around the three of us, and glanced at the crowd. "Someone get Michael."

"I don't need a doctor."

"You don't know that." Sherrie tugged Lillian's dress down to cover her knees and looked at me. "What happened?"

"Her dance partner got a little rough, and I tried to step in. He didn't appreciate it. Shoved me, and I accidentally knocked Lillian down." Fact was, if I'd kept my nose out of her business, none of this would've happened. "I'm sorry, Lillian."

Her eyes teared up. "For what? It's not your fault Nathan's mama never taught him the meaning of the word no."

"Nathan?" Sherrie growled, her gaze darting above us as if searching for the offensive man. "Y'all find Nathan and make sure he doesn't leave. The fool will probably drive off and get someone killed." A few men assured Sherrie they'd take care of it as Josh showed up.

"What in the world...Lil, are you hurt?"

She groaned. "Just my pride. Tell them to let me up, will you? There's nothing broken." She glared at the guests still hovering over her. "And I'm sure y'all can find something more interesting to do than gawk at me."

Sherrie shooed the guests. "Go on, now. Y'all heard Lillian. Give the girl some air."

"Michael's here." Josh stepped aside to make room for a tall, lanky man. Couldn't have been any older than me, but he took charge like he'd been born to it.

"You hurt anywhere?" He crouched down beside me and took hold of her wrist to check her pulse.

She groaned. "No, sir, I'm right as rain. And if y'all would let me get up, I'd be a whole lot more comfortable."

Michael chuckled. "Don't bite the hand that feeds you, Lil. I let you up without checking that nothing's broken, you could come back and sue me."

She scowled but allowed him to poke and prod until he was satisfied.

"If anything changes," Michael told her, "you get yourself to the emergency room, you hear?"

"I'd worry more about Nathan if I was you," she said as Michael and I helped her stand. "He's got a bad case of being obnoxious while drinking. Could prove fatal if he's not careful."

"Don't you give it another thought," Sherrie said. "I'm fixin' to give him a talking to he won't soon forget." She marched off like she was going to do just that.

I touched Lillian's arm. "You want me to take you home?"

Face flush, she swiped at the wrinkles in her dress. "I can't leave yet, Luca. But you should go on. I'll be fine."

Before I could protest, she snatched her shoes from the floor, spun around, and got lost in the dispersing crowd of onlookers. These were her people, and she sure didn't need me coming to her rescue. Still, it was my fault she'd landed on her backside, and the least I could do was see she got home safely. Even if I had to hide away in the corner until she was ready to go.

Chapter Eleven

Flashes of the night before went off in my mind the moment I pried my eyes open. Didn't matter the sun was peeking through my windows proving it would be a glorious day, I had a bad case of the gloomies. My face grew hot as I pictured myself sprawled across the floor with a crowd of witnesses to my humiliation. Most especially, Luca.

Burying my face with the sheet, I groaned. Another one let loose as I climbed out of bed. Muscles I didn't even know I had were pitching a hissy fit over being slammed against the floor last night. It would be so easy to sink back onto the mattress and use being sore as an excuse to shirk my responsibilities. But was clear as sin on the drive home with Luca after the wedding that he was toting a load of guilt over the whole thing, and I wasn't gonna add to it.

What I needed was to cool off, loosen my muscles, and get my head in the right place. I'd start with a few laps in the pool followed by some time in the Word. Nothing I'd go through could hold a candle to what the Lord allowed the Old Testament heroes. And if that wasn't enough to remind me of my blessings, a reading through the book of Job certainly would put things into perspective.

After slipping into my swimsuit, I stepped out the French doors from my bedroom onto the patio. Blessing number one—a front row view of the rising sun. There were fluffy clouds a plenty to paint a spectacular blend of orange and vibrant pink. The air was warm and moist, and I caught a whiff of white yarrow, reminding me summer was knocking at the door—blessing number two. A swimming pool smack in my backyard (even if it was a temporary one) was number three. A safe place to live. Daniel, Chase, and Matty. Luca's protection of me last night, even if I didn't need it. If I put my mind to it, I could count to a hundred before I finished ten laps.

By the time I was heading back inside to shower and dress for church, the gloomies had drifted away like dandelion dust—*Thank You, Jesus*—and I was ready to attend to my chores. I'd promised the boys they'd get something a sight better than cereal on Sundays. Might not know my way around the stove any more than I did a backhoe, but I'd found a pancake batter recipe quick as a lick on my phone. Flour, baking powder, sugar, eggs, vanilla, and salt. Even I couldn't make a mess from such a simple collection of ingredients.

The house was quiet as a whisper as I moved down the hallway on bare feet. I'd just get breakfast started before waking the troops. With a little luck, and a whole lot of prayer, we'd get to church with time to spare. Good thing it wasn't my week to teach Sunday School. What with learning the boys' schedules, working at the library, and the last-minute tasks for Sherrie's wedding, there was little time left to sleep, let alone prepare the lesson.

My feet braked when I stepped into the kitchen, like they had a life of their own, and my heart did a little flip. Luca stood at the stove tending to a perfect row of pancakes on the griddle. His dark, wavy hair was damp, face clean-shaven. How could his plain, white t-shirt and low-slung sweats look a sight better than the suit he'd worn at the wedding? Last thing I wanted was to find him attractive. Liked it better when he came across as stuffy and boring.

"Morning."

My gaze jumped from his wide chest to eyes that held a hint of amusement. Just when I had my embarrassment under control, something else came along to trip me up. "Hey."

"I saw you swimming, so I'm guessing you're feeling okay this morning. Any soreness?"

"A little." I fought the urge to run off like a scared little rabbit. Instead, I crossed to the cupboard to collect what was needed to set the table. "I was planning on taking care of breakfast today. Guess I'm gonna have to get an earlier start to beat you to it." Made it a lot easier when I didn't have to look at him.

"Got something else you can do for me, if you don't mind." He tucked the spatula under a pancake and flipped it.

"Oh?"

"You have any plans for tomorrow?"

"Other than taking the boys to and from school?"

A smile tugged at his lips. "Yeah, other than that? I was hoping you'd hang out here. I've got some furniture being delivered, but I need to be in Nashville. I know it's your only day off, so—"

"No, that's fine." For just a heartbeat, I thought he was going to ask me to do something *with* him, not *for* him. "I don't mind. Besides, that's what you're paying me for."

He nodded. "Thanks. The sales lady helped me pick some pieces out, but I don't have any idea where everything should go. This place could use a woman's touch."

Talk about the blind leading the blind. I'd have expected him to ask me to go frog gigging before that.

"What's with the face?"

I set the stack of plates on the table. "Just so you know, Daniel could probably give you better decorating advice than me." Although even I could see his family room would be a good fit for a monastery.

He stacked four pancakes onto the spatula and tucked them into the oven. "I don't know about that. You unpacked what was left of the boxes. Didn't need any direction for that."

Throwing him a grin, I shrugged. "It's kind of what I do every day. But you won't catch me furnishing the library."

"Still, I'd appreciate the help if you're willing."

Sure as the sun rises in the morning, there wouldn't be a lack of women willing to give him a hand—like Chloe the night before. Bet she'd jump at the chance to arrange Luca's furniture—or anything else he might need arranged.

I slid a pile of napkins toward me and focused on folding them just so. "What'd you think of Chloe?" Kept my tone casual as a Sunday morning. Just making conversation. "Did you know she's Sherrie's cousin?"

"So she said." A low sizzle accompanied his words as he poured more batter onto the griddle.

I rounded the table, placing a napkin and fork to the left of each plate, but kept an eye on him to gauge his reaction. "Voted most popular in high school."

A muscle jumped in his jaw, like he was clenching his teeth. Maybe I was pushing my nose in where it didn't rightly belong. Just didn't want him being taken in by the likes of Chloe. She left a trail of broken hearts clear across Bedford County and into Rutherford. Wouldn't surprise me one little bit if there weren't a few in Nashville, too.

"Rather not rehash last night, if you don't mind. Feel bad enough as it is." He turned and dropped the empty batter bowl into the sink. Braced his hands on the edge, the muscles in his shoulders flexing, and hung his head. "Can't apologize enough for knocking you down, Lillian. I'm just grateful you weren't hurt."

So he said about a hundred times on the drive home last night. Wouldn't even let me stop at the church to get my car. "It was Nathan who knocked me down, Luca." Which is what I'd told him every time he apologized, but it wasn't sinking in. Maybe I should just tell him the whole truth—it was as much my fault as Nathan's. I would've never gotten myself into that pickle if I hadn't been trying to show off a little. Just one more example of me not thinking things through before jumping into a whole mess of nettles.

But it wasn't on him that I acted like a fool, and if it cost me a bit of pride, so be it. "The thing is, when I saw you with Chloe last night—"

He turned to face me, hands held up. "Stop right there. You don't need to warn me about her." His face was flushed. Was he blushing? "I might not be an expert when it comes to women, but her type?" He cocked an eyebrow. "Let's just say I'm well-versed in the art of manipulation."

Interesting. Was he talking about the boys' mama? First he'd ever mentioned her. He'd left the door wide open, and I was itching to dive in. "You never did say what happened—" Rocket came barreling into the kitchen, dancing between me and Luca. Wherever he was, Daniel was sure to follow, which put an end to the questions just waiting for a place to land.

There was nothing more alluring to me than a mystery, and Luca was surely that. And more.

Had I known walking into church with Luca and his boys would turn some heads, I would've thought to go in alone—and maybe sat in a back pew where I could blend in. It didn't take much to get tongues wagging like a roomful of happy dogs, and I had me a feeling there'd be more than a few ready to spread gossip. Once it got around that I was living at his house, it'd fuel most every imagination. But apart from standing up at the altar and declaring the truth, there wasn't anything I could do. Unless I told Elsie Chambers. The woman could spread the word faster than fiberoptic Internet.

Matty sat next to me in the pew and whispered, "Why's that lady over there staring at us?" He started to point at Elsie, but I took hold of his hand.

"Pay her no mind." Could hardly tell him she was probably wondering what the Sam Hill was going on between Luca and me. It was sure to be a disappointment to the romantics in the congregation that there was nothing here to get excited about. Jilted Lillian hadn't found herself another beau—just another job.

But what if I had? The random thought popped into my head, and I ruminated on it during the organ interlude. I had Matty snuggled up on one side of me and Chase on the other like I was their mama. Brought a rush of pleasure that was immediately dashed by cold reality. Thinking this was anything more than what I signed up for would lead to nothing but heartache. I wasn't willing to go down that well-worn road again, so I flipped open my Bible and attended to the service. If only I could ignore Matty's warm little body leaning against my side.

After church service ended, I collected my car from the lot and headed back to the house where Luca was already pulling out the fixings for sandwiches. I slipped down the hall to my bedroom and changed into shorts and a t-shirt before joining him. The boys were itching to go swimming, so they were hounding him to hurry it up. It didn't seem to bother him any, but their nagging at him plumb drove me crazy.

I snatched up a dishrag and wiped up crumbs left on the counter this morning. "Instead of fussin' at your daddy, why don't y'all help out? Daniel, get some glasses from the cupboard and fill 'em with ice. Chase, rustle up some plates and napkins while Matty collects the pitcher of sweet tea and takes it out back. It's too nice a day to be inside."

As the boys hustled, Luca threw me a smile. "You've definitely got skills. Too bad they don't include laundry."

Without thinking, I lobbed the rag across the island. It smacked him on the forehead and dropped onto the sandwich fixings. I snickered along with the boys.

With a chuckle, he set it aside. "You never did tell me how it's possible a woman your age doesn't know how to run a washing machine."

I slid the griddle into the lower cabinet. "It's just been a minute. Sherrie and I split up the chores—she did the laundry, and I did the cleaning. When I lived at home, we had us a basic machine, not some futuristic monstrosity." *If he thinks I'm incompetent with the wash, wait until he gets a taste of my cooking.*

As we gathered around the patio table, Luca set out the platter of sandwiches while I passed around a bowl of Fritos and another of watermelon. The sun was warm on my back, and the air held the scent of summer. A mockingbird sat high in an old cottonwood tree in the corner of the yard singing his heart out for a mate. The boys were getting along for once—no snide remarks or putdowns. Luca was laughing at something Chase said, his dark eyes sparkling with mischief. Had me a feeling this was a moment I didn't want to forget.

"Excuse me a sec." The legs of my chair scraped against the concrete as I scooted it back.

"Everything okay?" Luca's voice followed me across the patio as I slipped into my room.

I'd stashed my box of art supplies in the walk-in closet, and I dug through it until I came up with a small sketch pad and charcoal pencils. Only thing Mama thought was more foolish than me getting a degree in library science was me going after one in art. But that didn't lessen my love of drawing, even if no one except me would appreciate the finished product. I had me four new subjects sitting outside, and I wasn't going to let them go to waste.

When I stepped back outside, Rocket was waiting for me. It was kind of hard to not fall for his silly doggy grin, even if he was a big oaf half the time. "You wanna be one of my subjects, too, boy?" He made five. I ruffled his ears and padded back to the table, Rocket close behind.

"What'cha got there?" Chase pointed to the supplies I was carrying.

"I'm gonna draw y'all." I dropped back into my chair, and Rocket rested his chin on the arm of it. He really was very sweet.

Daniel squinted at me. "Why?"

Wasn't about to share a children's book that'd never see the light of day. I tended to stumble on all kinds of ways to humiliate myself without offering up more. "I like to draw, is all. It's a perfect day, so why not?"

Luca wiped his mouth with a napkin. "Didn't know you were an artist."

A snort broke free before I could stop it. "I'm not an artist, believe me. I'm a dabbler."

"What's a dabbler?" Matty popped a Frito into his mouth.

"Another word for a hobbyist." I pushed my full plate aside. Drawing would fill me up just fine. "You know what a hobby is, don't you? I'm sure your daddy has one or two." I glanced at Luca who was frowning. Surely, he played golf, or worked with wood, or... "Don't you?"

He cleared his throat. "Not a lot of time what with raising the boys and working." He shifted his gaze to Matty. "You know how Grandpa likes to putter in his garden and Grandma likes to knit? Those are hobbies. Things we do for fun."

Chase wrinkled his nose. "You mean you don't have time for fun?"

Daniel snickered. "We're Dad's hobby." He shook his head and popped the last bite into his mouth. "Done. Can I go swimming now?"

"I'm done, too." Matty dropped his half-eaten sandwich onto his plate and jumped up.

After the boys ran inside to change into their swim trunks, I set the sketchpad aside. "Everyone needs to relax now and then. Maybe now that I'm here to help, you can find time to do something for yourself."

He tossed the napkin onto his empty plate. At least he ate everything. "Yeah? Like what?" His gaze was piercing, and I slid the pad back in place, so I had somewhere besides his chiseled features to focus my eyes.

"I don't know. Are the boys into any sports? You could volunteer to coach them."

A chuckle slid across the space. "Can't say the coaches I've seen seem all that relaxed when they're sprinting up and down the field, screaming instructions at the kids. Perfect setup for a heart attack." Point taken.

"Wasn't there anything you liked to do when you were a kid? Model cars or playing ball?" I couldn't imagine a person not having an outlet—creative or otherwise. "Maybe photography or gardening, like your dad."

He folded his arms onto the table. "It's a season, Lillian. Doesn't the Bible say something about a time for every season?"

"Ecclesiastes," I mumbled. Not the most uplifting book. "This so-called season of yours," I let my gaze rest on his, "did it start when you lost your wife?" Or maybe *lost* wasn't the right word to describe it. Did they get divorced? And if so, why didn't she have visitation? Maybe she died, or—

"I lost my wife long before Daniel was even born." He pushed his chair back and rose. "Better get the food inside or Rocket'll be table-surfing." He stacked plates with the same efficiency that he did everything—including dismissing me.

CHAPTER TWELVE

Lillian

If I gained nothing else from my master's degree, I was a whiz at research. I had me quite a collection of easy recipes, but until now, I hadn't had a spare moment to dig through them, let alone put together a grocery list. Luca had been generous with pitching in, since I'd been juggling Sherrie's wedding along with learning the ins and outs of the boys' schedules and such. But when he walked out the door that morning, I was on my own. Somehow, between the furniture delivery and collecting the boys from school, I'd need to get myself to Kroger's and pick up supplies for the week. Could hardly admit to him I didn't know the difference between a scallion and a shallot. Seemed like every meal required research appropriate to a dissertation.

Hadn't been back from dropping the boys at school ten minutes when a furniture truck pulled into the driveway, its squealing breaks putting Rocket into quite a lather. His raucous barking fired a shot of adrenaline through me.

"It's okay," I assured him as we moved together to the front door. He must've taken me at my word, because he allowed the strange man into the house with nothing more than a sniff and a tail-wagging welcome. That was a tad concerning.

"Where d'you want the stuff, Miss Giordano?" The burly man ruffled Rocket's ear and peered into the family room. "My guys are unloading now."

"I'm not Mrs. Giordano. Just the…" What? "Nanny," I finally managed. "Mr. Giordano purchased everything on his own, so I'm not even sure what all you have."

He flipped through the paperwork attached to a clipboard. "Well, let's see. Maggie broke things down by room here on the order form." He scratched his chin. "Says here we got two recliners, an end table, and a console that goes in the family room." He flipped another page. "Then we have an upholstered chair, another end table, a floor lamp, and a couple bookcases that go in Lillian's room." He shot me a look.

That didn't make any sense. "You sure it doesn't say Luca's room?" I grabbed hold of the clipboard and tilted it so I could see.

He pointed with a beefy finger. "Nope. Say's Lillian, clear as can be. Might not be the sharpest knife in the drawer, but I can read. You don't gotta Lillian here?"

Frowning, I sighed. "I'm Lillian. But why—"

"I'm just the delivery guy." He turned away and Rocket escorted him out the door. "You figure out where you want the stuff, and we'll put it there," he threw over his shoulder. "Get it wrong, and I'm sure Mr. Giordano will fix it."

I nabbed Rocket's collar before he could take off and put him in the backyard. I'd just reopened the front door when two more men came up the porch, one on each end of a large, leather recliner. They maneuvered it into the family room, set it on the floor and stared at me.

"Well. Where does she go?"

I wasn't lying when I told Luca Daniel would be better at figuring this stuff out. "Just stick it over there." I waved a hand on the far side of the sectional. "You can put the other on this end with the side table, and the console can go along the back of the couch."

The taller of the two swiped a hand across his sweaty brow. "And the rest of the stuff?"

I waved him to follow me down the hall to my bedroom. Why Luca would go to the expense to furnish it made no sense, but I'd get myself a copy of the order form so he'd at least understand I wasn't taking liberties.

When the burly man carried the chair in, I had me a feeling it wasn't a mistake after all. The upholstery was cream with variegated pink blooms and nail head trim. No man would be caught dead with that pattern in his room. What followed were two tall bookcases and a matching end table. Maybe he saw the mess of books I had stacked against the wall and took pity on me. But the chair? That was something else altogether. Of course, none of it was *mine*. He was fixing up the rooms, and he must've figured the one I was using needed more than my dismal bedroom set.

Once the men were gone, I slipped back into my bedroom and stared at the bookcases. I didn't dare fill them until I was sure they were meant to be in here. How embarrassing it would be if Luca said they belonged in his bedroom, or maybe one in each of the boys' rooms. Then I'd have to unload them while he watched with a pitying gaze. Instead, I sunk into the chair and sighed. What a perfect place to curl up with a book.

No time to daydream. It was a blessing the delivery was early because it would take me an obscenely long time to buy the groceries on my list. The only aisles I was familiar with were the frozen foods section and the produce. Limited produce, at that. I could whip up a good salad, but anything that required more preparation than a paring knife was beyond my limited capabilities.

Had me just enough time to unload the grocery bags before the kids needed to be picked up. I was fixin' to go out when I spotted Rocket with his nose pressed against the patio door. He was more pathetic than a one-eyed cat, and it pricked my heart. Didn't matter that he was used to being alone, I just couldn't bring myself to walk out on him.

I opened the French door and stepped back. "You wanna come with me?" He bounded in and spun in circles like he understood what I'd said. "That's fine then. Just try and keep the shedding and window slobbering down to a minimum, you hear?"

Rocket pranced to my car and didn't hesitate to hop into the back seat the minute I opened the door. His seventy-plus body wasn't gonna leave a whole lot of room for Matty with his booster seat and Chase, but I had me a feeling they wouldn't mind.

There was only a minor skirmish when I reminded Daniel he had to sit up front—the normally coveted position. Amazing how the presence of one lovable dog could change a kid's perspective. By the time I'd gone through the ridiculous pickup line at Thomas Magnet (Luca could probably come up with a better strategy for them) and collected Matty, I'd lost almost ninety minutes.

"Y'all need to remember Miss Meghan is gonna collect you from school the rest of the week and drop you at the library," I told the boys as I turned my car into the driveway.

"I don't see why we can't just come home," Daniel mumbled. "It's not like we'd be alone."

"We've been over this, kiddo." I killed the engine and turned to him. "Your daddy needs to be able to work, and it's hard to do with y'all fussing at each other." At least I could keep them separated at the library.

"I wanna go to the library." Chase unbuckled his seatbelt and fumbled with the door. "Come on, Rocket." He climbed out and tried to latch onto the dog's collar before he took off, but he wasn't fast enough.

By the time we stumbled into the house, Rocket in tow, I'd lost another ten minutes. The day was slipping away faster than a slimy fish. If I was fixing to cook dinner tonight—which would be my debut performance—then we needed a little luck and a whole lot of organization.

"You boys collect your homework while I find you a snack." I dropped my purse onto the entry hall table and made a beeline for the kitchen.

Matty trailed behind me. "I don't got any homework."

"You don't *have* any homework." I threw him a smile over my shoulder.

"I know. So, I wanna go swimming."

Matty was so precious, it would've been easy as apple pie to give him whatever his little heart desired. But I'd made a vow to myself and God that if I was gonna be a stand-in mama to these boys, I'd do it right.

I crouched in front of him with a sigh. "You remember what I asked you to do Saturday morning?"

His blue eyes met mine without even a hint of guile. "No, ma'am."

"Asked if you could please pick up your room. Remember? You got a bunch of those Legos spread all over the place along with Tinker toys and a pile of clothes. Can't hardly find the floor. You get it all cleaned up right quick, and when your brothers are done with their homework, you can go swimming with them."

Don't know if Matty didn't have it in him to pout or if he was too young to know how, but without batting an eye, he said, "Yes, ma'am," and marched out of the kitchen. Hopefully to do as I'd asked.

I got the other boys set up on the back patio with snacks and their homework before I pulled tonight's recipe up on my phone. The print was so small, a body would need a magnifying glass to see it. Luca had given me permission to use the wireless printer in his office. Just needed to get the rice started—even I could do that without the recipe. Once that was going, I headed upstairs for the copy I'd sent through Air Print and a quick peek at Matty to be sure he was on task.

I'd only ever been in Luca's office when he'd given me a tour the first time I came to the house. Matty hadn't inherited his messy ways from his daddy, that was for sure. If I remembered correctly, the master bedroom was every bit as tidy, too. Didn't know any other man who lived by the saying, "A place for everything, and everything in its place." Made me wonder what kind of mama raised him.

Late afternoon sun poured through the window that faced the front yard, giving the otherwise austere room some much needed warmth. Luca's desk was one of those L-shaped deals, and if I wasn't mistaken, made outta real wood. Not particle board and veneer like everything I'd ever owned. The only personal items in the room were some framed photos of the boys—and a couple of the four of them. It was the same in the living room. I'd yet to see any of the elusive wife. It was like she'd never existed.

The printer was on a wide file cabinet tucked behind the desk. One sheet of paper sat in the tray—my recipe, I hoped. As I reached for it, I couldn't help but notice the open file sitting next to the printer like it had been forgotten. Spread out were copies of the boys' birth certificates.

I started to close the file when I noticed the birth parents' names. Father: Luca Giordano. Mother: Bridget McCullough. *Huh. Guess it's not so unusual for a woman to keep her maiden name.* Or maybe they were never married. But it was proof right here that she existed, or at the very least, had existed.

"What are you doing in here?"

I twirled around at the harsh voice, knocking the file to the floor. Papers flew into the air before scattering all over the carpet while Luca pinned me with an angry glare.

Luca

Shock at finding Lillian snooping through my stuff made my words harsher than intended. Her eyes held that same fear and dismay Rocket's had the only time I'd swatted him with a newspaper. I was angrier at myself than I was with her. What had I expected? Knew better than to drop my guard, especially when it came to pretty women. Didn't matter that I thought Lillian was different.

"I...I'm sorry." With shaky hands, she scraped the hair back from a face that was now bright red. "It's not what it looks like." Where had I heard that one before?

"Really?" So much derision in one word. Not my finest moment. "It appears from where I'm standing that you're going through a private file."

"It was laying open, and—"

"Which doesn't make any difference!" Did she not grasp the obvious? "Why are you even in here?"

Eyes now suspiciously bright, she waved a hand behind her. "You said I could use the printer, and I had this recipe..." Her excuse drifted away. Maybe because it sounded as lame to her as it did to me.

I drew in a deep breath, willing the anger to dissipate. Never could execute good judgment when I was viewing things from a haze of red. It wasn't implausible that I'd left the file open, but that didn't give her the right to intrude.

"I'm truly sorry, Luca. I didn't mean to—"

"Miss Lillian!" Daniel's scream came from downstairs. "Stove's on fire!"

Fire?

Bolting from the office, I hit the stairs at warp speed and nearly took a header. Adrenaline running through my veins, first at Lillian's betrayal and now at Daniel's screams, was enough to stop a heart. I skidded into the kitchen where Daniel, Chase, and Rocket were entranced by two-foot flames engulfing the stove top.

"Go out back and take Rocket with you!" I lunged at the cabinet beneath the sink to retrieve the fire extinguisher and caught Lillian out of the corner of my eye with Matty in tow. She hustled everyone outside while I sprayed at the base of the flame.

"Should I call 911?"

I glanced up from the mess to find Lillian hovering on the far side of the island, face pale, a hand pressed to her belly like she was going to be sick. Shaking my head, I hit the stove with a couple more shots from the extinguisher. It didn't need it, but a safer target for the anger building to volcanic proportions. A scream sat at the base of my throat—accusations and insults that would inflict more damage than the fire.

"I'm sorry." Her apology got caught up on a sob. I'd been manipulated by the best with tears, and I was immune.

Staring at the high-end stainless steel stove top now blanketed with foam, I took a couple of breaths. *Count to ten before you speak.* Wise words from a dad who'd dealt with his short-tempered son. Losing it never fixed anything and often made the situation far worse. I'd learned that the hard way, not always wise enough to channel my father when needed.

"You were cooking?" Rather than look at her, I snatched up a hot mitt and took hold of the pan. It was then I caught sight of what appeared to be a partially foamed-over dish towel near the gas burner.

"I was making rice. Had me a casserole recipe—the one in your printer." Her voice was wobbly like she was holding onto control by a thin wire. Join the club.

Jaw clenched, I turned on the hot water and let it run. First, snooping in the file I'd stupidly left out. Should've known better. But now this? The boys could've been hurt. Might've even burned the house down. She was a menace in the kitchen, and I couldn't trust her alone in the house. Did I need to install a lock to keep her out of places she didn't belong?

No. This was *my* house, and she was in *my* office. I shouldn't have to hide my private files away because she didn't have the common decency to mind her own business. And I was about to tell her so when the boys stumbled back inside.

"Is the fire gone?" Matty's eyes were wide, his bottom lip trembling.

"Yeah." I blew out a sigh and slid my gaze to Daniel. "You did the right thing, son. Let this be a reminder for all of you that the stove and oven are off limits. Never can tell when something like this might happen."

"We weren't the ones cooking, it was—" Chase shot a quick glance at Lillian then ducked his head like he realized he was about to throw her under the proverbial bus.

"Your daddy already knows it was me." Lillian's tone was gentle. No surprise there. Might be a snoop, but I had no doubt she'd lay down her life for the boys. More than I could've said about their own mother. Maybe that was where I should keep my focus—on her relationship with the boys instead of on her failures. Wasn't without quite a few of my own. A short fuse, for one.

Lillian straightened her shoulders and made a beeline for the sink. "Why don't y'all go about your business, and I'll get this mess cleaned up? See if maybe I can start over here with supper." Her motives might be right, but she was another accident waiting to happen.

"Better not to use the stove tonight," I said. "Needs to be good and dry after it's cleaned up. And I want to assess the damage first."

"Oh." She came to a stop not ten feet in front of me, eyes landing anywhere but on mine. "Well, I'll see what I can put together without—"

"I'll order takeout." Why in the world was I bent on making her job easier? I needed to get out of the kitchen before I offered to clean up the mess for her. "Be sure to use rubber gloves and hot, soapy water." I threw the instructions over my shoulder as I escaped. Could feel the boys' eyes boring into my back until I was out of their sight.

I hadn't noticed the new furniture in the family room in all the excitement. Filled the room up some, although the placement needed work. Imagined the pieces I bought for Lillian were safely tucked in her room. Unlike her, though, I wasn't about to cross the boundary of privacy to find out.

I made my way up to my office with Rocket on my heels. I would've thought the dog had more smarts than to want to be in my company. Didn't he sense what a foul mood I was in? We entered the room, and he went to his favorite corner, turned in a few circles, and plopped down with a sigh.

The contents from the file folder were strewn all over the floor. How much did Lillian see? I knelt and gathered the papers one by one. Several pages of the last statement of my retirement account, bank statements, stock certificates, the boys' birth certificates, deed for the house—my hand froze as it hovered over the lab results from Health Street. Had I accidentally put them in the wrong folder, or had Lillian done more than glance through an open file? Maybe she'd gone through my desk after all.

Ridiculous. I was letting my fears get the best of me. Lillian might have crossed a line, but she was no spy. I'd need to get a hold of the paranoia before it got a hold of me.

Had the papers tucked safely away and was going over my calendar when there was a light tap on my open door. Glanced up to find Lillian standing at the threshold like she was fearful of stepping inside without permission. Now that the red haze had cleared, a pang of guilt shot through me. She wouldn't be the first person to leave a stove unattended with a dishtowel close by. It was just another unfortunate strike against her while I was still processing the first.

She cleared her throat. "Can we talk?"

I waved her inside. "I apologize for raising my voice."

She perched on the edge of the leather chair facing my desk and folded her hands. "You have every right to fuss at me. Should've kept my nose out of your business." Her gaze flitted about like a nervous bird. "Also, shouldn't've left the stove unattended like I did. And if you'll give me another chance, I promise neither of those things will happen again." She dared to glance at me.

Last thing I wanted was to search for someone to take Lillian's place. She might be challenging in some ways but couldn't fault her with the boys. "Clean slate?"

She sighed and offered a tentative smile. "Clean slate." She hopped from the chair, her demeanor much lighter than when she'd come in. "Almost forgot in all the excitement. The furniture came in, and the delivery man put some of it in my bedroom. I didn't know if it was a mistake, but—"

"No mistake." Although I'd been rethinking that decision before she'd come in. Emotions were capricious, which got me in trouble more than once. "Thought you'd want to have a space all your own that was comfortable. The saleslady picked everything out and said we could exchange anything you don't like."

Her eyes widened. "Oh, no. It's perfect. I appreciate you being so thoughtful. I'll take real good care of it while I'm here." She clapped her hands together. "Better check on the boys. Promised them they could go swimming once their homework was finished."

"Hang on, Lillian." I folded my arms on the desk. "Something I never thought to ask until now. Just how experienced are you in the kitchen?"

She twisted her face into a grimace. "I cook about as good as I do laundry. But I'm willin' to learn."

"But you made that lasagna for the church potluck a few weeks back." Had two helpings of it myself.

"No, sir. Stouffer's made it. I just heated it up in the oven."

Should've known. I'd just have to readjust my expectations. And maybe stock up on Tums.

Chapter Thirteen

Lillian

Some people found themselves a life verse from the Bible. Not me. Being a librarian, it seemed appropriate mine came from the Lemony Snicket series, *A Series of Unfortunate Events*. It was one bad decision after another that landed me where I was today—single, indebted, and working a job worthy of a high school graduate. To top it off, I'd moved in with a man who thought I was nuttier than pecan pie and three boys who'd surely break my heart.

Couldn't fault Luca for pitching a duck fit after catching me riffling through his file and nearly burning the kitchen down. Thought for sure he was gonna throw me out on my hind end, leaving me homeless and broke, which would be a sad addition to my list of achievements. Would serve me right, too.

So twisted up over the previous day's mishaps, I couldn't hardly keep my focus on the library patrons. It didn't help that I was always a little scattered the first day of my work week. Course, it wasn't an unfortunate accident that Luca caught me sticking my nose where it didn't belong—that was pure bad luck. Or maybe divine consequences. And the stove fire? Now that was a mishap. Then again, maybe not. If I hadn't lingered where I shouldn't have, then I'd've been back in the kitchen before the dish towel caught fire.

"You doing okay, Lillian?" Carrie's question pulled me from my mental flogging. "You're not your usual perky self today." She might've been ten years younger than me, but I'd bet Carrie wouldn't find herself in such a predicament.

"Just got a lot on my mind is all." Carrie was a sweet girl, but I wasn't about to let her see what a hot mess I truly was. No doubt, she'd look at me like I'd escaped the crazy asylum. I had *some* pride left. Besides, it was gonna be hard enough to confess my downfall to Sherrie, the only person who knew the authentic, pathetic me. And it was another week before she and Josh were scheduled to return from their honeymoon.

Carrie plopped a stack of returned books onto the library cart I was fixing to re-shelve. "Kathleen says your boys are gonna be spending some time with us starting this afternoon."

Your boys. Had a nice ring to it, even if it was a temporary assignment. One more strike, and I'd be out on my keister for sure. Didn't help that every now and again, when Luca set those dark eyes on me, my heart took to fluttering some. Another blot against my character. Going down that road would only lead to a dead end. "Yeah. Meghan Marshall's gonna pick them up for me." That was one thing I got right, at least.

Choosing books for Story Hour was a task I took to heart. Reading aloud was the easy part—finding those with a strong message to engage conversation with the children was a little trickier. Something for everyone was my motto. I had me a copy of *Koala Lou* by Mem Fox and the well-loved *The True Story of the 3 Little Pigs* by Jon Sieszka. Some might be too young to understand the theme of deception, but they had to start somewhere. Could do with a reminder myself, considering I'd basically been dishonest about the skills I brought to the Giordano household. But when I'd told Luca I was willing to learn, that was the God's-honest truth. And I would, or die trying. Just hoped I didn't take anyone down with me.

When the after-school kids started trickling in, I kept an eye out for the door. Wanted to do whatever I could to make this new experience for the boys an enjoyable one. Otherwise, the chore of collecting them would fall to Luca again, and I knew firsthand what a time sucker that was.

I spotted Matty first, surrounded by two of Meghan's girls, Chase close behind, and Daniel trailing in with Meghan's oldest—Chelsea. She was talking to him a mile a minute, but either he was playing it cool or not the least bit interested.

Meghan followed behind chatting with a woman who seemed oddly familiar. Short, dark hair, high cheekbones, and model thin. I'd bet what little I had left in my savings account that I'd never seen her before, so she must've had one of those faces. Although who could tell with all the makeup she was wearing?

I shot a quick text to Luca, as promised, to let him know the boys had arrived safe and sound. It was a wonder he didn't have an ulcer with all the worrying he did. Then I gave the boys a quick hug and greeted the girls as they passed on their way to the Story Hour carpet.

"Hey, Meghan," I said when she was close enough to hear. "I really appreciate you doing this for me." I offered her friend a smile. "I'm Lillian Murphy. Don't believe we've met before."

She flashed a perfect row of white teeth. "Jamie Rogers. Nice to meet you." Must be one of the recent transplants, because there wasn't a hint of southern in her voice.

"Where're you from, Jamie?" Never was good at deciphering an accent unless it was strong enough to knock a person over.

"Originally from Kansas City, Missouri, but I've lived all over the country."

"Jamie's a creative consultant for a new record label," Meghan offered. "Don't you think that sounds like a dream job? Gettin' to work with all kinds of music artists."

"You're in the right place, that's for sure." I checked my watch. "Sorry to cut this short, but I need to get to work. Hope to see you again, Jamie."

I joined the children. Along with Meghan and Luca's kids, there were an additional seven or so, which made a nice little group. Always enjoyed reading to a larger crowd, as long as they were engaged. Nothing worse than playing to an uninterested audience.

There was plenty of discussion about *The True Story of the 3 Little Pigs*. It seemed to appeal to a wide range of ages. Fact was, I had me a friend who taught middle school that used it even in her classroom. And since it'd been around for almost twenty years, I'd never yet met a child who hadn't heard it before.

It was when I started reading *Koala Lou* that my delight took a bit of a dive. It was a simple story about a soft, round koala bear named Koala Lou. She was loved by everyone, but it was her mama who picked her up a hundred times a day to tell her just how much. It was when I scanned the group of kids before turning the page that my heart tripped. Daniel's face was red, his fists clenched in his lap. This wasn't a sweet little story to him. Maybe a reminder of his own mama? How could I have been so thoughtless, especially since I didn't have any idea what had happened to her or when he'd seen her last?

I stumbled my way through the rest of the book, holding back a wince every time I read Koala Lou's mama's words to the little bear. Felt like I was driving a nail into Daniel's broken heart with every verse. Soon as I was done, I snatched up a book I hadn't planned to read. But I wasn't about to launch into a discussion about a mama's love when there were at least three little boys in the audience who were missing theirs.

After I finished up, I thanked Meghan again for collecting the boys and told Jamie how good it was to meet her, when all the time my mind was on Daniel. It took me a few minutes to find him sitting in the back corner staring at a math worksheet. I'd've bet the farm he didn't see a thing in front of him.

I slipped into the hard, plastic chair next to him and laid my hand on his where it was clenched on the table. "I wasn't thinking when I picked out that story."

His mouth tightened, but he didn't say anything.

"You must miss your mama, huh?"

A quick nod.

"Wanna talk about her?" Chase and Matty didn't seem to be affected by the story. Could be they were too young to remember her.

He shrugged. "Nothing to talk about. She was there one day and then she wasn't." He pulled his hand from beneath mine and stuck it on his lap.

Did that mean she passed away? Or had she abandoned them? I couldn't imagine a mama leaving her kids like that, but it happened. Oh, I wished I'd asked Luca about her before. Could hardly do so now that he thought I was a busybody.

"How old were you when she...when you saw her last?"

He shrugged again. "Don't know," he mumbled. "It was before I started kindergarten, 'cause she wasn't around for that."

"Guess I need to be more sensitive when choosing stories to read." Although, it would be impossible to know what triggers would set a child off.

"It wasn't just the book." He slid a glance at me, his mouth twisted. "Dad was real mad yesterday." He didn't know the half of it.

"He was scared is all. The fire—"

"Last time I remember seeing my mom, he was yelling like that. Think they had a big fight." That was a clue.

"So, your mom...she didn't pass away?"

"Not unless something happened after she left, like a car wreck or something."

How could Luca keep the whereabouts of the boys' mama from them? "Don't you ever talk to your daddy about her, Daniel? Like about memories y'all have or anything?"

He shook his head. "Don't remember anything else about her."

How strange. It brought to mind one of the *True Crime* stories I'd recently read. Always loved me a mystery, but this one was hitting a little close to home.

Luca

Every relationship required compromise at some level, but it took me filling out my calendar for the following week to remind me Lillian was doing a fair bit of it herself. Her culinary skills were non-existent, which came as a colossal disappointment. However, on the plus side, she found a way to give me an additional three hours every afternoon. Fifteen hours a week. Sixty hours a month. That was worth a little chaos in the kitchen. And if I needed to sacrifice one of those hours now and then to put dinner—or *supper*—on the table, then that seemed fair.

I didn't want to delve too deeply into why I found it necessary to make excuses for her. Maybe because I'd overreacted when I found her in my office. If the situation was reversed, and I came across her personal papers, I might or might not remember Jesus' words, "If your right eye causes you to sin, gouge it out and throw it away." Easy to judge others, but curiosity was a compelling motivator.

Err on the side of grace. It's what my dad would say whenever I was faced with responding to someone else's failures. God knew I had enough of my own, so I wasn't about to hold Lillian accountable for this one slip up. Now, if she had been in my office for the express purpose of snooping, then it would've been a different ballgame.

After Lillian's text that the boys had arrived at the library, I made a few phone calls, jotted down the appropriate changes in the coming weeks, then transferred everything to the wall calendar in the dining area. By the time Lillian and the boys had arrived home, I had burgers ready to go onto the grill, steak fries seasoned and awaiting to pop into the oven, and was working on a salad.

"What's all this?" Lillian set her bag on the counter and peered into the salad bowl, the flowery scent of her shampoo tickling my nose. "You didn't have to make supper."

I quirked an eyebrow at her. "Better that than letting you burn down the house."

She scowled at me. "Just so you know, I'm a gifted salad maker. It's just applyin' heat to anything that gets me into trouble." She dug into her bag and pulled out her phone. "But I subscribed to a YouTube channel that teaches cooking basics, and I'm gonna learn, just like I promised."

Leaning toward her, I glanced at her phone. "Do they have one of those channels for laundry, too?"

She backhanded my arm. "Now you're just bein' ugly."

Chuckling, I slid the sliced tomatoes into the salad bowl. Things were back on an even keel. "Where are the boys? You did remember to bring them home, didn't you?" I'd heard them greeting Rocket when they came in, but ribbing Lillian was surprisingly fun. She was a good sport.

"Very funny. Just keep it up, and I'll put starch in your underwear." No sooner were the words out of her mouth, her cheeks turned red. Imagine, a grown woman embarrassed over the idea of my underwear. Crazy as she might be, she was a breath of fresh air.

She snatched her bag off the counter and stepped back. "I told them to take their backpacks up to their rooms. Homework's all done, so they think it earned them the privilege of going swimming before supper."

I ducked so I could see the sky out the open kitchen window. Black clouds were rolling in, and the scent of rain was tangible. "Even if it wasn't too cool out, it looks like we're about to have a storm."

"That's what I told them, but I have me a feeling they think I'm a soft touch. It'd be better coming from you."

"Hey, Daddy!" Matty came tearing into the kitchen, Rocket at his heels, and jumped onto a bar stool. "Miss Lillian read *three* books today at Story Hour. And Miss Annalee says that we're gonna have a grad..." He squinted. "A gradiation in two weeks. Can you come?"

I ruffled his hair. "Hello to you, too, son."

He slapped a hand on his forehead. "I forgot. Hi, daddy. Can you?"

"Graduation, huh? From *pre*school?" It was either cute or ridiculous—couldn't decide which. "Sure, kiddo. You let me know, and I'll put it on the calendar." I motioned toward the dining area.

Lillian caught her bottom lip between her teeth as she scanned the updated wall chart. "Guess I didn't realize how soon the boys'll be outta school." She glanced at me. "You have any idea what you're gonna do with them then?"

I snatched up a dishtowel and joined her. "As you can see," I pointed to it, "We're going to be in Wheaton for a week the second part of June. My parents will want to spoil them, so I'll be able to get some work done while we're there.

And they'll come out for a week before the boys go back to school. Other than that, I'll need to accommodate my schedule and hope for the best."

Her eyebrows hitched. "How flexible of you." She chewed on a thumbnail. "I have two weeks' vacation coming, so why don't I plan on taking one of them the first week they're out?"

I frowned. "I can't ask you to give up your vacation to work."

"Don't be silly." She waved a hand toward the kitchen. Matty was listening to our conversation with rapt attention. "I love hanging out with the boys. And besides, you've been more than generous with me, and now you're doing some of the cooking, too."

"It's called self-preservation," I said with a grimace.

"Ha, ha." She folded her arms. "I don't feel like I'm earning my keep as it is, so I'd feel a whole lot better if I can do at least this. Besides, what else am I gonna do? Jet off to the Bahamas or take myself on an Alaskan cruise?"

I shrugged. "Why not?"

She stared at me like I'd grown two horns. "'Cause if I could afford to do that, I wouldn't be living here with y'all."

The mere thought of Lillian leaving was like a punch to the gut, even though there had been tense moments and plenty of frustration. She was basically working for me, but while bantering with her just then, the natural line between employer and employee blurred. It would complicate things. How would I get it back? And the bigger question—did I even want to? Hadn't felt this sense of companionship since I'd first gotten married, which really didn't count. It had all been a lie, which nullified everything that came from that relationship, except the boys.

Pounding footsteps drew my attention only moments before Chase and Daniel came in, both wearing swim trunks. "We're gonna go swimming." Chase headed for the patio door.

"I wanna go!" Matty hopped off the stool, and I nabbed his arm before he took off to get changed.

"No one's going swimming." On the tail end of my announcement, thunder rumbled across the sky, sounding like a runaway train. "You hear that?"

"So, it's gonna rain." Daniel shrugged. "Big deal. We're gonna get wet in the pool anyway."

Lillian raised her hands. "I told you boys in the car that it's not warm enough to swim."

"Duh." Daniel rolled his eyes. "A heated pool." His tone implied that she was being obtuse.

"Lose the attitude." I raised my brows at him. "You owe Miss Lillian an apology."

His eyes held a challenge for a beat before common sense kicked in. "Sorry," he mumbled. "But if the water's warm, why can't we go swimming?"

"Because summer storms often include lightning, and if it hits the water when you're in it, you could be electrocuted. So, unless you're willing to get barbecued, I'd suggest you table the idea for tonight."

"Aw, Dad," Chase whined. "Now what're we gonna do?"

Lillian's trill of laughter lightened the mood as she threw me a conspiratorial wink. "Goodness, but y'all act like your best friend up and died. Why don't we eat on the back patio, if it's okay with your daddy, and then we'll play a couple board games? Might even have something special to read to y'all at bedtime if you're good."

Switch out the English accent for a Southern drawl, and she'd be the modern day Mary Poppins. We could all use a little positivity around here. Wouldn't surprise me at all if she started belting out "Supercalifragilisticexpialidocious."

CHAPTER FOURTEEN

Lillian

It was a sad commentary on my social life that I was excited as a kid on Christmas morning when Sherrie and Josh returned. While I was still finagling my calendar for a time we could meet up, Luca invited them over for a barbecue. It reminded me that he was still new in town, and his social life was even more pitiful than mine. When he told me about the invitation, it caused a little flutter in my belly. Such a normal "couple" thing to do—except we weren't a couple, and knowing that was a bit of a letdown. It must've been the idea of being single that caused the pang of loneliness—had nothing to do with Luca.

"We're going to keep it simple." He handed me a handwritten menu first thing that morning. "Think you can handle a green salad and a fruit salad?" Wasn't a hint of sarcasm in his tone, so I decided to not be offended by the question.

"You're in the South now, Luca." I set his list on the counter and snatched the pen from his hand. "We don't do fruit salad. We do congealed salad."

He made a sour face. "*Congealed*? Doesn't sound at all appealing."

I scratched "fruit salad" off his list and wrote in my substitution. "It's a version of Jell-O salad is all. Nothing to get all twisted up about."

"Then why don't you just call it Jell-O salad?"

I handed his pen back with a grin. "We Southerners like to be different. Best get used to it if y'all plan to stay here."

His lips twitched, which I knew meant he was fixin' to tease me. "Does it require using the stove?"

I turned my nose up and pretended to be offended, although I hadn't earned the right. "Easy as boiling water."

"Same could be said for making rice, you know." He chuckled at my sneer. "But in the spirit of Christianity, I'm going to give you a little grace—and a second chance. Give me a list of what you need, and I'll run to Kroger's."

When I started working on the congealed salad, Daniel wandered into the kitchen. Had me a feeling he was spying for his daddy to be sure I didn't light anything on fire.

"You wanna help?" If he was fixin' to hang out, the least he could do was be useful.

"What're you making?" He moved up to the stove and peered into the red goo.

"Congealed salad." Looked just like his daddy when he made a face. "Or Jell-O salad for you Northerners. Take over for me and keep stirring while I pour in the Dr. Pepper."

He took charge of the spoon and sniffed the concoction. "Dr. Pepper? That sounds weird."

"Don't matter what it *sounds* like. Only what it tastes like." I popped the soda tab. "And trust me, you're gonna love this. Besides, it doesn't take the whole can, so you get to finish it off if you want."

"Really? Dad doesn't let us drink pop."

"I don't think this little bit's gonna hurt you, and what he doesn't know—" There I was, fixin' to lie to Luca over something as silly as a couple sips of soda. "I'll be sure and tell him it was my idea."

Working side-by-side with Luca throughout the day with the boys running in and out, only gave flight to my fantasy of us as a family. Was it really a fantasy though? Crazier things had happened, right? But on the tail-end of that thought, I pictured Daniel's pinched face when he'd talked about his mama and not knowing what happened to her. I couldn't ignore the wave of uneasiness that washed over me every time it came to mind. It was overlooking red flags in the past—or the Holy Spirit's nudge—that landed me in my current predicament.

Rocket's deep bark alerted me to Sherrie and Josh's arrival almost a half hour earlier than expected. Didn't surprise me the least little bit, though, because Sherrie's internal clock always did run a little fast. Had me a feeling Josh's would be synchronized along with hers right quick if it wasn't already. I grabbed hold of Rocket's collar before opening the front door, even though he hadn't bolted once in the last week.

While Josh was greeting Rocket with a healthy ear-scuffing, I hugged Sherrie. "Feels like y'all have been gone a lot longer than ten days." Gave Josh a hug then waved them inside.

Sherrie stopped in the family room, her gaze sweeping across it. "The place looks some different than the last time we were here."

"New furniture?" Josh dropped into a leather recliner. "If I had me one of these, I'd never get any work done."

Sherrie grabbed his arm and tugged him up. "Reason right there not to invest in new furniture."

He wriggled his eyebrows at me. "There's a method to my madness. Ever hear a woman trying to talk her husband *out of* redecorating?"

"Come on out back. The boys are in the pool, and Luca's tending to the smoker." Heat stole up my cheeks when I caught a look between Sherrie and Josh. I sounded like an old married lady, and if I wasn't careful, I was gonna make a fool of myself all over again.

Sherrie hooked her arm in mine as we walked out the French doors to the patio. "You and me need to sneak off and talk before we leave." Knowing Sherrie, she saw right through me and was itching to get every detail.

The boys, splashing around in the pool, barely took the time to wave. "Y'all come out and say a proper hey to Miss Sherrie and Mr. Josh." A combination lesson in proper manners and the chance to reapply their sunscreen.

Luca crossed to shake Josh's hand and give Sherrie a hug. "Glad you guys could make it. What can I get you to drink?"

I made sure the boys were slathered again in SPF 50 before letting them escape. Daniel and Chase were already turning a golden brown, which I'd expected from their olive complexions and dark eyes, but Matty wasn't as fortunate. His skin was lighter, and it wouldn't take much for him to get burned. I was gonna have to keep a closer watch on him.

"You getting all settled in?" Sherrie's probing tone broke my focus on Matty. There was a deeper question in her eyes than the one she voiced.

"I should be the one asking you that. Feel any different bein' married?" Another month, and it would've been my one-year anniversary with Billy. It should've made me sad.

Sherrie cut a quick glance at the men then tilted her head toward the house. "Why don't you show me what you've done with your room?"

Either she had some juicy tidbit to share or she was fixin' to interrogate me. If I had to lay odds, I'd bet on the latter. Sherrie wasn't one to kiss and tell, not that I had any desire to hear about it if she did. It wouldn't do me a lick of good to fight what was coming, so I might as well get it over with.

"Luca?" I waited for him to glance at me then motioned we were going inside so he'd keep an eye on the boys.

Sherrie walked beside me as we crossed the patio to my bedroom. It really was extravagant living to have a swimming pool right out my back door, even if it was only for a season. I'd taken to swimming most mornings and even found myself puttering in the yard once the boys were down at night. Dead-heading the roses and other blooms, pulling the weeds that had the nerve to sprout up here and there. All the while reminding myself not to get used to it.

"What's this?" Sherrie's eyes roamed the new furniture. "I expected there would be a bookshelf or two but didn't think—" She clamped her mouth closed like it just occurred to her that she'd tattled on herself.

"Now why in the world would you expect I'd have bookshelves in here?" What did she know that I didn't?

She ran her hand across the back of the chair Luca had bought and shrugged. "Last time we were here, you were on the phone with your mama, and we got to talking about how you could use a little more furniture in this monstrous room of yours."

Heat climbed up my neck. "*You* told Luca I needed these things?" How embarrassing. "Really, Sherrie, I—"

"It wasn't like that." She raised her hands like she was holding back an ambush. "He was sayin' how the house was bigger than he'd expected, and he could use some things to fill it." She shrugged. "I might've let it slip that you could use someplace to put your books is all." She patted the chair. "But the rest is all him." Then her gaze slid to the side table. "What's this?"

Too late, I caught sight of the sketch pad I'd left out and the charcoal rendition I'd drawn of the boys and Luca hanging around the pool. Daniel was standing in the shallow end, Matty on his shoulders, while Chase was splashing them. Luca sat on the edge, laughing, with his head thrown back. I hadn't needed to imagine the muscled chest and dark V of hair that covered it, because I'd seen it for myself when he'd been swimming with the boys.

"I've just been doodling." I stepped up and snatched the pad from Sherrie's hand and hugged it to my chest.

"Doodling?" She quirked an eyebrow at me. "Are you gonna finally write that children's book you've talked about since we were in middle school?"

I slipped the sketchpad into the drawer of the side table. "Been thinking on it, but this isn't about that. Like I said, I was just doodling."

She folded her arms and sighed. "You're starting to have feelings for him, aren't you?"

A fist clogged my throat. "Doesn't matter one way or the other. I keep messing up like I have, and I'm gonna be looking for somewhere else to live." The thought of it was enough to make me cry.

"You mean because of that little ol' fire you told me about?" She snorted. "Not likely. I'm good at assessing a person, and I wouldn't be the least little bit surprised if he was attracted to you, too."

A flicker of hope flared then died just as quick. "There are a whole lot of things neither of us knows about him that make me uneasy—like what happened to his wife?"

She threw her hands in the air. "Well, why don't you just ask him?"

I plopped into the chair and blew out a sigh. "Because he already caught me peeking at a file in his office." Her mouth dropped open, and I rushed ahead before she could ask for details. "And what if he won't tell me? What if he did something so horrible, he *can't* tell me?"

"Oh, Lil." She knelt beside me. "You don't really believe that, do you?"

It would just be my luck that I'd fall for someone who had a dark past. "Then you tell me why his boys don't know what happened to their mama."

Luca

"Hey, Dad? Look at me." Chase waved his arms to catch my attention before he cannonballed into the pool. He dispensed a wave of water over Matty, who sputtered and swiped his eyes clear.

"Be mindful of your brothers." Matty wasn't much of a swimmer, but he could dog paddle with the best of them. Still, we didn't need the drama of the kid choking on pool water.

Josh chuckled. "Did y'all have a swimming pool at your last place?"

"No. I'm not so sure having one now is a good idea. Too much temptation and not enough sense." Daniel dunking Chase right then proved my point. "Daniel!"

"Yeah?"

"No rough housing." I blew out a breath and looked at Josh. "See what I mean?"

"Guess boys will be boys. My brothers and I got into quite a few scrapes when we were little. Imagine if my mama knew the half of it, she'd've been gray before we reached high school." Josh took a pull from his beer.

"I grew up with an older sister—Lisa—but my friends and I got into enough trouble, I can see the hand of God was all that kept us safe." It was too bad I hadn't been on better terms with him when I met Bridget. Then again, if not for her, I wouldn't have the boys. Fair trade off.

"Appears you and Lillian are gettin' on okay." There was an intensity to his gaze that put me on alert. That lawyer brain of his probably didn't miss much.

"As long as I keep her out of the kitchen." I was only half joking. Didn't trust her to even make a Jell-O salad without causing a mishap. Had to send Daniel in to keep an eye on her.

Josh grinned. "So I heard. Guess I should've warned you that she's cooking-challenged. But I've also heard she's getting real attached to your boys. That's gotta account for something."

More than he could understand. "It definitely makes up for any inconvenience. Thought when I was looking for someone to help out, it was about maximizing my work hours. Since Lillian's been here, I've come to realize that wasn't the half of it. She's great with them—a healthy combination of nurture and discipline." I rubbed my chin. "In fact, I think she's a lot better at both than I am, which is humbling."

He didn't appear at all surprised. "I've known Lil almost as long as I've known Sherrie. They don't come much better than her. It's just too bad—" He shook his head. "Never mind."

"Don't just leave me hanging again." He did that to me last time he was here. I forced a chuckle to lighten things a bit, but I was figuratively sitting on the edge of my seat. *It's gossip.* The thought struck me with the force of a blow. How was me prying Josh for information on Lillian any different than her snooping around in my office?

He cleared his throat and threw a glance toward Lillian's room as if making sure they weren't within earshot. "It's good for her to have the boys to focus on. Maybe remind her it was a good thing Billy left her at the altar like he did."

I winced. "It's none of my business, Josh." If Lillian wanted to share her past with me then she would.

"It's not a secret. The whole town knows. Billy Runyon's his name," Josh went on. "And she's better off without him. Sherrie and me never did like the guy, but what're you gonna say, right?" He shrugged. "She was in love, and we all know love is blind—deaf and dumb, too. But the worst part is that he pushed for an extravagant wedding, at least by Shelbyville standards. I mean, we're not in Nashville or Franklin. A catered affair, live music, open bar. The whole shebang."

That had to cost a small fortune. And despite the guilt nipping at me, I blurted, "I don't get it. How can he walk away from that without any recourse?" Lillian's best friends were lawyers, and they couldn't do anything about it?

He waved the question away. "Don't even get me started. Sherrie's tried to get her to see reason, but she refuses to go after him. Not sure it doesn't have to do with feeling embarrassed. Her mama certainly rubs it in every time they talk. Between that and her school loans, she's living at poverty level."

"No wonder she was willing to take this job." Even if Lillian's past wasn't a secret, like Josh said, I couldn't imagine she'd be comfortable with me knowing about it. Guess that put us on an even keel—her seeing my personal papers and me knowing her embarrassing situation. Kind of made us even if I was to keep score.

It was time to change the subject. "So, you did such a great job referring Lillian to me, maybe you can give me another referral."

Josh pushed his beer bottle aside and folded his arms on the table. "I'll do what I can."

"I need to redo my trust, and I was hoping you might have the name of a good family lawyer."

He grinned. "Josh Cummings comes to mind."

Of course, he would expect me to ask him, which is where things got a little sticky. "I appreciate that, but there are some...sensitive aspects to it that—"

He held up a hand. "You don't have to explain. If you're not comfortable with me, that's fine. Truly. It's not always easy mixing business and friendship—and I do consider you a friend."

The muscles in my shoulders eased up. "I appreciate that."

"But just to remind you, a lawyer-client relationship is privileged. Anything you tell me can't go beyond me—not even to Sherrie." He shrugged. "But I get it if it's uncomfortable to—"

"It's not that." Wouldn't it be better to work with someone I knew and respected than a stranger? "I just don't want to put you in a tenable situation."

His eyes narrowed slightly. "It's the nature of the business. I'm happy to take care of your trust or anything else you might need. But I also have a couple people I would be confident to refer you to, as well. Whatever you prefer."

I nodded. "Thanks, Josh. Appreciate it. I'll call your office Monday and make an appointment."

"Cool." He leaned his elbows on the table. "Now I have a question for you. We have a men's Bible study that meets every Thursday morning. You interested in joining us?"

One way to kick up the faith walk, and it'd give me a chance to meet other like-minded men. "Sounds good," I said as the women appeared. "What do you say we get the food on?"

Better to keep the hands and mind occupied and not think too much about Lillian's dilemma. I had half a mind to find this Billy Runyon character and see if I couldn't persuade him to do the right thing.

CHAPTER FIFTEEN

Lillian

The boys' last two weeks of school flew by with a whole lot of activity and planning—at least on my part. Even if I was only gonna be off with them for a week, I figured we'd start on projects that might could last throughout the entire summer. Soon as I had Luca's permission, I used up my lunch hours at the library to research and coordinate my ideas. Even had a schedule all written up that would make Luca proud. By the time I got off work on Saturday, I was happier than a dead pig in sunshine.

When we got home from church on Sunday, I helped Luca put together a quick lunch and urged the boys to finish up. "I need y'all to get changed and meet me in the backyard. We got ourselves two chores that need to get started."

Daniel's squint had a definite hint of suspicion. "Chores? Are you gonna make us paint the fence?"

Laughter burst from me. "I wouldn't do you that way, kiddo." This was what came of reading *Tom Sawyer* to him and Chase before bed every night. "I promise y'all, you'll enjoy what I've got planned, or we can come up with something different. This is your week."

Matty rounded the table and leaned up against me. "I like to paint."

I fingered a swath of hair from his forehead. "We can do that, too, but not the fence. Got us some canvasses and water paints so you can make a picture for your daddy. But that's for another day." I clapped my hands. "Let's go. Time's a-wasting."

As the boys took off, I glanced at Luca. "You think they'll have fun? If not, what else am I gonna do to keep them all happy."

He carried a stack of plates to the kitchen sink, and I lagged behind with the partially empty glasses. "You've put a lot of thought into this week, and I really appreciate it. I think they will, too. But you can't worry about keeping them happy all the time. That's way too much pressure to put on yourself."

I stepped around him and started rinsing the dishes. "I know, but—" How pathetic would it sound if I told him I wanted his boys to like me? If I was gonna be completely honest, I really wanted them to love me. It didn't make sense, not really. I was just a glorified babysitter—not their mama.

Luca rested a hand on my shoulder, and the warmth of it spread throughout my whole body. Just showed how desperate I was for a man's touch. "Lillian." His deep voice resonated clear to my heart. "You're the best thing that's happened to them in a long time. Just hanging out with them is more than enough."

It was near impossible to catch a breath.

He stepped away to load the dishwasher. "As soon as I have this done, I'll get changed and join you outside with the drill and containers."

Couldn't speak a word to save my life, so I just nodded and scurried off to my bedroom to get changed. Maybe I shouldn't have let Luca help set up the containers for the worm farm. The reason I took vacations was to give him more time to work—not more time with me. But when I asked if he had a drill I could use to make holes in the containers, he took it upon himself to lend a hand. What could I do but accept? With my pitiful luck, I'd miss the container and drill a hole in my hand.

On the positive side, I'd taken to doing all the laundry without a mishap, and I'd cooked supper five times in the last week without once even starting a spark of a fire. The meals weren't anything to brag to Mama about, but they were edible.

And speaking of Mama, it'd been a while since we'd talked. She'd called three times, and I'd screened every one of them. Felt a little guilty over it, but not enough to call back. Not yet, anyway. Wasn't ready for a piece of humble pie, and that's all she seemed to serve up these days.

When I stepped outside in my ratty jean shorts and t-shirt, Luca, the boys, and Rocket were all waiting on me by the picnic table where the drill and two plastic containers sat.

The moment Matty spotted me, he started jumping up and down. "What're we makin'? Daddy says it's a surprise."

I kept my focus on the boys rather than their daddy, who somehow looked better in a plain, white t-shirt than a body ought to. "Today, we're gonna make us a worm farm." Their little faces went from excitement to a whole lot of bewilderment in the span of a heartbeat.

"What're we gonna do with a *worm* farm?" Chase said. "Are they for fishing?"

I grabbed hold of the instructions I'd stuck in my back pocket. "Not for fishing, although if y'all wanna go this week, I can take you over to Tims Ford Lake to do that." Wouldn't say it was a favorite pastime of mine, but this was about them, not me. "What else are worms good for?"

Daniel crossed his arms. "Last year, when I was in Earth Science, my teacher said we need worms to make the dirt good for growing stuff."

"Your teacher was right. Worms give nutrients to the *soil*, which is a little different than dirt. Soil has dirt in it, but it also has lots of things that help to feed the plants, so they grow big and strong. Worms are super helpful to make some of these nutrients."

"What's a worm farm?" Leave it to the youngest one to ask the critical question.

"It's where we're gonna grow our worms for the garden by putting together these here containers." I tapped them. "Your daddy's gonna drill holes for us so the worms can breathe. Then we'll put it together with some newspaper, cardboard, and food for them to eat. And before you know it, the worms will reproduce, and we'll have tons of them."

That started a whole slew of questions. Where would the worms come from to start with? Why do we need a farm if we're gonna buy some from the nursery? Can't we just use *those* in the garden? And Matty, again, came up with the critical question—what garden were we talking about?

That was my cue to point out the twelve-by-twelve section at the back corner of the yard where we'd plant tomatoes, zucchini, and green beans. "That's about all we're gonna have room for here. We'll pick up the plants along with the worms tomorrow."

I sent Chase and Matty to gather whatever old newspapers and cardboard Luca had stacked in the garage while Daniel helped me mark where the air holes would go. As Luca handed him the drill, his eyes met mine, and I swore my heart missed a beat or two. Was the admiration I saw staring back at me all in my head?

Maybe Sherrie was right—he was attracted to me, too. But even if I could believe that, there was still the issue of his wife, or ex-wife, or late wife. There wasn't the teensiest doubt in my mind that he loved his boys fiercely. Didn't suppose there was a limit to what he'd do for them, like breaking the law in order to protect them. *Dear Lord, please don't let him have done something foolish. I know I'm not the best judge of character, but it would plumb break my heart if he's not who I want him to be.*

"Earth to Lil." The rumble of Luca's deep voice sent a shiver down my spine. It was the first time he'd used my nickname, which might could mean that ol' professional wall he'd stuck between us was teetering some.

Luca

A bank of windows in the master bedroom overlooked the backyard—and the swimming pool. The rising sun painted the partially cloudy sky in hues of pinks, reds, and yellows. Some would say it was captivating, but it couldn't hold my gaze—not when Lillian was cutting laps through the water below with barely a ripple from the measured movements of her tanned, toned limbs.

Peeping Tom.

Guilty as charged. In my defense, it wasn't animal attraction that drew me to her, although no one could deny she was pretty. Not stunning like Bridget. But real. No artifice. What first drew me to Lillian was her affection for the boys, and it continued to be a factor for sure. Reading to them every night before bed, laughing at their silly jokes, encouraging their individual talents. But there was so much more to her than I'd expected.

My eyes swept over her as she climbed from the pool. *If your right eye causes you to sin, gouge it out. It is better to enter into life with one eye than have two eyes and be thrown into the fire of hell.* Spent a lot of time meditating over that scripture verse lately. Not that I was stumbling into sin. *But if it isn't lust that holds your attention, then what? Love?*

"Don't be ridiculous," I muttered, turning from the window. Love? I hardly knew the woman. How could I possibly be in love with her? And what did that mean, anyway?

You know her a lot better than you knew Bridget.

It would be self-destructive to do anything that might push Lillian away. Even if I could live with the consequences, the boys would never forgive me. She'd given up her vacation to make theirs special. Never would I have expected the boys would be so excited about worms procreating or watching for the appearance of new leaves on the tomato plants, or the zucchini blossoms beginning to sprout. She'd taken them fishing at Tims Ford Lake, set up an impromptu art studio on the back patio so they could paint, and even helped them make a batch of chocolate chip cookies—with no mishaps. Just last night, she announced that she'd ordered an ice cream maker on Amazon.

"Can't hardly call yourself a Southerner if you're not able to make homemade ice cream," she'd told me when I asked her why.

A glance at the clock reminded me I needed to be out the door in twenty minutes if I was going to make it to Josh's Bible study on time. A little instruction on the Word of God was just what I needed to combat these irresponsible ideas that kept nudging the line of better judgement.

The boys were still sleeping, but Rocket was lying at the threshold of Daniel's open door. When he caught sight of me, his head popped up and his tail started thumping on the floor.

"Good boy," I whispered before slipping into my office to grab a notebook and Bible. A quick trip to the kitchen for a cup of coffee, and I'd be off.

But I was stopped short by Lillian who stood staring out the kitchen window, cup in hand, wearing a robe—most likely over her swimsuit. Her long damp hair was held up by some kind of clip, strands coming loose and hanging down her back, just beginning to curl as they dried.

"Morning," I mumbled.

She turned, a smile in place. "Morning. You're up and about early. Got yourself a meeting?"

I retrieved a travel mug from the cabinet. "Josh invited me to his Bible study. Thought it'd do a sinner like me good to be in the company of more learned men."

A giggle cut loose, and I couldn't help but smile in response. "What's so funny?"

"The way you talk. Sometimes you sound old as Methuselah."

I barked out a laugh. "*I* talk funny? You ever hear your y'alls and might coulds? And don't even get me started on the fixin' tos and hissy fits."

She wrinkled her nose. "You got me there. Want some cream for that coffee?" Without waiting for me to respond, she pulled the milk from the refrigerator and set it on the counter.

"I want to thank you for everything you've done for the boys this week."

She took a sip and swallowed. "You already did. Several times."

"Just goes to show how grateful I am." I screwed the lid onto my cup. "It's a shame you don't have a family of your own." The words were out before I could stop them. Before I remembered what Josh told me about her being left at the altar last year.

Lillian turned back toward the window, but not before I caught the pain in her eyes.

"Hey, Lil." I reached a hand out but dropped it before I made a bigger fool of myself and touched her. "I'm sorry. I wasn't thinking."

She shrugged and raised a hand to swipe a strand of hair from her face. Or maybe she was crying, and it was tears she was clearing away. "About what? Why would you assume I'm wanting a family? Some women aren't cut out for marriage and kids, you know." But she wasn't one of them.

"You're good with the boys." That was an understatement. "Great with them, in fact. You don't expect me to believe it's just part of the job, do you?"

Silence.

Rubbing the back of my neck, I let out a breath. "Well, I guess I'd better go." I didn't want to leave her like this, but if she wouldn't talk to me, what choice did I have? "See you later."

"See you," she mumbled, without turning around.

The entire drive to The Coffee Break, my thoughts were on Lillian. How would I feel if I was in her situation? Yes, I'd been deceived just as she had, but I wasn't left with a financial burden that wasn't mine to carry. On top of that, she had little choice but to accept the job I offered her just to have a roof over her head. She got a raw deal, but I'd never heard a word of complaint. Not when Daniel was disrespectful, or Chase was needy, or Matty asked a million questions in a row.

There was an available parking space in front of the courthouse, and I pulled in. Maybe it was good we'd be in Illinois next week—give Lillian a little breathing room and me time to get my head on straight. Brother Paul had mentioned in passing that there were a few tongues wagging because Lillian was living under my roof. Could be he was exaggerating. We knew there was nothing inappropriate going on, but if I started having feelings for her, then that would all change—at least on my end.

Josh told me that he and the four other men in the Bible study met in the upstairs loft. Felt a little guilty bringing coffee from home—what had I been thinking?—so I bought a muffin before heading up. They all sat around a large table, Josh at one end. Bibles were open, but it didn't appear they'd started yet. Recognized two of the guys. One was Meghan Marshall's husband—Pete I think his name was. The other I'd seen sitting alone at the back of the church.

"Hey, you made it." Josh hopped up and shook my hand. "Y'all, this is Luca Giordano. Luca, I think you know Pete Marshall. This here is Kevin Johnson, Greg Barker, and Sam Collins."

I shook hands all around before taking the only vacant seat. "Good to meet you guys."

Sam, the back-of-the-church loner, nodded. "Good to have you. Josh tells us you're from Chicago?"

"Close enough. Wheaton, actually. Single dad to three boys ages five to nine. Thanks for having me."

Josh slapped the table. "Now that we're all here, what d'you say we get started?" He slid a copy of the study book down to me. "What did y'all think of the week's reading?"

An hour later, we were all dispersing when Pete pulled me aside. "Didn't wanna say anything in front of the other guys but thought you should know." He rubbed his chin, blew out a breath. "It's about a few petty church members talking about Miss Lillian living with y'all."

A fist lodged in my belly. Guess Brother Paul wasn't the only one hearing things. "So I've been told. But just so you know, we're not doing anything inappropriate. I would never—" Clenching my jaw, I shook my head. "You know that, right?"

"Of course, I do. Just wanted to make you aware. It's a few mean-spirited people—nothing to trouble yourself over." He gave me a couple light punches to the arm and grinned. "There's one way to stop the tongues from waggin'."

Didn't have to be a mind reader to know what he was thinking, but I'd play along. "Yeah? What's that?"

"Make an honest woman outta her. Two birds, one stone." He walked away, chuckling.

Chapter Sixteen

Lillian

Growing up on the outskirts of town, we'd had us a humble little crafts-man-style house. It was the typical three-bedroom, two-bath with little to no elbow room, but I liked it just fine. Could've fit three of them into Luca's place. When he and the boys left for vacation on Thursday, I kind of thought it'd be nice to have the house to myself. It didn't take but two nights alone to change my mind. It was too big and too quiet. Or maybe I was just missing the sound of the boys' laughter and Luca's deep voice.

I tried filling the silence with busyness—even started on that children's book that'd been rattling around in my mind. Watered the boys' garden, did laps in the pool, and walked Rocket. Thursday and Friday evening moved slow as a three-toed sloth. Showed up at the library Saturday morning before Kathleen and had to use my own key to get in. Another five days of this, and I'd go stark-raving mad. Maybe it was time I got me a life.

Meghan and her girls—Molly, Emily, and Chelsea—showed up at the library that afternoon while I was working the front desk. Now that school was out, Story Hour was on hiatus, so I hadn't seen them in a while.

"Hey, Lillian." Meghan leaned on the desk as the girls wandered off to search for books. "Came in last week, and Carrie said you were on vacation. Do anything fun?"

"Just hung out with the boys so Luca could get some work done." Most fun I'd had in a while. "Made a worm farm, planted a garden, did some fishing." I laughed at the look of horror on her face. "You know, boy stuff."

"Makes me relieved I have girls. Gardening?" She waved a hand. "That I could get behind. Fact is, I've been after Pete to fix me up a raised flower bed so I can grow a few things. Nothing better than fresh tomatoes."

"We'll see how they come out. It was a little late to plant, but I think it'll be just fine. Y'all going anywhere this summer?"

"Maybe. Pete wants to go down to Gulf Shores, but I think it's too stinkin' humid this time of year. The girls don't even like the beach. Afraid of sharks and complain about the sand. All they like to do is go swimming. Told Pete we should forget about vacations and invest in a swimming pool instead."

"Can't hardly get the boys out of theirs, that's for sure." Then inspiration struck. "Luca took them to visit his mama and daddy for a week, but if you think the girls would like to go swimming, y'all are welcome to come over on Monday." It'd give me something to look forward to other than work.

Her eyes widened. "Really? That's awful generous of you. I mean, I'm sure there are a lot better things you'd rather do on your day off."

"Not really. I feel like I'm rattling around in that big ol' place, and I could use the company. Besides, I'm sure Rocket would love the attention." If I was lonely, Rocket was downright pitiful.

"Seriously? A week on my own would be a dream vacation. If I were you, I'd eat whatever I wanted, binge-watch rom-coms, and work on my tan."

Not a one of those things appealed to me. I supposed everyone thought the grass grew just a tad greener on the other side of the fence.

Meghan slapped the counter. "Hey, if you don't have anything going on this evening, why don't you come over for supper? Nothing fancy, just hamburgers and potato salad, but it'd be nice to get to know you better."

"I'd love that. Just give me your address, and the time, and I'll be there."

Meghan and Pete lived only a few blocks from the library, so I didn't even need my GPS to find their place. Their house wasn't as big as Luca's, but it was still substantial. Boxwoods lined the front porch where a hanging glider sat along with a couple rattan chairs. Used to be, most everyone sat on their front porch and greeted their neighbors. Nowadays, it was more for aesthetics than practicality, along with the required "Welcome" sign hanging by the door.

Wasn't halfway up the walk when Meghan came around the side of the house. "Hey, girl. Come on out back. We got everything set up there."

Pete was working the grill on the patio while the girls were carrying plates and bowls of food from the house. "Lillian. Glad you were able to make it. Meghan and me were just saying the other day it'd be good to get you, Luca, and the boys out here sometime soon."

Was it my imagination, or were people starting to clump us together as a family?

"What can I get you to drink?" Meghan touched my arm. "We got us some lemonade, sweet tea, soda…"

"Sweet tea is just fine. Can I do something to help?" Felt like a useless dead limb just standing around with everyone else having something to do.

Pete pointed to the table. "Grab that there platter, would you? I'll just get these burgers off the grill. Don't wanna overcook them."

I handed him the plate. Now what? "Luca mentioned you're in Josh's Bible study. Y'all been meeting together for long?"

"Goin' on two years." He slid the burgers onto the platter and covered them with foil then glanced at me. "Hope I didn't rile him with that whole gossip thing goin' on at church. It's really just a couple of people with nothin' better to do than stir up trouble."

"Gossip? Afraid I don't know what you're talking about." Seemed like every muscle in my body tensed.

Closing his eyes, he blew out a breath. "Me and my big mouth. I just assumed—"

"Who's sayin' what?" Had me a feeling I already knew. Elsie Chambers and that group of hens couldn't help but ruffle a few feathers.

"Few of the folks are talking like you living under Luca's roof doesn't look good."

"Pete!" Meghan stepped out of the house with a glass of sweet tea. "What're you doin' telling her about that nonsense?"

"Thought she already knew. Was just sayin' I hoped Luca didn't take offense at me telling him." He turned back to the grill. Probably to escape Meghan's scowl.

"Don't mind him, Lillian. And don't mind what other people say." She handed me the frosty glass. "You'd think we were livin' in the 19th century the way some of those women go on."

I wasn't one to listen to gossip, but when it was aimed at me, it wasn't so easy to ignore, either. And I'd had more than my share after Billy dumped me. Everyone had an opinion about what happened, because the truth wasn't worth going on about. Instead, some claimed Billy had a girlfriend on the side he'd gotten pregnant. Another group of busybodies decided my family wasn't good enough to marry into his (which was a hoot.) The truth was more likely Billy didn't want to get himself married to someone who couldn't cook and clean to his liking, but I might never know for sure.

Chest tight, I took a couple sips of sweet tea to wash down the bitterness that wanted to take root. "Don't know why I'm surprised. Guess I'm just naive enough to think people claiming to be Christians would know better than to spread lies." Instead, gossip was cloaked in seemingly pure motives. No doubt Elsie Chambers was telling anyone willing to listen that I was in desperate need of prayer.

Pete closed the grill and carried the burgers to the table. "Might be a good time for Brother Paul to give us a sermon on gossip and slander."

Meghan snorted. "Wouldn't matter. The worst offenders never see themselves as such. All of us are nothing if not experts at justifying our sins." Wasn't that the truth?

"Are we gonna eat?" Chelsea's question put an end to our discussion, but it didn't stop me from thinking on it.

Me living in Luca's house was feeding the gossip mill. That stemmed from a long line of choices I'd made that went against the Bible. Getting myself in debt. Agreeing to marry a man without praying on it first—and getting myself into more debt. Wasn't that what Mama had been going on about from the beginning? She could've been a little more subtle, but she wasn't wrong. And now my foolishness was gonna affect Luca and his boys, too.

Luca

Aside from my parents and Lisa (and her kids), there wasn't much I'd missed about Wheaton. There were too many dark memories that overshadowed the good, and it didn't take long for the oppression to press down on my chest, making it hard to breathe. Wasn't there two days before I was wishing we'd planned a shorter trip.

Saturday afternoon, Mom took the boys to a movie, leaving Dad and me to play a round of golf. I would've preferred to play first thing in the morning to beat the heat, but Dad wasn't a planner. By the time we agreed on the activity, it was too late to get a decent tee time. A year ago, his casual attitude would have irked me. I was maturing or Lillian was rubbing off on me. Either way made the experience more pleasant.

We'd finished the third hole and slid into the cart. Dad released the brake and swung onto the cart path. "You've been quieter than usual these last couple days. Got a lot on your mind?"

I dug my feet into the floorboard as he swerved around a brazen squirrel. "No more than usual."

"That's not saying much." He knew how to play the long game. Always had. Mom would've been peppering questions until she was satisfied. "From what I gather, the boys have grown fond of your...Lillian." No one quite knew how to label her, myself included.

"I think the feeling's mutual." I grunted. "If I can trust my instincts. We both know they've failed me in the past."

"You're not the same man now that you were then." He veered off the path and parked before turning to me. "And you've always been too hard on yourself. We've all made unwise choices, Luca. It's what we take away from them that counts."

One of the components of golf I enjoyed was the respect for quiet contemplation. The moment Dad suggested the game, I knew there would be an interrogation of sorts. A question, an answer, and time to process. Dad was good with the one-liners—wise advice, a scripture verse, or an old adage that fit into the conversation.

We finished nine holes, put our bags in the car, and headed for what Dad referred to as the 19th hole for a beer. After washing up, I joined him at the bar. It was the quiet time between lunch and the Happy Hour rush.

"Thanks for this." I held up my pint glass in a casual toast. "Playing golf with you is definitely one of the things I miss."

Dad smiled. "It's been hard on your mom, not having those boys around every day. If it wasn't for your sister and her kids, she'd be nagging me to move down your way. Still might, come to think of it."

"They miss her, too. Thought for sure Daniel was going to hitch a ride back here. But they're settling in, thanks to..." Her name popped up more than was comfortable.

"Lillian?" Dad's eyebrows rose. "We've heard a lot about her from the boys, but you've been quiet on the subject." Good thing he couldn't read my mind. "Does that mean you don't care much for her?"

"It's complicated." That much was true. "She works for me and lives in my house, so I need to maintain a professional distance." Which was becoming impossible.

He shook his head. "This is me you're talking to here. And feeding me the company line isn't going to cut it." Turning, he pinned me with a glare. "What's going on, really? Do you have feelings for the girl?"

I rubbed the back of my neck. "It doesn't matter, Dad. Not surprisingly, a few people from church are taking issue with her living under my roof. Their dirty, little minds are making something out of nothing, and Lillian's the one who will get hurt. And I don't know what to do about it." A rock and a hard place.

"You didn't answer my question, son." His eyes cut to mine. "Do you have feelings for her?"

If only it were so simple. "I think so." I ran my thumb down the condensation on the glass. "I'm attracted to her. She's different from anyone I've ever known. Worthless in the kitchen, but she sparks the boys' imaginations in ways that amaze me. She's gotten herself into a financial situation, which is why she's working for me and living at the house."

"She's a librarian, right?"

I nodded. "Doesn't pay well. And if living at the house is going to hurt her reputation, then the right thing would be to ask her to leave. But that would put both of us in a bind."

"Well, let's look at your options." He slid his glass aside. "You could find someone to take her place."

I frowned. "Which would go over like a lead balloon with the boys and still leave her homeless."

"You could have her move out and pay her more."

I groaned. "Even if that could work, it would be financially irresponsible."

He threw his hands up. "Which leaves you with only one other choice." I didn't like the sly grin on his face.

"Which is?"

"Marry the girl."

A bark of laughter exploded from me. "You're a riot, you know that?" First Pete and now Dad. "I've known her less than two months, and she didn't even like me at first."

"Laugh all you want, it's the perfect solution."

"Wait. What? Are you serious, Dad?" He couldn't be. It was a completely insane suggestion.

"One date with your mom, and I knew she was the one. Doesn't always have to make sense. God's in the story." He raised his glass in a salute and took a drink.

"Well, I'm not you and Lillian isn't Mom." He must've been out in the sun too long. "You forget what a disaster my first marriage was?"

"We warned you about Bridget, remember? I'm sure Lillian isn't anything like her, or the boys wouldn't love her like they do."

I shook my head hard enough to dislodge the insane idea. If I were to propose such a thing to Lillian, she'd no doubt walk out and never look back—and I couldn't blame her. *Marry the girl*. No one in his right mind would consider it to be anything other than ludicrous.

Still, the thought of it kept popping into my head, and I needed it to stop before it took root and grew. That was the only reason I slipped into my bedroom to call Lillian that night after I put the boys down. A dose of reality would do the job.

"Luca?" There was an edge to her tone—concern or surprise? "Is everything okay?"

"Yes, of course." Had an excuse for the call already planned out. "Thought I should just check and see how Rocket's doing. He's not used to being left behind." Somehow, it sounded better in my head.

A puff of laughter came across the line. "Well, he's right here if you wanna talk to him. Although, I gotta warn you, he's not much of a conversationalist."

Quick thinker that I was, I improvised. "I forgot to leave the vet's name and number with you. Just in case."

"Oh. Well, let me get a piece of paper, and I'll write that down." I could hear her rustling in the background while I frantically opened up the contacts in my phone. "Okay, shoot."

I rattled off the information. "Everything's going okay then?"

"I have to admit, it's awful quiet around here. Except for the creaky noises houses always seem to make when you're alone. How are the boys doin'? Bet they love bein' with your mama and daddy."

"They're good. Although, I wouldn't be surprised if they don't start feeling homesick here in the next day or two. They have my parents thinking you're a gift straight from God." Because she was. "Have you done anything fun since we've been gone?" All of two days.

"Meghan invited me to supper this evening. Had a nice time getting to know them and the girls better. I think Chelsea has herself a crush on Daniel."

"What is she, nine?" Did kids really start thinking about the opposite sex that young?

"I think so. Just a case of puppy love, is all. Nothing to concern yourself over." A soft sigh reached my ears. "There is one thing I wanted to ask you."

"What's that?"

"Why didn't you tell me there's been some gossip goin' around church about us? Pete and Meghan say it's nothing, but if I'm causing problems for you by bein' here—"

"You're not." I wished Pete would've kept his mouth shut. "And they're right, it's probably nothing. We aren't doing anything wrong. Let's just table that until I get home, okay?"

Silence.

"Listen, Lil, if you're worried about it—"

"I'm not worried, but I'm fixin' to share a few key scripture verses with the busybodies in our church. No doubt, Elsie Chambers is the one stirring things up."

I chuckled. "Don't do anything you're going to regret later. We'll tackle it together when I get home."

"I suppose." That wasn't very convincing. "Oh, I wanted to make sure it's okay with you that I invited Meghan and her girls to come swimming on Monday."

"You don't have to ask permission, Lil. It's your house, too."

"Thanks, Luca. I appreciate you sayin' that. Give the boys a hug for me, won't you?"

"Sure thing."

I disconnected the call and slid the phone onto the bedside table. So much for dislodging Dad's asinine idea about marrying Lillian. Short of a lobotomy, I wasn't sure it was even possible now.

Chapter Seventeen

Lillian

Despite feeling a bit lonely, the weekend flew right on by. After Sunday School and church, I'd spent the rest of the day with Sherrie and Josh, which only shined a big ol' spotlight on my single status. The two of them couldn't seem to pass the other without a tender touch or sharing a look that made me feel invisible. Didn't fault them for it, although, I did have to battle a bad case of envy. It brought Luca to mind. Was that because there might could be something between us or because he was the only decent single man I'd been around?

Monday's forecast was rain, but I woke up to bright sunshine with only a few puffy clouds on the horizon. That could change right quick, though—heat and sunshine to a torrential downpour accompanied by thunder and lightning in the span of a few minutes. But according to the weather app, the storm wasn't supposed to hit until after four. Not that anyone could count on that. Meteorologists and politicians were the only ones who could get things wrong more than right and still keep their jobs.

Rocket and I took us a long walk before it got too hot. I could see why people loved having dogs. Not only was he a good companion, but I could talk till I was blue in the face, and he listened better than any human ever—except maybe a monk who'd taken a vow of silence.

"Are you excited as me to have company today?" I asked him as we got back to the house. If his tail wagging was any indication, he was.

Meghan and I had agreed they'd come for lunch, so Rocket helped me put together a deli tray—by taste-testing the turkey—and a congealed salad. I fixed a pitcher of lemonade for the girls and had a gallon of sweet tea, too, just in case. Had a bowl of Fritos and store-bought pimento cheese and cookies. Wasn't fancy, but no one would go away hungry unless they chose to.

When Rocket and I answered the door right at noon, my welcoming grin slipped the least little bit. Meghan had texted earlier and asked could she bring one more person. I'd assumed it was Pete. Instead, standing behind the girls was Jamie. Why the sight of her flipped my mood, was a pure mystery. She was friendly and likable. Beautiful, too. Might could be that was the issue right there, but I didn't wanna think too hard on it. Made me feel petty and insecure.

I compensated with a brighter smile and more enthusiasm than the situation warranted. "Hey, y'all. Come on in." Gave Meghan, Molly, Emily, and Chelsea a hug as they came in the door. Rocket greeted each of them with a spastic tail-wag and a big doggie grin. But when Jamie crossed the threshold, he stiffened and growled. What was that all about? I'd never seen him be anything but friendly.

Jamie's smile faltered some. "He must smell my dog." She put her hand out for Rocket to sniff, but he was having none of it.

"Rocket, that's not at all nice," I said, taking hold of his collar. But there was a smidgeon of glee I had to tamp down. Proved right there I was still a sinner in need of grace. "You behave yourself, boy, or we're gonna have to lock you up." I kept a close eye on him as we went through the house. Didn't need him causing a lawsuit or a fight with animal control.

"Can we go swimming?" Seven-year-old Molly asked the moment we stepped outside.

"That's the plan. If you wanna change into your swim—" Before I could finish, the girls had their shorts and t-shirts off, revealing swimsuits, and were heading for the water, Rocket following close behind to keep a watchful eye on them.

Meghan laughed. "They're not at all excited." She glanced at the food-laden table. "Gracious, Lillian, you didn't have to go to all this trouble."

"No trouble. Only thing I fixed was the congealed salad. Rest is store-bought." Caught the raised brow Jamie aimed at the food. "In fact, I should've maybe put on the dog a bit more."

"Nonsense. This is perfect." Meghan snatched up a Frito then scooped a dollop of pimento cheese. "This here is my absolute favorite. Can't have it around the house or I'd be big as a horse." She wriggled her eyebrows and grinned. Hit me then that if it was good enough for the one actually invited to this party, it was good enough for me.

"Can I pour y'all some sweet tea or lemonade?" I had me a cooler at the end of the table with a bag of ice I'd collected from the freezer.

"Ooh. Sweet tea sounds great," Meghan said. "What about you, Jamie?"

"That's fine."

I filled three glasses with ice and sweet tea then Meghan and I chose seats at the table facing the girls. Whether they were good swimmers or not, things could go sour right quick. I felt some better knowing Rocket was keeping a close watch as he darted around the pool. It was the same he did with the boys—ready to jump in and prove he was as good a rescuer as Lassie.

"This is a real nice place you have." Jamie took a sip of tea. "How long have you lived here?"

I darted a glance at Meghan. Hadn't she told Jamie I was just a glorified sitter? "Goin' on a month now." I popped a Frito into my mouth to give me a little time to work out how much I was willing to share. "Luca hired me to help out with the boys, so this isn't my place. I'm like the housekeeper Alice on *The Brady Bunch*." I giggled at the picture. "Except I'm not a great cook"—I swept a hand across the food—"as you can see, and I'm not a housekeeper."

Meghan waved away my humility. "You bring a whole lot more to the table than cooking and cleaning." She glanced at Jamie. "This girl is a wonder with kids, let me tell you. And I know first-hand how much those boys love her. Last time I picked them up at school, Matty went on and on like she'd hung the moon and stars all by herself." She reached over and patted my hand. "Luca and his boys are blessed to have you, that's for darn sure."

Could feel my cheeks heating at her praise. "I appreciate the vote of confidence, but it's me who's blessed to have those boys. They're easy to love." The thought of not being around them was enough to cause an ache in my chest. How could three little boys become so important to me in such a short amount of time?

"So where are these charges of yours?" Jamie deigned to dip into the pimento cheese with a Frito.

"They're with their daddy visiting his family in Illinois."

"Mommy! Look what I can do." Six-year-old Emily stood at the edge of the pool, Rocket right beside her, and did a perfect cannonball, displacing way more water than her little body should've been able to.

"That's great, sweetie. Y'all getting hungry? Miss Lillian's got some good food over here. Lemonade, too."

Chelsea wiped the water from her eyes. "Can we get back in after we eat?"

I chuckled. "Y'all can stay and swim until you turn into little prunes as far as I'm concerned."

While they climbed out of the pool, I set three paper plates out for them to fill.

Jamie stood. "You mind if I use the ladies' room?"

"Not at all." I jumped up. "Let me show you where it is." I took her through the family room and pointed down the hall past the entry hall. "Just at the end before it veers off to the right." Would've been easier to have her go into my bathroom, but I felt funny about her being in my bedroom. Reminded me of Luca wanting his private space kept private.

When I stepped back outside, the girls were all sitting at the edge of the pool, their legs dangling in the water, plates of food in their laps. "Y'all be careful that Rocket doesn't snatch a bite or two from you." He was pretty good about behaving himself, but he was still a dog.

I plopped back into my seat and fingered the sweat from above my lip. It was getting to be hot, even under the patio cover. "I'm so glad y'all came over, Meghan. Your girls are adorable."

She swiped at the condensation on her glass of tea. "I'm sorry about springing Jamie on you like I did."

Although I appreciated the apology, it wasn't very hospitable of me to be irked at Jamie's presence. "Don't worry about it."

"She just showed up at the house, and when I said we were heading here for the afternoon, she all but invited herself. Didn't know what to do."

"Really, Meghan, it's all good. Any friend of yours—"

Molly ran up to me. "Can I have some lemonade, Miss Lillian?"

"You most certainly may. You think your sisters might want some, too?"

By the time I got the girls their drinks, Jamie had come back outside, and there was no more talk about her.

They left just as the predicted storm blew in, and it was while I was cleaning up the kitchen, I realized it had been some time since I'd seen Rocket. Didn't need to go outside to know he wasn't there. The least little sign of thunder, and he was at the door wanting in. Could he have gone up to one of the boys' rooms and hidden himself under a bed? Wouldn't be the first time I'd found him there.

Dish towel in hand, I walked through the family room, glancing in every corner for a sign of him then headed upstairs. Other than putting away the folded laundry, I hadn't been up there since Luca and the boys left. I searched Daniel's room first since that was the most likely place. Got down on my hands and knees and looked underneath the bed. No Rocket. Next, I moved into Chase and Matty's room. Nothing.

When I stepped back into the hallway, I felt the first glimmer of concern. Rocket couldn't have gotten out the back fence, and he hadn't been with me when I saw Meghan and the group out. So, where had he gotten to? My room, maybe? But as I stepped off the first tread to head that way, I noticed the door to Luca's office was open. Strange. *I know it was closed.*

The thunder rumbling in the sky was loud enough to wake the dead, so I hadn't heard Rocket at first when I stepped into Luca's office. But there he was, roaming the room, his nose to the floor, like he was sniffing out prey. Why was he in here? And more importantly, how'd he get through a closed door? Even Lassie wasn't talented enough to do that.

I'd read enough true crime novels to jump to conclusions right quick. Didn't take but a tiny shred of suspicion, and I had me a dark scenario playing in my mind with the speed of a Japanese Maglev train. It's near impossible to stop something moving that quick, and it was everything I could do to catch my breath as I called Meghan, a trembling Rocket plastered to my side.

"Hey, Lil." The crack of thunder muffled her voice. "Crazy storm, isn't it?"

"Yeah." *Just breathe.* Running my hand over Rocket's head soothed the runaway thoughts. Another reason right there to have a dog.

"Thanks again for having us over today. The girls about talked Pete's ear off goin' on about it. Now, on top of us getting a pool, they wanna dog."

My mind was too distracted for small talk. "Look, Meghan, I know you and Jamie are close, and I don't wan—"

"We're not close." Meghan was quick to clarify. "In fact, I hardly know the girl. That's what I was starting to tell you today when she went to use the bathroom. But then the girls distracted me, and she came back out before I could finish."

Hardly know her? "I don't understand. When y'all came into the library that day, you introduced her as your friend, so I just assumed." Should know better.

"But I didn't. Introduce her, I mean. I'd run into her at the coffee shop before I picked up the boys, and we got to chit chatting. When I told her I had to collect the boys and carry them to the library, she asked if she could tag along. That's the first I met her, though. Since then, she's been calling now and then, popping in on occasion, which is what happened this morning."

"You don't find that a little...odd?" I wanted to say suspicious because I *was.*

"At first, yeah. Then I got to thinking if I had to move to a new place for a job and didn't know anyone, who's to say I wouldn't do the same?" True. A confident person could make friends anywhere she went. And if there was one thing Jamie exuded, it was confidence.

"So, would you say you're friends now?"

Meghan hesitated a couple of beats. "We've got nothing in common, except maybe the fact I appreciate music. Never did feel like she connected with my girls—not like you do. And I kept getting the feeling that she looked down her rhino plastic nose at me."

Despite the sick feeling growing in my stomach, I couldn't help but grin. "She is a little too perfect, isn't she?"

She snorted. "Let's just say I wouldn't want Pete comparing the two of us. What's this all about, anyway?"

Suspicious or not, it wouldn't be right to tarnish a person's view of another without facts. "Maybe nothing. Forget I called, okay?"

"Ha! You've got me all kinds of curious now, but I'm not gonna press. You'll tell me if it's important, right?"

"Absolutely."

Sherrie always did kid me about reading too many true crime stories, and it causing me to have a suspicious mind. If anyone could give me a shot of reality, it was her. Picked up my phone and texted her.

Hey girl. Can I drop by 2night for a few or you stop here after work?

It didn't take her a minute to reply. *I'll be there 5:30.*

Gave me an hour to stew over the possibilities. I started to work on my children's book but had me a better idea. If things didn't work out with Luca, and I had every reason to believe they wouldn't, then I needed to find myself a job that could support me. Didn't wanna spend my life depending on the kindnesses of others or living with a pauper mentality.

I carried my laptop to the kitchen table and pulled up a couple different sites and noted possible positions I was qualified for. All of them started at salaries almost double what I was being paid. Just needed to put together my curriculum vitae, update my resume, and see what God brought my way. Loved my job, but having a roof over my head I could afford and three meals a day was important, too.

When the doorbell rang, Rocket jumped up from where he was sleeping at my feet and raced through the house to bark at our guest. Another reason to have me a dog—great security system. I did a quick glance out the sidelight to be sure it was Sherrie before opening the door.

"Goodness, boy, you gave me a fright." She petted Rocket's wriggling body before giving me a hug. "No one's gonna mess with you as long as he's around."

"Right? Was just thinking of all the reasons for having a dog, and that one's on the top of my list. Especially since I'm here by myself." I led the way to the family room. "Can I get you something to drink? Got some sweet tea and lemonade."

She set her purse on the coffee table and dropped into the corner of the sectional. "Depends on why I'm here and how long it's gonna take."

Sat myself down and shifted so we were facing each other. "Need you to talk me down off a ledge of suspicion. You know how I can get myself all worked up over nothing."

She swiped at a piece of lint on her slacks. "This about the gossipmongers at church? 'Cause we already talked about that yesterday. And if you keep worrying yourself over—"

I waved a hand to shush her. "It's not that. Remember I told you about Meghan and her girls coming over today?"

"Yeah?" She leaned toward me like she was fixing to give me her full attention. "Were they here?"

"Came just as planned. But Meghan brought this woman along with her. Jamie's her name. Thought they were good friends, but it turns out Meghan hardly knows the woman. She's just sorta insinuated herself into Meghan's life. Then she invites herself to come along today."

Sherrie smiled and slumped back against the sofa cushion. "Probably doesn't know many people. Is she new in town?"

"So she says. Couldn't get a whole lot of personal information outta her." Rocket, lying at my feet, shifted with a groan. "But all that's beside the point.

She came inside with the excuse to use the bathroom and was gone a while. Didn't think anything of it until after they left when I went searching for Rocket." At the sound of his name, he popped up and started wagging his tail. I ran my hand along his neck while looking at Sherrie. "Found him in Luca's office. I *know* that door was closed. Closed it myself when he left for vacation." Was actually surprised he didn't lock it to keep me out.

A wrinkle formed between Sherrie's eyebrows. "What're you saying? You think this gal Jamie was in there?"

I nodded. "And it was weird. When they all showed up, Rocket was his usual friendly self with everyone *except* her. He was growling at her and wouldn't let her near him. Don't you think that's odd?"

She frowned. "I don't know, Lil. Just because Rocket didn't like her—"

"And he was sniffin' around Luca's office like he was tracking a scent, like one of those police dogs."

She held up both hands like she was trying to put a stop to my suspicions. And even though that's what I'd wanted her to do, saying it all out loud made me think I was right—there was something off about the whole situation.

"I know what you're thinking, but I'd swear on my life Luca's door was *closed*. You gonna try and convince me Rocket opened it?"

She blew out a breath. "Well, is it possible one of the girls wandered up there when they came inside?"

I shook my head. "They headed right for the pool. I'm telling you, that woman was snooping around in Luca's office."

"But why would she, Lil?" She arched a brow. "I mean, if you believe she was looking for something, then you gotta believe that she positioned herself into Meghan's life for that purpose. It just doesn't make any sense."

"But—"

"I'm not sayin' she wasn't in there. Could be she's some kind of kleptomaniac or maybe a tad unstable. Was there anything missing?"

I blew out a breath. I wanted to believe her version of the story, but I knew deep down there was more to it. But what? "I don't know. Only been in there once or twice myself. Can't hardly remember what's sitting on my own nightstand. And what about all the files he has in there? Would've been easy enough to snap pictures with her phone."

Her eyes widened. Probably thought I was certifiable. "For what purpose, Lil? I mean, you got means and opportunity, but you're missing the crucial motive part of the situation."

Crossing my arms, I glared at her, even though I knew it was unfair of me. She came over after a hard day of work, gave me the courtesy of listening to my story, and was offering sound, wise counsel. It didn't make me feel the least little bit better, though.

She sighed. "Okay, how about this? You get me her last name, and I'll see what I can find with a *legal* search. But if I don't find anything, you'll drop it, right?" Sounded fair.

"I'll get her last name from Meghan, but maybe you should at least jot down a description of her. That way, if she's stolen some old lady's ID, you'll know it."

As much as I fought for Sherrie to take my suspicions seriously, I truly hoped they proved false. The alternative was just too disquieting to consider.

Chapter Eighteen

Lillian

The week dragged by while I waited on pins and needles for Sherrie to ease my fears some. It didn't help that she was wrapping up a big case, so I couldn't expect her to put my paranoia at the top of her list. Filled my evenings with activities to help take my mind off whatever it was Jamie might've been up to. Worked on my children's book, meandered through the aisles of Walmart to find the boys a little something special, and took Rocket on early-morning and late-evening walks.

When there was still no word by Wednesday night, I put together an enchilada casserole (without any near mishaps, I might add) to heat up for Thursday's supper. Luca and the boys would be home, and I wanted to earn my keep. Wouldn't hurt to get on his good side in case Sherrie told me that I'd invited a criminal mastermind into his house. And I'd thought church gossip was something worth getting ruffled over. I'd take Elise Chambers over the mysterious Jamie any day of the week and twice on Sundays.

Thursday afternoon was quiet at the library, so I went into the back room to get started on a collection of broken book bindings. It didn't take a whole lot of focus, which left my thoughts to wander where they shouldn't. On Luca and his crooked smile—hard to believe I ever thought he was stiff as a broomstick. On what Jamie could've been searching for in Luca's office, and if she found it. Was just fixing to pull a new stack of broken books from a box on the floor when I glanced up to see Sherrie standing in the doorway.

"Carrie said I could come on back." Her smile slipped as she slid into a chair across from me and fingered the frayed edge of a cloth-bound cover with a loose book block. I was saving that one for when I could give it my full attention.

"I know you've been busy, so should I assume since you took the time to stop by rather than call it's because you've got bad news?" My heart thumped clear into my throat.

"Not bad news." She shrugged. "Not good news, either. Couldn't find anything that matched Jamie's name *and* description. Had my assistant call the recording company you said she works for, and they never heard of her."

The air was sucked clear from the room, and it became near impossible to breathe. "But that *is* bad news," I gasped. "Don't you see? It means she lied about who she is." I swiped a hand over my face that had gone hot. "And I was right about her snooping in Luca's office."

Sherrie took hold of my hand and squeezed. "You're borrowin' trouble, Lil. Just because she lied about her job doesn't mean it has anything to do with Luca. Could be she's stalking Meghan for some reason." As if that should make me feel any better.

"But she was in—"

"Luca's office." She sighed. "I know you believe that, but you can't be sure the door wasn't already open or that she ever went upstairs. I mean, it could be Rocket wandered in there 'cause he missed Luca and was searchin' out his scent."

I wanted to believe Sherrie, but I knew in my gut there was more to it. "Rocket didn't like her." Definitive proof right there. "He was sweet as could be with me the first time I met him, and I didn't even like dogs." Now if anyone dared to lay an angry hand on him, they'd have to go through me first.

Sherrie closed her eyes for a moment like she was counting to ten. Wouldn't be the first time she'd had to muster a little more patience with me. Then she looked me straight in the eyes. "What d'you wanna do? You wanna go to the police and file a report?"

I dropped my gaze to a ragged cuticle and picked at it. "And what would be the charge?"

"You tell me. You can't prove criminal activity or even intent." Her lawyerly language put a distance between us I didn't care for. Reminded me how much smarter she was—and practical.

"I don't know." I abandoned the cuticle and focused on Sherrie again. "Maybe she was casing the house and plans to break in."

"For?" Sherrie's eyebrows arched so high, they disappeared behind her wispy blond bangs. "Does Luca have any valuables around? Expensive artwork, jewelry, rare coins?" She made her point.

I spread my arms wide. "You're right. It's just another case of Crazy Lil overreacting once again." A lump of disappointment lodged in my throat. Not because Sherrie proved Jamie to be a non-threat, but because she didn't believe me. And why should she? It wasn't the first time I'd cried wolf.

Couldn't tell whether it was sympathy or pity in Sherrie's eyes. "When does Luca get back?"

"This afternoon. Could be there now for all I know." I plopped my elbows on the table and dropped my chin into my hands with a sigh. "What am I supposed to tell him?"

"Nothing." She stood up and slung her purse strap over her shoulder. "Or you can share everything with him and see what he thinks. Might could be he has someone in his past who comes to mind. We just don't know enough." She started for the door.

Someone in his past. "You mean like this mysterious wife of his?"

Turning, she narrowed her eyes at me. "You're not thinking this Jamie person is his ex-wife, or late wife, or whatever she is."

"Unless she's dead, it's a possibility, isn't it?" I rose from my chair and grabbed a piece of scratch paper. "Her name's Bridget McCullough." I scribbled down the name and handed it to her.

Sherrie stared at it for a moment, a wrinkle forming between her brows, then glanced at me. "McCullough? Where'd you get the notion her last name is different from Luca's?"

She knew I'd got caught snooping in Luca's office, but I didn't need to confess *everything*. "Just do is all."

"Okay, but why would she go to all the trouble of creating a fake persona just to get into his house?"

"I don't know. But will you check it out anyway?"

Frowning, she looked at it again. "This is bordering on crazy, Lil. Maybe you should share your concerns with Luca first."

"Please? If you don't find anything on her then I'll let it go."

"Wait a minute." She readjusted her purse strap. "Didn't you say the first time she came in with Meghan, they were with Luca's boys?"

"Yeah. So?"

"Wouldn't they have recognized their own mother?"

I thought about what Daniel had said about his mama that very day. "Daniel told me he was four the last time he saw her, and he hardly remembers anything about her."

"Okay, here's what I'm gonna do." She pointed the scratch paper at me. "I'll look up this Bridget McCullough, and if nothing comes of it, we're done with Crazy Town. Swear?"

I blew out a breath and smiled. "Promise."

After Sherrie left, Carrie poked her head in the door while I was gathering the supplies. "It's near five, Lil. Just wanted to remind you we traded days so you could go home early."

"Thanks. I hadn't forgotten. Just want to get this mess cleaned up first." Giddiness at seeing Luca and the boys warred with more than a little trepidation. Even if the mysterious Jamie wasn't an issue, we still had the church gossip to contend with. I'd submitted a few job applications, which I should tell Luca about. If any of them came through, it would give me the freedom to move out on my own. But the thought of it didn't bring me the relief it should've—just a whole lot of indecision.

When I stepped outside the comfort of the air-conditioned library, the heat and humidity was nearly breathtaking. And not in a good way. There wasn't a cloud in the sky, and the sun blinded me as I moved from the protection of the covered walkway toward the parking lot. There were few cars left besides mine—Carrie's, Kathleen's, and a few probably belonging to the library patrons who were still inside.

I caught movement in one of the vehicles as the driver backed out of a spot. Was that Jamie? Same short, dark hair and small build, but I couldn't get a clear look at her face between the oversized sunglasses and the tinted windshield. I stepped forward to get a better view, but she sped out of the lot, and my opportunity was gone. Didn't matter. I knew in my gut it was her.

Despite the ninety-degree heat, my whole body went cold. Something bad was coming my way, and I didn't have the first clue how to fight it.

Luca

An eight-hour car trip with all the fussing (as Lillian would say), griping, and bathroom breaks was enough to wear a grown man down to the point of exhaustion. Figured driving would be easier than flying—and take about as long with all the requirements that entailed—but being a prisoner behind the wheel in my own vehicle made me rethink the wisdom of that choice. It was bad enough on the way up to Wheaton, but the boys' patience with each other was wearing thin by the time we headed home.

We pulled into the driveway a few minutes to four—cranky, hungry, and tired. It took a lot of energy to maintain control in a confined space. Couldn't wait to unpack the car and maybe take a quick swim before needing to start on supper. If we hadn't already loaded up on junk food on the drive, I'd have considered ordering a pizza. What I hadn't taken into consideration was Lillian.

"You boys let Rocket in then take your bags up to your rooms and get them unpacked." I dropped mine in the foyer and headed for the kitchen for a glass of water. Had no idea what I'd face being gone for a full week with Lillian left to her own devices. What I hadn't expected was a plate of what appeared to be homemade chocolate chip cookies, a wrapped gift for each of the boys, and a note for me.

Luca, I know y'all must be worn out after the long drive, so don't worry yourself about supper. I've got it covered. And I promise no harm came to any of your appliances in the making of this meal. Ha ha. Got the boys a little something to welcome them home. I switched my hours with Carrie, so I'll be there a little after five.

Lillian

It felt normal and intimate at the same time. Dad's ludicrous idea popped into my head. *Marry the girl.* But I never jumped into a situation without considering the consequences from every angle—not anymore. I'd done that with Bridget and learned my lesson. Mom told me once that you can never truly know a person until you've lived with them. I don't think she meant just residing under the same roof—although that afforded plenty of insight—but living life day in and day out. The ups and downs, joys and sorrows. It's where true faith was built or revealed. Isn't that what Paul was referring to in Romans?

"What's this?" Daniel reached past me to snatch up one of the wrapped gifts. "Says it's for Matty." He slid it back.

"And this one's for you." I handed him the package blocked by my body. "Lillian was kind enough to get you boys a welcome home gift."

"Cool." He shook it. "Can I open it?"

"Depends. Did you get your bag unpacked?"

He nodded.

"And put everything away? Clothes in the drawers, toiletries in the bathroom?"

He rolled his eyes. "Aw, Dad. Can't I do it later?"

I grunted a laugh. "No, son. You can do it now. How hard is it to move folded clothes from one spot to another?" Thanks to Mom insisting on laundering everything, there wasn't a dirty sock in the lot. "Besides, I think it would mean a lot to Lillian if you opened her gift when she can be here to watch."

He moaned and stomped his way out of the kitchen.

Filled a glass with water then perused the contents of the refrigerator as I drank it. There was a large foil-covered baking dish inside, which I assumed was supper. Peeled back a corner and tried to decipher what it was. A casserole of some sort.

"Can I go swimming?"

I shut the refrigerator door and there stood Chase in swim trunks. Guess I needed to supervise the unpacking if I expected it to get done. "Let's go upstairs and see what's left to do first."

By the time Lillian arrived home, everything was put to order and the four of us were in the pool while Rocket kept a keen watch. When I caught sight of her standing in the kitchen door, Rocket rushing to her side, I could've sworn my heart skipped a beat. A reaction to seeing her after a week or an early indicator of a cardiac episode? Neither was preferable.

I'd never claimed to be a keen observer of women. Fact was, Bridget had accused me of missing whatever gene a man needed to clue into emotional cues. But even I could sense there was something off about Lillian. Her arms were wrapped around her middle like she was holding herself together, and the smile she flashed didn't reach her eyes.

"Hey, guys. Welcome home."

"Miss Lillian!" Matty clambered out the side of the pool and about knocked her over with a wet hug. Didn't seem to bother her in the least. In fact, her eyes finally caught up with that smile.

"I missed you boys." She rubbed his back as Chase joined them, Daniel hanging back just enough to let everyone know he wasn't quite the baby his brothers were.

I climbed from the pool and grabbed the towel I'd left on a lounge chair and started drying off. "It's too bad they didn't miss *you*." Maybe she'd just had a bad day or an emotional phone call with her mom. As far as I knew, there hadn't been much communication between them, but when there was, it seemed to leave her deflated.

Her gaze didn't quite meet mine as she wrapped an arm around Daniel's shoulders. "I swear you've grown an inch in the last week."

"Yeah, right." But he couldn't quite contain a grin. "It was a heck-of-a-long drive home today."

"I'll bet." She fingered a strand of wet hair from his eyes. "Just let me get changed, and I'll put dinner in the oven. Hope y'all like enchilada casserole." But she didn't wait for an answer—just slipped back inside.

While Chase and Matty jumped back into the pool, Daniel moved to my side. "Hey, Dad, is there something wrong with Miss Lillian?" So much for my pride in catching a clue. It was clear even to a nine-year-old that something was amiss. And he expected good ol' dad would have some insight into a woman's mind.

"I don't know, bud. Might just be tired from a long workday." I tossed the towel aside. "I'm going to get dressed and see if I can help with dinner. Why don't you stay out here with your brothers a while longer, and I'll call you guys when it's time to get out."

He nodded. "Okay."

By the time I changed into dry clothes and was back downstairs, Lillian had the casserole in the oven and was working on a salad. A hot day like this, grilling would've been preferable, but I'd be an idiot to complain.

I tapped one of the wrapped gifts on the counter. "It was nice of you to get the boys something."

"It's not much. Just wanted them to know I was thinking about them."

"Still." Wasn't the conversation starter I'd hoped for. Now what? "Can I help? Maybe cut up some veggies for you?" I stood with the island separating us—literally and figuratively.

"I've got it covered." Her gaze slid to mine for a brief second before she focused on tearing lettuce like it took all her attention. "Maybe you could gather the boys' dirty clothes, and I'll get a load started after supper."

"My mom did it all before we packed." I dared to move closer. "You have a hard day at work?"

She shrugged. "It was fine."

"Everything okay with your parents?" Maybe if I asked enough questions, I'd catch a clue.

"Don't know. Haven't talked to Mama in a while." She reached for a tomato. "Did you have a good visit with yours?" We were easing back into normalcy.

"Yeah. Even got a lot of work done while we were there. Have an appointment with a recording company in Nashville Monday morning."

Her head shot up, and her eyes narrowed for a split second. "Oh, really?" Was there a thread of panic in her tone? "I didn't know you worked with the music industry."

I reached over and snatched a slice of cucumber from the cutting board and pointed it at her. "What's going on with you, Lillian? You look about ready to jump out of your skin. Did I do something to upset you?"

Her eyes went wide. "No! Not at all." Shaking her head, she scooped up the sliced veggies and dropped them into the bowl. "Guess I'm a little worked up over this whole church gossip thing. It's got me on edge."

Relief pulled a chuckle from me. "Is that all?"

She pushed out her chin. "It's not nothin', Luca. Last thing I wanna do is cause you trouble. I know it's just a bunch of busybodies, but it doesn't hurt any less."

Why did I have the feeling there was more to it than that? "My dad has a solution to that little problem." I grinned at her, hoping she'd reciprocate.

A smile tugged at her lips. "Oh, really?"

"Yeah." I forced a lightness to my tone, even though the moment called for the opposite. "He said we should get married. Isn't that crazy?"

Her shoulders stiffened as her eyes filled with tears. Then before I could unscramble my brain, she rushed from the kitchen. Bridget's accusation about me being incapable of reading emotional cues was the one thing she'd been right about.

Chapter Nineteen

Lillian

If Luca hadn't already thought I was nuttier than a pecan pie, running off like an emotional tween last night would've cemented it. And that wasn't even the worst of it. I still had to face him during supper and act like it'd never even happened. Made it some easier when we could focus on the boys tearing into their presents—at least that's where I kept my attention. Not Luca. Could feel his eyes assessing me off and on, like he was waiting for me to implode.

After supper, I showed the boys how much their vegetable plants had grown since they'd been gone. Matty was especially excited to know that each of the blooms was the start of a real tomato or zucchini. Then we checked on the worm garden, which we'd moved into the shade of the patio before they left for their trip so they wouldn't get too hot.

Soon as Luca told the boys it was time to get ready for bed, I jumped up to do the dishes while he tended to that. Got it done right quick, too, so I could escape to my room. It was early, but I just couldn't pretend anymore that everything was just fine. It was bad enough I was fretting over the whole Jamie situation, but now the crack about his daddy saying we should get married? Made it even worse that he thought it was a big joke—like marrying me was crazy as a June bug. Billy had already made that clear, and I certainly didn't need Luca reinforcing it.

Next morning, I slipped out of the house before anyone was up, feeling a tad guilty. But if what I suspected about Jamie was true, Luca wouldn't want anything to do with me once he found out. The sooner I figured out a way to detach my heart from those three little boys, the better. I didn't wanna think too hard about Luca. Even if I didn't have myself a habit of making foolish decisions, I knew it wasn't possible to fall in love with a man in such a short span of time. It was chemistry—a heavy dose of dopamine or some such nonsense. And nothing else.

Stopped by Dunkin' Donuts on my way to the library for caffeine and a sugar fix—iced coffee and donut holes. With the Billy heartbreak, it was a pint of Ben & Jerry's Chunky Monkey. But even I couldn't indulge in ice cream first thing in the morning.

The library parking lot was empty, as it should've been when the sun was just peeking over the horizon. Had me two hours before I clocked into work, and I'd use the time to fill out more job applications. Maybe expand my search outside of Middle Tennessee. There were plenty of opportunities in Knoxville, and I did love the Smoky Mountains.

I'd gotten a call to go for an interview in Murfreesboro on Monday, but I was keeping it to myself for the time being. There were too many conflicting emotions tied up in the possibilities. If I got it, I'd need to find myself somewhere else to live, which might be the wisest (and hardest) move I could make. With the commute and hours, I'd be of little use to Luca and the boys. But the thought of leaving them was too painful to consider.

Had just gotten my food stash set out on the table in the staff room when my phone buzzed. Who'd be wanting to chat this early in the morning? Checked the Caller ID—Mama. Of course, she'd have a *sick* sixth sense about me getting myself into another fix.

The thought that something could've happened to Daddy had me answering. "Mama?"

"Goodness, Lillian." A sigh reached my ears. "I was fixing to call Sherrie if you didn't answer."

My heart thumped like a bass drum. "What's wrong? Daddy okay?"

"What's wrong?" Her voice pitched. "You tell me. I've been leavin' messages for weeks. Was beginning to think you fell off the face of the earth."

Is that all? The muscles in my shoulders released, and I blew out a breath. "I've just been busy, Mama. With working and taking care of the boys."

"So, how's that goin'? You gettin' on okay with them and their daddy?"

Her question threw me off. I'd spent so much of my time playing defense, I wasn't expecting casual conversation. Always seemed there was an agenda with her, but it appeared this time I was wrong. "It's goin' just fine." For the moment. But that could change right quick. "Been applying to other libraries, though. It makes sense to keep my options open." Telling Mama upfront was like killing two birds—she'd see I was maturing and be forewarned if I suddenly changed jobs.

We chatted a few more minutes before another call came through—Sherrie. "Hey, Mama, it's been real nice catching up with you—" and I actually meant it "—but I gotta get this other call coming in. Could be important. Love you, and give Daddy a hug for me, will you?"

I thumbed Sherrie's call on the fourth ring, relieved that she hadn't hung up. "Hey, Sherrie."

"Did I catch you at a bad time?" Sounded like she was clanking pots and pans in the background.

"No. You didn't find out anything already, did you?" I popped a donut hole into my mouth and let the sugar calm me—at least for the moment.

"Nothing definitive. You know how many Bridget McCulloughs are in the U.S?"

"A lot?"

She laughed. "Yeah. A whole lot. I did find a wedding photo of Luca and his bride from ten years ago in the newspaper archives. Even though the picture is grainy, it's clear to see Luca's Bridget was a stunning blond. Didn't you say Jamie's a brunette?"

I closed my eyes and sighed. "Yes. Definitely a brunette." The sick feeling I'd been carrying around in the pit of my stomach melted away. Still didn't know what Jamie was up to, but I couldn't think of anything worse than giving Luca's ex-wife access to his house. When I saw him later, I could excuse my emotional meltdown last night on worrying over gossip and his lame crack about marriage.

"So, we're gonna let it go as promised?" Sherrie's lawyerly voice broke into my thoughts.

"Yes, ma'am."

It was amazing how a person took boring and uneventful for granted. Felt as if I was floating on air the rest of the day just because I didn't have to share my fears with Luca. I'd tell him about Meghan bringing a stranger to the house, and how I'd mistakenly thought she was a friend. Just in case something came of it. But I wasn't gonna borrow trouble, like Sherrie had accused me of doing.

After I checked out the last patron, Carrie walked him to the door to lock it while I tidied things up. Inevitably, there were books left out and a few things for the lost and found box.

Kathleen wandered out from her office, sweater and purse over her arm. "Okay, y'all. We'll see you bright and early in the morning. Don't forget we have Susan Grogan stopping by before lunch to talk to us about starting a mobile library here."

After she left, I rolled my eyes at Carrie. "A mobile library? They're gonna need to hire more people for that, which means we'll be making squat for the foreseeable future. Can't imagine there's anything left in the budget for raises as it is." Another reason right there it was wise of me to send out those job applications. We walked to the door, and I dug in my purse for my keys.

"I don't know why you're still here, Lil. You could get a job anywhere." It wasn't the first time she'd said so, but until one of those jobs was a sure thing, I was staying quiet.

Carrie headed toward her car at one end of the lot while I went in the opposite direction. Rounding the corner of the library, I stopped short. The pit I'd been carrying around earlier was back the moment I spotted Jamie leaning up against my car. A quick glance confirmed what I feared—we were alone.

Straightening my shoulders and holding my head high, I moved forward. Didn't know if the same held true for a person sensing fear like dogs did, but I wasn't taking any chances. She couldn't know I was aware she'd lied about everything, so I'd just play along and see where it took me.

Forcing a smile, I hit the fob on my keys to unlock the door. "Hey, Jamie. This is a surprise. What're you doing here?"

She folded her arms and jutted out one hip. "Was hoping you could help me out." She didn't look the least little bit like someone who needed help.

"With what?" A couple of teenage boys walked down the sidewalk, laughing and nudging each other. They wouldn't be any help if things took a turn.

"My name isn't really Jamie Rogers." She tilted her head. "But you probably figured that out, didn't you?"

A bead of sweat trickled down my lower spine as I squinted at her, but I wouldn't give her the satisfaction of cowering. "Had me a feeling. Especially since you were snooping through the house the other day." I clenched the key fob so hard, it cut into my hand.

"I'm Luca's wife, Bridget." She wrinkled her nose. "Ex-wife, I suppose. I have a proposal for him, and I think you're the person to help convince him it'd be wise to accept."

I scowled. "You're not Bridget. I know for a fact she's a blond."

She had the audacity to laugh, and the amusement in her eyes appeared genuine. "Easily changed. For a college-educated girl, you're not real bright." She combed her fingers through her hair. "Couldn't have Daniel recognizing me, even if I didn't think he would anyway. He was just a toddler when I left."

"He was four." And he had her cheekbones. Chase's nose tilted the tiniest bit like hers, too. But it was her eyes that had me thinking she looked familiar the first time—Matty's eyes. "How could you be around your babies and act like they meant nothing to you?"

She shrugged. "Never mind about that. All you should concern yourself with is convincing Luca that it's in his best interest to wire a tidy sum into my bank account."

Now it was my turn to laugh, but there wasn't the least little spark of humor in it. My crazy wasn't even a close second to hers. "And why should he do that?"

"Because if he doesn't, I'll be sure to take Matthew from him."

Hot anger surged through every nerve ending. "No one's gonna take a boy from his daddy and hand him over to an absentee mama. Especially one who's trying to extort money from him."

"That's where you've got things backwards, Lillian." She reached behind her and pulled a card from her back pocket. "Matthew isn't his son. You only have to look at him to know that. And it's only going to cost him fifty thousand dollars." She held the card out and wiggled it. "Take it. You tell Luca to give me a call, and we'll work out the details."

Luca

Didn't get much work done, despite having things in place to occupy the boys. I continually revisited the night before and the distance I'd caused between Lillian and myself. Why had I ever revealed Dad's cockamamie marriage idea? I wasn't serious. Well, not really. I'd hoped we could share a chuckle over it or possibly plant a seed for the future. Hadn't expected her to fly out of the room in tears then spend the rest of the evening avoiding eye contact and conversation. Didn't bode well that she was already gone when I got up this morning.

I owed her an apology, and the sooner I could give it and get us back on solid ground, the easier I'd be able to breathe again. *Marriage.* What had I been thinking? Hadn't been thinking is more like it. At least not with my head. Sure, she was great with the boys, and I was attracted to her. But other than that, we had nothing in common. *They say opposites attract.*

"Hey, Dad." Matty stood at the threshold of my office door. So focused on Lillian, I hadn't even heard him come upstairs.

"Yeah, bud. What d'you need?" I closed my laptop. Wasn't getting any work done anyway.

"Can I have one of Miss Lillian's cookies? I'm hungry."

I glanced at my watch. Almost five. "She'll be home in just a bit, and I'll light up the barbecue. Think you can wait?"

He shrugged his little shoulders and meandered inside, working me with his blue eyes. "I don't think so. It's just one cookie. I can still eat a ham-bugger, I promise."

No doubt, Daniel and Chase had already eaten their fair share—without benefit of permission. Matty couldn't sneak or lie to save his life, which was a miracle, given his DNA. "Okay. I'll come on down and get you a cookie if you'll feed Rocket. Deal?"

His face lit up with a grin. "Yeah. Deal."

As I rounded the table, he slipped his little hand into mine. These were the moments I never wanted to take for granted. Being a single father made every one of them worth it.

"Where are your brothers?" We started down the stairs, and I slowed my steps to match his.

"Playing with Rocket in the backyard." He looked up at me as we reached the foyer. "We wanna know if we can go swimming."

The boys would live in the pool if I let them. "Sure. I'll get your cookie, and you let them know it's okay."

I could just as easily keep an eye on them while waiting for Lillian to get home. The moment she showed up, I'd squire her away to my office so we could talk without an audience of three. But when 5:30 came and went, my optimism over mending things took a deep dive. Called her cell, but it went to voicemail. Had she left us? Only way to know was to step into uncharted territory—her bedroom.

A knot formed in my belly as I moved down the hallway toward her closed door. Hand on the knob, I tried once more to call. The ringing of the phone coordinated with the peppy ringtone coming from her bedroom. Had she snuck in while I was in my office or did she leave this morning without her phone?

I rapped on the door with a knuckle. "Lillian? Are you in there?" Could hear movement, but it was a full ten seconds before the door was opened a mere crack.

"Can't talk right now." She croaked more than spoke, and her words were punctuated by a sniffle. Was she crying?

The knot grew. "Look, Lil, I know you're upset with me. Have every right to be. Can we please just talk about it? Clear the air?"

She hung her head. "You didn't do anything. I did."

Couldn't imagine what. "Well, let's talk about it." It wasn't appropriate for us to meet in her bedroom. "Come on up to my office."

Sniffle.

"Please."

When she opened the door, I got the first real glimpse of her. It was clear she'd been crying, but there was more. Pain, dejection, fear. Took everything in me to keep from pulling her into my arms like I did with the boys when they were hurting. What could possibly have transpired in the last twenty-four hours to bring this on? Or had it been longer? She hadn't been her normal self since we got home from Wheaton.

"Come on." I placed a gentle hand on her back and guided her down the hall and upstairs to my office. Once there, I closed the door and indicated she should sit in one of the two chairs in front of my desk. I opened the window overlooking the pool to keep an ear out for the boys before sitting next to her.

Bending forward, I rested my elbows on my knees, narrowing the physical distance between us. What I wanted to do was pull her into my arms and promise everything would be okay. "Did something happen while I was in Illinois?"

Her eyes, now swimming with tears, darted to mine, and her chin quivered. I took that as yes. So, she was being honest—it wasn't what I'd said the night before. Was I going to have to play a childish game of twenty questions to get to the bottom of all this?

Hands wringing, she cleared her throat. "You remember I asked you about having Meghan and her girls over to swim?" Deciphering her garbled words took all my attention. Her voice was pitching worse than a storm-riddled boat.

"Yes." I opened my mouth to ask another question but got the sense she needed to do this at her own pace. As much as I liked to control things, this wasn't the time or place.

"When Meghan showed up, she had a friend with her." Her mouth twisted in a grimace. "At least that's what I thought. She'd brought this woman by the library the week before and introduced her to me, so I, of course, assumed she was a friend." She shrugged. "I mean, wouldn't you?"

All I could do was nod. Despite wanting to allow Lillian to tell things in her own way, I had to clench my jaw to keep from firing questions at her. One thing I'd discovered living in the South for an entire two months—kind as these people were, they tended to use a lot of words when fewer would do.

"There was something about this woman that put me on edge." She clenched her hands. "Should've listened to my gut."

Although the last words seemed to be aimed at her rather than me, a fist grabbed hold of my heart and started a slow squeeze. No more tiptoeing through this conversation. "What happened?"

Her tongue flicked out to wet her lips, and she jumped up. "She asked if she could use the bathroom, so of course I let her." Stopping, she glanced at me. "I mean, what else could I do?"

The blood rose up to pulse at my neck. "Who was she?" But the question was moot. I already knew.

"Found out when I left work that she's your ex-wife." Hands shaking, she dropped back into the chair while all the air left my lungs.

"Bridget." The name was an expletive and just saying it out loud had my blood boiling.

"She said her name was Jamie." Lillian grabbed hold of my arm and squeezed. "But when I figured she'd been snooping in your office instead of going to the bathroom, I knew there was something off."

Bridget was a con artist and a manipulator. And she'd been good at biding her time. "So, what's her endgame?"

Tears were coursing down Lillian's cheeks. "I should've never let her in, Luca. It's all my fault."

"Tell me." Didn't realize how harsh the words came out until Lillian flinched. "Dragging it out isn't going to change anything."

She swallowed a couple times and took a deep breath. "She was waiting on me when I came out of the library tonight. Said Matty's not your son." She reared back the moment the words were out as if she expected me to strike her. "She's lying, Luca. I know she is."

I barked out a humorless laugh. "It's probably the only thing she's ever been honest about."

Her mouth dropped open. "You mean he's not?" Then her eyes narrowed. "And you already knew?"

I rubbed a hand down my face. "I've always known. Had a DNA test done years ago, but that was just a formality. Doesn't matter who fathered the boy, he's every bit mine as Chase and Daniel are."

She folded her arms and hung her head. "Which she surely knows."

I shrugged. "Maybe. The minute he was born, she took off with some other man—might've even been Matty's sperm donor. Haven't had any contact with her since, other than through lawyers in order to finalize our divorce." *So, what's her angle now?*

Heart hammering in my throat, I nudged Lillian. "I know she didn't connive all this just to let me know I'm not Matty's biological father. What's the rest of it?"

Her face crumpled like a limp tissue. "She says I've gotta convince you to give her fifty thousand dollars or she's gonna take Matty away from you."

Now I knew why she was going through my office. Looking for financial records so she'd know just how much money she could squeeze from me. Either she wasn't thorough in her search, or she had no concept what a father would pay to secure his boy. Matty was worth a heck of a lot more than what she was demanding.

I would've been willing to give my life for him.

Chapter Twenty

Lillian

Whenever I messed up, the least I could say was I hadn't hurt anyone else. It wasn't like I needed Daddy to pay my rent—although I had been willing to move in with him and Mama—or put anyone else in a tight spot. That consolation went right out the window with the Jamie/Bridget fiasco. Luca was nice enough about it, even going so far as to say it wasn't my fault at all. In fact, he said it was on him for not being *forthcoming*—his word—about his ex-wife. Maybe if he had been, I'd have been forewarned. And maybe that was true. I already walked a thin line between suspicion and paranoia, so the moment she appeared, I would've trusted my gut that there was something off about her.

But I saw his face when he didn't know I was looking. What she was doing broke him, and me allowing her into his house was a betrayal of sorts—even if it was unintentional. Just the thought of Bridget getting her claws into Matty was enough to make me see red. Don't get me wrong. If she loved the boy like a mama should, I'd be the first one to say she had every right to spend time with him. But she had evil in her heart, and it didn't appear there was a whole lot of room left over for love.

Me being in his house on the tail end of learning about my betrayal would be rubbing salt into his wound. So, I did us both a favor and invited myself to stay with Sherrie and Josh for a night. I just couldn't go home Saturday after work and pretend with the boys that everything was fine. Gave me a whole new respect for married couples going through a rough patch. Not that Luca and I were married. Or would ever be married.

"You think ignoring it for one weekend is gonna fix everything?" Sherrie tossed the question at me as we settled onto her back patio that evening. Wasn't as nice as Luca's yard—there was no swimming pool, or rowdy dog running around, or three adorable little boys. And instead of Luca standing at the grill, it was Josh.

Tucked my bare legs underneath me and took a sip of my sweet tea. "Just giving him a little space to work through his anger." And maybe hiding from the shame of bringing all this on him for a short bit.

"But you told me he didn't seem at all upset with you."

I shot a quick glance at Josh, who was flipping the steaks, to see if he was listening. But he had Air Pods in his ears and seemed to be engaged in a more interesting conversation than the two of us were having. "How many times have you told Josh you weren't mad about something, but deep down you were fuming?"

She wrinkled her nose. "That's different. Nine times outta ten, when I'm worked up, it takes me a little time to figure out why. Once I do, it's usually got nothing to do with him."

"Well, if I'm gonna be completely honest with you—"

"Please do."

"Then I gotta admit it's hard to look at Matty and Luca right now. I allowed the devil herself a foothold into their lives, and now they're at risk." If Luca lost that little boy on account of my foolishness, I wouldn't be able to live with myself. Best case, he'd end up losing a whole lot of money. I'd pay it myself if I had it.

"So, what're you gonna do, Lil?"

I shrugged. "What I don't understand is how she can get away with this. I mean, extortion's against the law, right?"

Josh plopped down next to Sherrie and took a swig from her beer. Apparently, the engaging conversation with his client was over. "What you got here is a case of he said/she said. It's just too bad you weren't wearing a wire."

"Doesn't matter," Sherrie said. "If Matty isn't Luca's biological child, it's gonna be quite a fight to keep him away from her." She frowned. "And Matty's the one who'll pay in the end."

It took me a moment to process what she was saying. "So, you think Luca should just give him up." My voice rose with each word along with the heat climbing my neck.

"Of course not." Sherrie glanced at Josh. "Tell her what you told me, babe."

He passed the beer bottle back to her. "What she wants is money. It's obvious from all that's transpired that she doesn't care at all about the boys. Last thing she wants is the responsibility and expense of raising Matty—or anyone else. She's probably a narcissist."

My heart rate slowed, and I could breathe again. "Then you're sayin' Luca should go ahead and pay her the money."

Josh shook his head. "I'm not sayin' that."

"Then what?"

"It's a tricky situation. There's nothing you can do here, Lil, unless you wanna get yourself deeper into the whole mess. Why don't you tell Luca to give me a call before he makes a decision? I can at least run through the legal options and give him my best advice." He pushed from the chair and moved toward the grill again. "And you gotta stop blaming yourself for this."

Sherrie hopped up. "Come help me get the rest of supper together. You can make a salad."

I followed Sherrie inside where the kitchen counter was cluttered with a stack of mail and a couple files. Typical mess, but after living with Luca's regimented organization for even a short time, I had to resist the urge to clear it up. He'd rubbed off on me, and the boys had a bigger part of my heart than I thought possible. The longer I stayed, the harder it would be to leave.

"Where did you go off to, Lil?"

"What?" It was just then I realized she'd been talking to me, and I hadn't heard a word.

"I asked you what you were thinking, but it's pretty clear you're not here with me." She pulled salad fixings from the fridge and handed them to me.

"Feels like I got myself into another pickle." I collected a cutting board and paring knife.

"You're beatin' a dead horse. There's nothing you can do about it. You heard Josh."

"It's not just that. I felt like God gave me this opportunity." I glanced at her. "I didn't tell you this, but I'd prayed for Him to guide my next step when I gave up looking for a roommate. And now here I am, fixing to get my heart broken again."

Sherrie paused from uncovering the congealed salad, her mouth forming an O. "You're in love with Luca."

I threw a scowl. "Am not." Sounded like a five-year-old. "In *like* maybe. But even if I was, which I'm *not*, I don't think he sees me that way." Wasn't about to tell her how his daddy said we should get married, and that he saw it as a big joke. Sherrie'd hear the word marriage and totally ignore the joke part of it.

"Well, it's only been a month. Give him time."

"That would be just fine if it was only the two of us. Course, if it was just the two of us, I wouldn't be living in his house in the first place. And the longer I live there, the more I fall in love with those boys of his. Can't stay there forever on account of them, now can I?" My throat went tight at the thought of leaving. But what else could I do?

"Didn't you tell me God opened this door for you?" Sherrie put an arm around me.

I nodded.

"Don't you think there's a reason He did it?"

"Of course, I do. But that doesn't mean it's forever."

"Forever?" She let out a soft laugh. "Goodness, Lil, it's been a few measly weeks. If you leave now, what was the point of bein' there in the first place?"

"I don't know. Yet. But God landing me with Luca doesn't mean He planned for me to fall in love and stay there. Might be another lesson entirely. Maybe it has to do with the boys, or maybe it's so I grow a backbone and do for myself what I couldn't before."

Sherrie folded her arms and quirked a brow. "Okay, then where will you go? You got enough money saved up to live on your own? What about rent? You get a raise in the last week or so I don't know about?" There she was, grilling me again.

"Put in quite a few job applications, and I have an interview on Monday." There. That should put a hitch in her giddy up. So much for keeping it to myself.

Her face lit up. "That's great, Lil. But you still need first, last, and security deposit." Sherrie was a natural at playing the devil's advocate. That's why she was such a good lawyer.

"Then I guess it's time I mustered up the nerve to pay a visit to Billy." And if that wouldn't take a whole lot of backbone, I didn't know what would.

Chapter Twenty-One

Luca

Lillian was gone one night, and to hear the boys grumbling, you'd think the world was coming to an end. Matty and Chase weren't satisfied with "because" when they asked why, and Daniel's reversion to his previous surly attitude told me he wasn't buying it, either. They'd sooner trade me in for her, and I couldn't blame them.

She showed up at the house Sunday morning in time to get the boys ready for church. They didn't seem to notice the tension emanating from her—probably too relieved she was back with them to notice. Wanted to talk to her about the situation, but she managed to keep the boys as a buffer between us the rest of the day, which was just as well. I had enough to deal with as it was.

I hadn't yet called the number Bridget gave Lillian. Ignoring it wouldn't make it go away. Praying for Bridget's demise was only slightly satisfying. Tried to justify it by recounting to God all the times King David asked for his enemies to be struck down in the book of Psalms. But even in my dejected state, I knew I should've been praying for her salvation instead. Couldn't quite get there yet.

Only thing Lillian shared with me once she got home was that I should talk to Josh before deciding. I agreed. But first I wanted to be armed with all the information possible, which required me to meet with Bridget. I didn't call, though. Couldn't stomach the idea of hearing her voice, and I wasn't sure I could keep from losing my temper. So, I texted. Was tempted to use all caps, but I refrained. No sense poking the bear before I had what I needed.

I told her to meet me at The Coffee Break at 6:30 Monday. She wasn't a morning person, but I didn't care—it would give me an advantage. And just maybe, the courthouse looming just across the street might give her pause, even if it was subconscious.

There was already a line of people waiting to order, but I wasn't there for the coffee. Just wanted a public place with plenty of witnesses so she couldn't pull a fast one—like accusing me of sexual assault. Wouldn't put it past her. After glancing inside to be sure she wasn't there, I sat at one of the tables set out front. The sun was high enough to warm the air, and the trees surrounding the courthouse were full of birds celebrating the morning. It grated on nerves that were already taut.

It wasn't more than a minute before I caught sight of a woman crossing the street. Took me a moment to recognize her as Bridget only because Lillian said her hair was short and dark now. Apparently, she'd been wearing a wig. Guess she didn't need to keep up the subterfuge anymore. I slipped my phone into the front pocket of my shirt and took a deep breath. Let the games begin.

She dropped into the chair across from me with a scowl and set her small bag on the table. Didn't appear she'd aged a day. Somehow, that didn't seem fair. "I don't know why we couldn't meet later in the day. Worried I'd interrupt your precious work hours?"

"Yeah, that's my highest concern right now. Not the fact that you're extorting money and using your own son as leverage."

Her head whipped around like she was checking to be sure no one heard me. Then she leaned in and hissed, "Keep your voice down."

Could she not see the irony? "Why? Are you ashamed of what you're doing? Because you should be." I pinned her with a glare. "This is low even for you."

Her gaze latched onto mine. "Consider it the alimony I never received." And there it was—her version of reality.

"Our lawyers hashed this out before you ever signed the divorce papers." Did she really need me to remind her? "We weren't married even six years, which precludes alimony in most cases. Plus, you never held a job and you abandoned your children."

"Which is why we're not going through the court system. Besides, you weren't making the kind of money back then that you are now."

"I wasn't raising the boys on my own back then, either." Although that wasn't technically true. Despite Bridget not working, she was rarely home. Instead, she'd insisted we hire a nanny to watch Chase and Daniel while she spent her days doing only God knew what.

"And if it weren't for me having those boys, you'd be alone today. I never wanted them, and you knew that." As if I forced myself on her. As if she didn't have access to birth control. As if she hadn't gone out and had an affair, which resulted in a third pregnancy.

But there was no point arguing the facts with her. She had a warped view of things, and I wasn't going to change that with one conversation. What she needed was years of intensive therapy, which was the reason right there I'd do whatever it took to keep her away from the boys. Not that she had any desire to see them.

"You haven't even asked about your children."

She shrugged. "I don't need to. I saw them for myself just a couple weeks ago. They couldn't stop talking about your girlfriend." Was that hurt I saw in her eyes? She couldn't possibly be jealous of Lillian, could she?

"Lillian isn't my girlfriend." I should be so fortunate. "She's an employee." I nearly choked on the words, even if they were true.

"Yeah, right. She's living in your house, Luca. Do you really expect me to believe there's nothing going on between the two of you?"

Why should I expect her to think otherwise when even some of the women in our church were suspicious?

"It's true. Lillian has nothing to do with this, so I'm not sure why you put her in the middle."

She shrugged. "She letting me into your house gave me a chance to see how much more you're worth today than when I left. Her doing so must have been quite the disappointment. We both know you have impossible expectations."

My blowup over Lillian going through the file in my office came to mind. If I was suspicious of others' motives, I had only my marriage to Bridget to blame. Rubbing my forehead, I sighed. We could go back and forth until Jesus returned, and we'd still be at opposite sides of the fence. "You need help, Bridget."

Her eyes hardened. "I'm done with the chitchat." She rummaged through her bag and pulled out a business card. "Here's the wiring instructions for my bank account. You know what to do."

"And if I refuse?"

"Don't test me, Luca. I don't need to see you with Matthew to know how much he's worth to you. I can prove he isn't your biological son, and it wouldn't take much to convince a judge that a boy belongs with his mother rather than a stepfather who never even bothered to adopt him."

My blood went cold as a shiver ran up my back. Thought I held all the cards, but this was one thing I hadn't expected. As far as I was concerned, the moment the nurse put Matty in my arms, he was my son. There was never even a question about it.

Bridget shoved the card toward me. "I expect the money to be in my account by the end of the day."

"I'm afraid that's not possible." Even if it was, I needed time to talk to Josh. Should've done that before meeting Bridget, like Lillian suggested. "It'll take a few days to liquidate it from my account, and another business day for it to be transferred." I was making it up, but it sounded logical enough to be true. Hopefully, Bridget didn't know different.

Her lips thinned. "Fine," she mumbled. "I'm here one week. If I don't have that money by next Monday, you'll be hearing from my lawyer."

I grunted. "Seriously? You really expect a lawyer to be party to illegal activity?"

She rolled her eyes. "You're so naive. Everyone has a price—including you." Snatching up her bag, she pointed a finger at me as a warning. "Don't test me, Luca. You'll lose."

If I hadn't been fuming mad, I would've laughed. Did she have any idea how comical she appeared? But funny or not, I didn't doubt she'd do whatever she could to achieve her goal.

Lillian

I had woken before the sun Monday morning after a night of tossing, turning, and praying. Could've blamed it on nerves, since I had me an interview at MTSU later in the day, but I was only fooling myself. Kept thinking about Sherrie saying I was in love with Luca. It'd been easy enough to deny, but I knew in my heart she was right. How could that happen so quick? It'd taken me months to believe my feelings for Billy were anything close to love, and that didn't turn out so well.

Finally gave up on going back to sleep and climbed out of bed. I'd have dark circles under my eyes for my interview, but there was nothing to do about it. It wasn't like anyone was gonna base my qualifications on a haggard appearance. Might could be they'd feel sorry for me, and I'd get the pity vote.

After a quick swim and shower, I went to the kitchen to get a cup of coffee and found a note from Luca: *Had an early morning appointment. Will be back soon.* Surely, he saw me out back, so why'd he leave a note instead of coming out? Then again, why would he when I'd done everything I could to avoid bein' alone with him? *Can't have it both ways, girl.* Sherrie's words in my head were clear as if she'd been standing there.

Luca and I had been antsy as show pigs at the state fair since he got home from vacation. And I didn't have the first clue how to change it. The fact that I wanted to was sort of telling. Guilt, shame, and a whole lot of sadness weighed on me.

"Where's Daddy?"

I whirled around to find Matty right behind me rubbing the sleep from his eyes. "I'm not sure, sweetie. Guess he had himself an errand. Want me to make you some breakfast?" By the time I had the griddle heated and pancake batter mixed, Chase, Daniel, and Rocket had joined the party. When I was their age, summers were for sleeping in, but this bunch was on Luca's internal clock.

Once their bellies were full and they'd changed out of their pajamas, we spent the morning pulling weeds, tending to the worms, and planting some annuals I'd picked up at Lowes.

Luca appeared mid-morning and stood apart from us while we were digging in the yard like whatever was eating at him might be contagious. The only thing I could imagine would put those dark shadows in his eyes was Jamie, or rather, Bridget. Guess the chance to get herself a payoff was worth an early meeting.

I stuck my hand-shovel in the soil and squinted up at him. "You okay?"

He shoved his hands into the front pockets of his jeans. "Fine. I see you have an appointment listed on the calendar at one. I need to go out again at four. Will you be back by then?"

"Yes." Even if I had to leave my interview early to keep that promise, I would. It was my fault all this was happening. Or at least I had a hand in it. Sherrie and Josh kept telling me I wasn't to blame, but it sure didn't feel that way.

"Hey, Daddy." Matty ran up to Luca and grabbed a hold of his hand with his soil-crusted one and tugged. "Come look at the 'tunias Miss Lillian got us to plant."

Luca crouched down and gave Matty a hug then kissed the top of his head before he stood again. "I'll come see them a little later, okay? Got a couple things to do that can't wait." His eyes lingered on the boy for a long moment before he escaped back inside.

The boys' joy from only a few minutes before vanished along with their daddy. There was a worry wrinkle between Daniel's eyebrows, and while Chase and Matty might not understand what was different about Luca, it still affected them. Even Rocket stood at the back door and stared as if keeping watch over him.

"Come on, boys." I infused as much energy into my voice as I could muster. "Let's get these flowers in before it gets too hot. We don't want them to wilt, now do we?"

"What's wrong with Dad?" Daniel mumbled low enough his brothers wouldn't hear.

"Oh, your daddy's just fine." I swiped at a bit of dirt on his cheek. "Probably has himself a difficult client is all." But beneath the cheery Mary Poppins positivity, I fumed. The idea that one thoughtless, self-centered woman could be the root of so much heartache was enough to make me pitch a duck fit. Mama used to tell me that beauty was only skin deep, and it was sure the truth with that woman.

About the time I needed to clean up for my interview, Luca came back out wearing swim trunks and carrying a towel. "Who wants to go swimming?" The darkness no longer surrounded him, so I imagined the good Lord ministered in the way only He could.

Leaving the boys to their daddy, I slipped into my bedroom where it was a sight cooler and quieter. Felt a tightness to my skin after being in the sun too long—and some queasiness, too. Course, that could be pure nerves. Hadn't been on a job interview in years, and I wasn't in the best frame of mind for this one. Shouldn't a person really *want* the position they were interviewing for?

Took a quick shower to wash away the sweat and dirt, slathered my reddening skin with lotion, and slipped into a yellow tank dress. Hadn't had time to wash my hair but twisting it up and clipping it looked more professional anyway. A little mascara and lip gloss added the finishing touches.

As I sat on the bed to slip into my sandals, my eyes caught on the sketchpad I'd been using to illustrate one of my children's books. Daddy told me once that if I got a job doing what I loved, I'd add five days of joy to my week. That was one reason right there I decided to become a librarian. Loved books, and I loved reading to children. If I took a university position, it'd be a whole lot of textbooks, which didn't appeal in the least, and no children. But it came with a bigger paycheck. Everyone had to make compromises, didn't they?

I flipped through the illustrations inspired by the boys and Rocket: Daniel holding up a juicy, red worm as if it was a prize-winning specimen; Chase with his nose buried in *Treasure Island* doing his best to sound out the hard words; and Matty with a huge grin watching Rocket clean up the mess of food that didn't make it in his bowl. They weren't just part of a story, they'd become a part of me, and walking away would be near impossible.

A quick glance at my bedside clock told me I'd best get moving if I didn't want to make a bad first impression. I'd have much rather changed into my swimsuit and spent the afternoon playing with the boys—and Luca, if I was gonna be completely honest. Seemed every time I caught him looking my way, my stomach took to flipping like a fish out of water. Couldn't even remember why I'd ever compared him to a broomstick.

The drive to Murfreesboro wasn't nearly long enough to clear my head. This position would be a foot in the door for something bigger—and it's what I had in mind when I'd decided to work toward a master's degree. It'd be plumb crazy not to do whatever it took to get myself hired. Would give me some financial stability, professional clout, and show Mama that my education wasn't a waste of money after all. Just the job a grown-up should have.

The campus was beautiful—lots of green grass surrounding brick-and-stone buildings, seating areas with nature views, and state-of-the-art facilities. I'd toured the library the year before when I applied the first time. It was a monstrous four levels a body could get lost in with just one wrong turn. Very impressive if that sort of thing appealed. And it had then.

Made my way to the administrative building and through the heavy glass doors. The blast of air-conditioning had goosebumps skittering up my bare arms. Should've thought to bring a sweater. Nausea hit me again, and I was lightheaded. Not only forgot my sweater, I forgot to eat. No sleep, no food, and moody as a hormonal teen. Could be I was subconsciously trying to tank my chances. If for some crazy reason I was offered the job, it would be by the grace of God.

Could be the reason right there I hadn't prayed for it.

Chapter Twenty-Two

Luca

I parked across from the courthouse for the second time that day. Josh's law office was between a nail salon and antique store. The entire square was peppered with lawyers, which made sense, given the courthouse was the center of it. I'd intended to make an appointment for Josh to amend my trust, not to advise me on extortion, or blackmail, or whatever law Bridget was breaking.

I stepped into the office to be greeted by a middle-aged woman. "May I help you?" She was pleasant but constrained. *Don't feed the animals.* Could only imagine the amount of drama clients walked in with and the need for staff members to keep a respectful distance.

"Good afternoon. I'm Luca Giordano, and I have a 4:00 appointment with Josh."

She smiled and stood. "Ah, Mr. Giordano. Mr. Cummings is ready for you. Come this way, please."

Dark wood-wainscoting topped by cream-colored walls went the length of the long hallway. At the end, a door with privacy glass had *Josh Cummings, Attorney at Law* painted in black.

Josh's receptionist tapped twice before opening the door. "Mr. Giordano is here."

"Thank you, Adele." Josh hopped up from behind his desk and came around to shake my hand as his receptionist closed the door behind her. "Have a seat, Luca. Can I get you anything? Coffee, water?"

I waved his question away. "No, thanks. I've had enough caffeine today to power a trip to the moon." Could be why my hands were shaking, but I suspected it had more to do with the visit. I'd only given him the bare bones over the phone and revealing the extent of my stupidity didn't sit well. But if he was going to be of help, he needed to know everything.

Josh resumed his position behind the desk. "So, what I know is your ex-wife is threatening to take your youngest boy from you unless she receives a hefty payoff. Does that sum it up?"

I nodded. "Which is illegal, right?" A surge of heat shot through my body. It wouldn't surprise anyone who knew me that I was all about black and white—didn't go in for shades of gray. A character flaw? Maybe. It certainly left little room for sympathizing with those who used others to get their way.

Josh grimaced. "Yes, of course it's illegal."

"I recorded the entire conversation on my phone. Thought maybe I could use it as proof."

"I'm afraid it won't hold up in a court of law. Any lawyer worth his fee would claim you doctored it. Can you give me a little history on your relationship with—is it Bridget?"

"Yeah." I snorted. "Or Jamie. Depends on who you ask, I suppose." I shifted to a more comfortable position. "Married her a little over ten years ago. Had Daniel ten months later. Two years after that, Chase was born. In hindsight, I'm confused about why she didn't do anything to prevent the pregnancies. Made it clear she hated everything about being pregnant, and she never connected with the boys."

Josh frowned. "When you say she didn't connect with them, what d'you mean?"

"Just that. Hired a nanny so she didn't have to take care of them." Closing my eyes, I blew out a breath. "I don't have the first clue why she ever wanted to get married. She had no love for me, she couldn't care less about the boys, so I don't know what she got from the deal."

"No doubt she'd need a therapist and a whole lot of hours to figure that one out." He rested his elbows on the desk. "I'd hazard a guess that even she doesn't know, so I doubt you'll figure it out."

"It's moot now. Can't go back and fix it even if I wanted to. The question is, what do I do about the situation now?"

"She says Matty's not your biological son?" He quirked a brow along with the question.

This is where things got sticky. "He's not. I knew that when she got pregnant. We hadn't been…intimate since Chase was born. She was out most nights partying, and I was planning for her inevitable request for a divorce. Then she said she was pregnant. Only have to look at Matty to know—" I clamped my mouth shut before finishing that thought. *He is my son. DNA doesn't matter.*

Slapping a hand on the desk, I leaned forward. "I raised him from the time he was born. Bridget was gone the minute she was released from the hospital, and I never heard from her again. I filed for divorce, and our lawyers handled everything from there."

"So, all she wants from you is money?"

"That's the size of it. Fifty-thousand dollars or she'll take Matty. Says it's in lieu of the alimony she should've gotten when we divorced." I shrugged. "She may have something there. I refused to pay her anything at the time, because we'd been married less than six years."

Josh pursed his lips. "You sayin' you're willing to pay the money?"

"I'm willing to do whatever it takes for her to leave Matty with me. If that's a payoff, so be it."

He tapped his hand on the desk. "The problem with extortion is that it's never enough. You give her money now, and she'll be back for more. Doesn't change her claim that Matty's not your biological son." His eyes narrowed. "Did you ever adopt the boy?"

My stomach dropped. "No. Never even considered it. As far as I was concerned, he was already my son—no different than Chase and Daniel." A thought occurred to me. "Even if I'd thought to adopt, I couldn't have gotten Bridget's consent. Didn't know where she was."

He shook his head. "Doesn't matter. If a parent abandons a child for two years, the court can find in favor of a stepparent adopting without permission. But that ship's sailed. What we need to do now is decide how to handle her demands."

I threw my hands in the air. "Give her the money. I don't care."

"And if she comes back for more next month or next year?"

No doubt, that's exactly what she'd do, too. She'd be like a wild animal with a taste for blood—mine. "What do you suggest then?"

"Well, you could take her to court to prove her an unfit mother. There's a lot of evidence to back it up."

"But wouldn't Matty be dragged into the whole sordid mess, too?"

He sighed. "Possibly." Rubbing his brow, he seemed lost in thought, then his eyes cleared. "I think you should call her bluff."

The words rocketed through me leaving a frisson of fear in its wake. "You mean deny her request entirely?"

"Yes. It's not Matty she's after. It's all about the money. Do you really think she's gonna pay a lawyer to go to court and fight for a child she never wanted in the first place?"

Not unless she was crazy, but I wouldn't bet Matty's life on it. "You don't know her, Josh. She might do it out of spite."

"Then I suppose you're gonna need to do some thinking—and praying—before you make a decision one way or the other."

Didn't care much for things being out of my control. Maybe Josh was onto something with the suggestion to pray. Hadn't the Lord brought Lillian when I needed her?

"There's something else," Josh said. He cleared his throat. "Lillian feels like she's to blame for this entire mess—"

"She's not. And I told her that."

"I know you have, and I hear you. But she's not convinced." He raised his hands. "It's none of my business, except she's a friend, and I hate to see her hurt again. I know when I'm working through something, I tend to shut down. Sherrie has to pry information out of me. Lillian? Well, whatever's between you is your business, but you might wanna consider how she's perceiving things."

He was right. But it wasn't me blaming Lillian that put up a wall between us, and I couldn't talk to her about it. At least not yet. "We still under client-lawyer confidentiality?"

Josh frowned. "Yes."

Even knowing it, I hesitated to open myself up. But who else could I confide in? "When I hired Lillian to care for the boys, it was only my concern for them I considered. Thought she'd be just the right person to give them both intellectual stimulation and a healthy amount of nurturing." I could've cited the studies to back up my approach but doubted Josh would care.

A line formed between his brows. "She's not workin' out? I know she loves those boys, and it seems to me she'd be perfect for the job."

"Oh, she is. Believe me." If only it were that simple. "Problem isn't her. It's me." Could feel heat climbing up my neck. "I've...well, I've developed feelings for her. The only way I can keep the proper distance is to erect a wall of sorts. That wall is what she's sensing. Not any anger on my part."

Josh's mouth dropped open. "Huh. So, why not tell her that? She might feel the same."

Thought about her running off in tears with the mere mention of marriage—even in jest—and I doubted that was something she'd be interested in. "Then what? There's enough gossip spreading through the church to hurt her reputation now when there isn't anything between us. And if she doesn't feel the same about me, then it makes things even more awkward, which would probably make her quit. She does that, and the boys are the ones who get hurt." As well as me. "It also leaves her in a financial bind with nowhere to go."

His mouth twisted. "Seems you've got yourself between a rock and a hard place." An understatement. "Of course, if she gets that job at MTSU, it'll ease up her finances a good bit, then you won't have that concern hanging over your head."

MTSU? News to me. My heart rate kicked up. Had Lillian been making plans to leave? And for how long? The thought of her lying to me was a punch to the gut—every bit as hurtful as Bridget's betrayal.

Chapter Twenty-Three

Lillian

There was a time I wondered how it was possible for married couples to avoid communicating for so long, their relationship disintegrating like an old newspaper. I mean, they lived day in and day out in the same house, ate supper as a family, and raised the kids alongside each other. Wouldn't one or the other crack under the pressure and call a truce?

But I hadn't taken into account how distracting kids could be. It was easy enough to shove aside Luca's coldness over the next several evenings because I had the boys to tend to. Luca managed to find things to keep them occupied while I was at work, but they were all mine after supper. Once I read to them and tucked them in at night, I'd slip away into my bedroom and dissect every word or glance Luca had thrown my way.

Just when I was falling for the man, he'd turned back into a stiff ol' broomstick. If he was mad about the fix he was in with Bridget, why didn't he just say so and get it over with? Instead, he only deigned to speak to me when asked a direct question, and even then the answers were short and not-so-sweet. The man needed to use his words—preferably those with more than one syllable—and grow up. At least it made me grateful I hadn't blown off my interview at MTSU.

By Friday evening, my patience was worn thin as a bride's negligee, and it was only the boys that kept me from pitching a hissy fit. But someone had to be the adult, and that little chore fell to me by default. It was my turn to cook supper—which of course was listed on the blasted chart/calendar—so I stopped by Kroger's on my way home from work and picked up a few supplies. Promised Daniel I'd make tacos, and I wasn't about to disappoint him. Might not be around much longer, so I needed my time to count.

I parked in the driveway and came in through the front door. Rocket, as usual, was there to greet me. I was gonna miss him almost as much as the boys. What was it about dogs that made a body relax? Could be their unconditional love. God spelled backwards.

"Hey, boy." I shifted the grocery bag to one arm so I could scratch his ears. "You miss me today?"

His tail thumped as he stared up at me with pure love in his eyes. Right at that moment, I'd take a dog over a man any day of the week. Never said a cross word, didn't care what I looked like, and loyal to a fault. Could anyone say the same about a man?

"Miss Lillian!" Chase bounded down the stairs so fast, I was sure he'd take a tumble. "You're home. Can we go swimming now?" The boy practically lived in his swim trunks.

I glanced up the stairs and gave a listen. "Where's your daddy?"

"In his office on the phone." He tugged on my hand. "He said we'd have to wait till you got home, 'cause he can't watch out for us in case we drown."

"And your brothers?" The three of us moved together through the family room, Rocket's nails clicking on the hardwood floor.

"Backyard. So, can we?" His eyes were lit up with excitement. If only life could be so simple again.

"Only until I have supper ready."

"Yay!"

Within minutes, all three boys were in the pool with Rocket keeping watch, and I had the ingredients for tacos lined up on the counter. Felt tense as a fiddle string waiting for Luca to show himself. Every day, I'd prayed he wouldn't be so cantankerous or at least be willing to talk to me about it, but so far, the good Lord hadn't come through. Used to be when things went sideways, I'd ask Him, "Why?" Learned over the last few months the better question was, "What?" There was a lesson in my trials, and I just had to dig deep enough to find them.

It was real convenient that the cook top was situated on the island—could work in the kitchen and keep an eye on the boys at the same time. Had a skillet with vegetable oil heating on the stove, a plate of corn tortillas next to it, and some paper towels to soak up the grease. I'd just slipped the first tortilla into the sizzling pan when Luca strode in.

He stopped short like he wasn't expecting to find me there, which was plumb crazy, because who else would be fixin' his boys' supper? His eyes narrowed on the tortilla as he came closer.

"What are you doing?" It about shocked me dumb that he not only spoke a full sentence, but it wasn't even in response to a question.

He left the door wide open to respond with sarcasm, but I was gonna be the bigger person. "I promised Daniel tacos for supper." I used two spatulas to flip the tortilla over then folded it in half before adding a second one.

"That's not how you do it." Was he itching for a fight or what?

"Actually, it *is* how I do it. Might not be how you do things, but I'm the one cookin' supper tonight." I pointed the spatula toward the ridiculous chart. "Says it right there in green."

"No reason to heat them like that when you can do it in the microwave." His nostrils flared like a bull fixin' to charge. What in the world was his problem?

I flung the spatula down and it hit the skillet, splattering hot oil onto the stove top and my hand. But I wouldn't give him the satisfaction of wiping away the sting. "Don't you come in here after ignorin' me for days and start throwing your weight around. I'm the one cookin' supper, and I'll do it however I see fit. You don't like it, do it yourself." I folded my arms and glared at him.

Hands on hips, he glared right back. "I might as well get used to it, since you're planning on leaving anyway, right?"

The accusation snatched the breath from my lungs. "Wh...What're you talkin' about?"

His face twisted up all ugly-like. "You're going to stand there and lie to my face? I know about your job interview, Lillian. The least you could've done was give me a heads up, so I can find someone else to help with the boys."

I dropped my gaze to the skillet where the tortilla was a burnt mess. Flicking off the burner, I took a deep breath to regain control of my temper. Fussing at him wasn't gonna get us anywhere.

"How d'you know about the interview?" Had he been spying on me?

"Had a meeting with Josh, and he mentioned it. Said you'd be making a good salary once you got the new job." He shook his head. "Of course, he couldn't know it was a secret—that you were angling for a new position behind my back."

"That's not how it is. You're takin' it outta context, Luca. I'm just keepin' my options open—"

He barked out a laugh. "You and Bridget—keeping your options open. Whatever works best for you, right? It doesn't matter at all that the boys'll be devastated when you leave. Ever think about that while you were interviewing for a better job?"

He had every right to question me about the interview. After all, he would need to find someone else to take my place. But what he didn't know was that I'd be every bit as devastated as they would. And it wasn't until that very moment I realized I had no choice—if I was offered the MTSU position, I'd have to take it.

"Nothing to say, Lillian?" The sneer in his voice shot straight to my heart.

Tears swimming in my eyes, I looked up at him. "What would be the point? You've already colored me with your ex-wife's paintbrush." I swallowed a sob. "You gonna believe me when I say the only reason I went looking for another job is *because* of the boys? You think I don't know they're attached?" I snatched up a dishtowel and swiped at the oil on my hands to give me somewhere to focus but on the condemnation in Luca's eyes.

"But you don't care." He passed through the kitchen and slammed out the garage door.

"I care," I whispered to the empty room. If I didn't, his distrust wouldn't have ripped a hole in my heart.

It was a losing battle. If I told him the truth—that I'd fallen in love with him—then he'd think it was a ploy to manipulate him. There wasn't the least little doubt in my mind that it was what Bridget did when they were together. He might've thought it was only his boys hurt by their mama, but he was far more damaged than them. And it would take a better person than me to convince him of it.

Luca

There were so many conflicting emotions roiling around inside, I didn't have a clue what to do with them or where I was going, so I drove with no destination in mind. Bridget was the only person who'd ever made me so angry—and I'd been fielding texts from her all week. *No one can* make *you angry. You need to own your feelings.* It wasn't what I wanted to hear, but there was no denying the Holy Spirit. Reminded me of the times I'd told Daniel not to allow schoolyard bullies control over his actions. Sticks and stones and all that.

Control. I was all about it and look where it'd gotten me. Maybe what I needed was to take a step back and allow God more access to my heart. No better place to pray than church. Hit me right then I'd been driving toward Mount Hermon Baptist since I'd peeled out of the garage like a petulant child. That couldn't have been a coincidence.

I pulled into the parking lot and pocketed my keys. If the church was locked, I'd sit on the steps instead. God was everywhere, wasn't He? But the door was open, and I entered the empty sanctuary. Old churches and libraries had a similar smell. Could be ancient wood, but it seemed more likely it was must and mildew. The stained-glass windows let in enough light to bathe the room in a soft glow. Closing my eyes, I drew in a deep breath. *I need to feel You here, Lord.*

"Luca?"

For a split second, I thought it was the voice of God, and I was having a Moses moment. But when I whipped around, Brother Paul was coming from the prayer room. Yeah, that made a lot more sense. "Hey, Paul. Hope it's okay that I stopped by."

Nodding, he said, "Was just getting ready to lock up, but there's no hurry." He was physically fit for a man in his late sixties—or maybe it was just the white hair that aged him. Could be ten years younger. "You want me to leave you to the Lord, or do you need another listening ear?"

Was about to dismiss him, but since Bridget's deadline was looming, he might be quicker with the advice than God. "Could use some wise counsel." I slipped into a pew and sat. Felt it rock slightly as Paul dropped next to me.

"You just take your time." He bowed his head and closed his eyes. Praying most likely.

"Not sure even where to start." Confession, maybe. Wasn't proud of the way I spoke to Lillian. But I could only tackle one problem at a time, and right now Bridget's scheme took precedence. "Found myself in a situation I'm not sure how to navigate."

He pursed his lips. "This about Lillian?" Logical conclusion.

Rubbing my forehead, I took a beat before answering. "Another matter entirely. You probably know I was married."

"Figured it was likely."

"Bridget." It was an effort to say her name out loud. "Married ten years and divorced six."

He nodded but didn't respond.

"I'm sure you see struggling couples all the time, and every complaint is a matter of he said/she said."

"True. Amazing how a different perspective changes a story." He shifted, making the pew groan. "You wanna tell me yours?"

I started at the beginning. Meeting Bridget and being charmed by her vivacious personality and beauty—only to find out she was a chameleon who changed to suit her circumstances. The sham-of-a-marriage, her disinterest in being a mother to Daniel or Chase, late-night partying, and ridiculous spending sprees.

"And then when I was expecting her to tell me she wanted a divorce, she casually announced that she was pregnant." Grunting, I shook my head. "We hadn't been...intimate since Chase was born, so I knew Matty wasn't mine. At least not biologically. He wasn't two weeks old before she left without a word. After a few months, I hired a lawyer to handle the divorce and never heard from her again. Until last week."

Paul had listened to my monologue in silence only nodding now and then to encourage me to continue. "Did she have a change of heart?"

I laughed, although there was no humor to it. "Hardly. What she wants is a payoff. And if I don't give it to her, she'll take Matty." A knot formed in my throat. Couldn't remember the last time I'd cried. "I don't know what to do. Josh believes if I pay her, she'll come back for more, and there will be no end to it."

Paul pinned me with a probing stare. "What do you believe?" His question gave me pause. Was he asking about just this situation, or something far more profound? "Have you prayed about it? Do you trust the Lord to guide your decision?"

"No." Abrupt but honest. "This is my *son* we're talking about." God wouldn't condone being a party to criminal activity—which is what I'd be doing if I gave Bridget the money.

"Let me ask you this." Paul cleared his throat. "Did you pray about marrying Bridget? Did you feel it was the Lord's plan?"

Wasn't so quick with a negative response to that one. "Never even considered it," I finally admitted. "Thought I knew what was best for me." And just maybe, I didn't want God interfering with my plans. "Could be this entire mess is a case of divine consequences." That was a humbling thought. Brought it all on myself.

"Natural consequences, maybe," Paul said. "It sounds to me as if Bridget wasn't forthcoming about who she was, and you didn't take time to find out before you committed yourself to her. You put your trust in her, and she let you down."

"Yes."

"But God won't, son. While you're struggling to figure out on your own what to do, he's already workin' out the details in the background. Doesn't mean there won't be disappointments, but no one can thwart His plans."

A thought occurred to me. "If that's true, then where does free will come into play? If he doesn't control people, then how can I trust that Bridget won't take off with Matty like she threatened if I don't pay her?"

"It's not Bridget you need to trust. You pray about this and see what the Lord puts on your heart, and then you trust Him to do the rest. That's what faith is all about."

Ever since Bridget left six years ago, I'd pushed God aside because I blamed Him for not healing my marriage. In hindsight, I'd run ahead and did what I wanted then expected Him to bless the outcome.

"I hear what you're saying." Wasn't sure I was ready to jump on board, though. "I think about what a fool I'd been marrying Bridget, but if I hadn't, I wouldn't have the boys now. Can't imagine my life without them."

Paul smiled. "That's the Lord's grace, Luca. We can mess up our lives something fierce, and He's still faithful to give us good gifts. You need to dig into the Bible, son. You'll find a lot of stubborn, hard-hearted people God used for His greater good. None of us is perfect, which is why we need Jesus. God looks at you, He sees you through the righteousness of His Son."

I nodded. How many times throughout my life had I heard that preached, and still suffered from faith-amnesia more often than not? "I appreciate the reminder." Didn't have the answer yet, but the tension in the pit of my stomach had eased up.

Paul stood and patted me on the shoulder. "Keep me posted, won't you? I'll give you some time alone. No rush. I'll lock up, and you just be sure the door's closed tight when you leave."

"Yes, sir. Thank you."

He'd gotten halfway down the aisle before he turned around. "I'm always here, Luca. You need a listening ear, don't hesitate."

Once he'd disappeared, I bowed my head to pray, but I couldn't stop the wayward thoughts bulleting through my mind. Lillian giving me as good as she got. Didn't even know she had it in her. The tears in her eyes—but that meant nothing. Bridget could cry on demand if it got her what she wanted. The betrayal. That one hurt. It wasn't about me, though. It was all about the boys. Wasn't it?

Stop! Had to clear my mind of the jumbled thoughts to focus on the Lord. *I'm slow in learning, God. Slow in trusting, too. I trusted Bridget and got hurt. I don't want to make that mistake again. I don't know what to do. Not about her, or Matty, or even Lillian. I've failed You, Lord, every bit as much as Bridget's failed me, so I suppose I shouldn't hold it against her. But I can't lose Matty. More than that, I can't expose him to a mother who is only using him as a bargaining chip. Brother Paul says I need to put my faith in You. Help me to do that. Please. Guide my thoughts and actions. Give me the wisdom to know what to do and peace in obeying it.*

Realized as I sat up straight, the knot was gone from my throat, and my face was wet with tears. Still didn't know what to do, but I would. God would see to it.

Chapter Twenty-Four

Lillian

The library was quiet on Saturday. Most people were probably out enjoying the beautiful sunshine while they could. According to the weather forecast, it was fixin' to rain the next day. I was in the mood for a good storm, too—lots of thunder and lightning—since I wasn't feeling particularly sunshine-y after the little set-to with Luca the night before. Did I know how to pick 'em or what?

I was re-shelving books near the end of my shift when Kathleen approached, clipboard in her hands. "Hey, Lil. Have you had a chance to finish your list of recommendations for the children's books you'd like to see us acquire?"

"Yes, ma'am. I'll go get it." I slipped around the book cart and headed down the aisle.

"Hold up, will you?" Kathleen drew closer to me. "Are you doin' okay? You seem a bit off today."

Could hardly tell her Luca and I had us an argument the night before over me trying to get another job. Way to kill my chances for advancement here if nothing else came through. But a half-truth was better than none at all. "Might have to find me another place to live. Things are a little tense at Luca's place. Guess that's been distracting me today. Sorry."

"Don't apologize." She offered a sympathetic smile. "I was hoping things would work out for y'all. It seemed like you were getting attached to those boys of his."

Tears bit at the back of my eyes. I'd always kept a respectful distance between Kathleen and myself—after all, she was my boss. But her concern closed that gap some. "That's what makes it so hard. I was getting attached to Luca, too. I surely don't wanna make *that* mistake." I tried to laugh, but it came out more like a sob.

Her eyes softened. "What mistake? Fallin' in love again?"

"Again?" I sniffled and reached for the tissue in my pocket. "I've had plenty of time to think about it, and I don't believe I was ever in love with Billy. I sure as heck know he wasn't in love with me. If he had been, he wouldn't've left me like he did." And stuck me with the wedding bill on top of the humiliation. Seemed he was as deceitful as Luca's ex-wife.

Kathleen gave me a quick side hug. "You're too nice if you ask me. A man does to me what he did to you, I'd make him at least pay for the wedding." She stepped back and sighed. "Anyway, you let me know if I can do anything."

I never told Kathleen about Billy's underhanded move, so how did she find out? Had I shared it with Carrie? Couldn't recall, but it brought to mind what Benjamin Franklin said about secrets—"Three can keep a secret if two of them are dead." Wasn't that the truth?

Billy was stuck in my head as I finished shelving the books. The more I thought about him, the angrier I got. When Luca'd told me about Bridget being a manipulator, I wanted to ask him why he'd allowed it. I mean, did he love her so much he couldn't see through her? Or didn't he have enough backbone to hold her accountable?

But here I was, still whining over Billy's deceit and doing nothing about it a year later. My own spine was wimpy as a shoestring. Hypocrite. That's what I was. Didn't bother to listen to Sherrie or Mama when they told me I should've made him pay. Sherrie had called it a breach of contract. Here I was, stuck for a second time with nowhere to go and nothing much to live on. Couldn't hold Luca accountable, because he'd done nothing wrong. Aside from being ugly last night. The same wasn't true for Billy. I'd told Sherrie a week ago it was time I had me a come-to-Jesus meeting with the man, and I hadn't done a thing about it.

Once I got off work, I sat in my car with the air-conditioning blowing for a full five minutes. My heart was pounding so loud it seemed to beat to an old tune—Joan Jett's "I Love Rock 'N' Roll" while I scratched together the courage to confront Billy like I should've done a year ago. Ever since he'd left, I'd convinced myself I was the only one to blame for the fix I was in. But that wasn't true. He had a part in it, too.

Billy had himself an auto garage in Murfreesboro, which was how we met. My car had broken down when I was shopping there one day, and his was the closest shop—and was as far as the tow-truck driver was required to go. Billy had been charming, but then so had the asp in the Garden of Eden.

Through the forty-five-minute drive to Billy's place of business, I talked to myself and prayed to God. I'd've gotten there sooner, but I'd changed my mind twice and pulled over. I was tempted to call Sherrie; she'd goad me all the way there and wouldn't let me chicken out. But it was important to do this one on my own.

Heart pounding and stomach flip-flopping, I finally pulled into A1 Auto & Tires. Both bay doors were wide open with vehicles sitting in the air on car lifts. Recognized Manuel working beneath the huge truck but didn't see any sign of Billy. Maybe he'd taken the day off, which would suit me just fine. I could take some comfort in knowing I'd tried, small as it might be. Of course, it might could take me another year to build up the courage to come back.

Then Billy came out of the office. His red cap was on backwards over sandy-colored longish hair. He was wearing blue coveralls, darkened in areas by what I assumed was grease. My belly clenched, and I thought for sure I was gonna throw up. *Don't be such a baby. He can't hurt you anymore.* That was true enough, but it didn't make it any easier to confront him. Face hot, I slipped outta my car and tried to catch my breath. Didn't know if it was nerves or the humidity that struck me as I walked on wobbly legs. Pathetic, that's what I was.

I'd almost reached the bay doors when Billy, who was laughing at something Manuel said, glanced my way. He did a double take before his smile melted away like ice cream in the August sun.

Had to unstick my tongue before I could speak. "I need to talk to you a minute, Billy."

He flicked a glance at Manuel then back at me.

"Hey, Lillian." Manuel waved. "You're looking good, girl."

Never did figure out if he was a flirt or just a really nice guy.

"Hey, Manuel." I moved closer to Billy, my heart galloping, as an air compressor kicked on. He didn't look any different—hadn't grown horns like I'd half-expected. "We can either do this here or we can go into the office." I was shocked at how strong my voice sounded. Billy must've been, too, 'cause he nodded toward the door like I should follow him.

It was quieter in the cluttered room—aside from the swamp cooler blowing cold air. Goosebumps skittered up my bare arms, and I folded them hoping it'd warm them some.

"Surprised to see you here, Lillian." Not as surprised as I was.

My eyes darted around as I scrambled for what to say. I'd rehearsed it a hundred times on the drive. Was strong and articulate in my mind. Somewhere between my head and my mouth, my genius dissipated.

There was a picture on the desk of Billy with his arms around a busty blond woman wearing a tight t-shirt with his business name stamped across the front. The newest flavor, I supposed. "I should've come a long time ago. Like right after you no-showed the wedding."

He cleared his throat. "It was a crummy thing to do. Guess I owe you an apology." He guessed? Too little too late as far as I was concerned, and not the least bit sincere.

I got up the nerve to pin him with a glare. "Not as crummy as leaving me with a $20,000 wedding bill."

He scowled. "The bride's family pays for the weddin'. Ever'one knows that." So much for the apology.

What did I ever see in him? His eyes were a pretty shade of blue. I'd give him that. But they had no depth. Not like Luca's. "I'm not gonna argue with you about this, Billy. I came here in good faith to ask you to pay at least half. By rights, you should foot the entire bill, because you walked out. Sherrie calls it a breach of contract, and—"

He snorted and threw his hands in the air. "Of course, your hoity-toity friend is gonna raise a stink."

"No one's raising a stink. Just pointing out the facts. If we'd been married and split up, the debt would've been shared. I'm just asking you to do the right thing." Should've listened to Sherrie and Mama and handled this when it was fresh.

"Can't." He crossed his arms. "Don't have me that kind of money."

No longer nervous, anger zinged through my blood. "And you think I do?" The interest alone was killing me. "I know for a fact you have at least three hot rods worth a whole lot more than that." Or had.

He barked out a rude noise. "Those are investments, Lil. I sell them off now, I won't get near what they're worth."

"Not my problem." I stabbed a finger at him. "Either you pay what you owe, or I'll go ahead and sic my hoity-toity friend on you. And she won't file for half, she'll go after the entire amount. Maybe get those cars of yours confiscated and sold." I had no idea if Sherrie could do such a thing, but from the way Billy's face fell clear to the floor, neither did he.

He glanced at the photo of him and Auto Mechanic Barbie with a growl. "Fine. I'll write you a check for the ten thousand."

"So I can watch it bounce from here to the moon? Not likely. What is it you liked to say—'I was born at night, just not *last* night'?" I huffed out a laugh. "If you have the money, you can just come along to First Commerce Bank down the street and transfer it from your account to mine. Otherwise, you'll be hearing from my lawyer. And I promise you, the stench she makes will follow you for a good long time."

A half hour later, I was giddy as a schoolgirl as I drove back to Shelbyville. Didn't even care that traffic was a slow crawl in an over-crowded city. I still had me more debt than was comfortable, but it had just gotten a whole lot easier. I'd faced Billy and reclaimed what was rightly mine—along with a little dignity.

I might not like moving away from Luca and the boys, but I'd survive. I was a fighter when I had to be. Just took me a good long time to figure it out.

Luca

I sat in my office and stared at Lillian's earlier text three times, as if I'd find some clue to what her state of mind was in the three simple words, *I'll be late.* Compared to previous texts, it was somewhat telling. Before it was, *I'll be* home *late,* and she always said why. Stopping by Walmart or meeting up with Sherrie or Meghan. Did she no longer consider this place as her home? And was the lack of explanation because it was a secret or because she was still angry?

Bridget had been the Queen of the cold-shoulder move. Said as little as possible, in person or by text, to let me know the effort to communicate wasn't worth her time. But here I was, doing exactly what Lillian had accused me of—painting her with the same brush as my ex. It wasn't fair to her. And it wasn't right that I'd thrown that comparison in her face before storming out the evening before.

Had some bridges to build, and I didn't have any blueprints to guide me.

"Hey, Dad." Daniel sauntered up to my desk with Rocket on his heels. "When are we gonna eat supper? I'm starving to death." *Supper*? He was picking up on Lillian's Southern vocabulary. "And where's Miss Lillian? She's always home early on Saturdays."

I pushed away from my desk and pocketed my phone. "She had an errand, and I don't know when she'll be back. How about we do a pizza night?" That way, when Lillian got home, she wouldn't feel guilty for not being around to fix dinner. Seemed as if she was always apologizing for not doing her part.

"Cool. I want pepperoni. Can we watch a movie while we eat?"

After ordering two large pizzas, the boys and I were scanning through the Disney+ app on the family room tv when Lillian came rushing through the front door.

"Sorry I'm late, y'all. I'll get supper started right quick. Just give me two shakes to get changed and—"

"We're doin' pizza night!" Matty shouted as he dashed across the room to give her a hug.

Lillian didn't hesitate to drop her things and crouch down to catch him as he flew at her. How could I have ever accused her of not caring about the boys? Pure joy lit up her face as she wrapped her arms around him. Chase followed behind Matty then Daniel.

"Y'all sure make a girl feel loved." She gave them one more squeeze. "Just let me get outta my work clothes." Her gaze darted to mine then slid away again, but not before I caught the sheen of tears in her eyes as she escaped.

I'd better figure out those blueprints *right quick*, as Lillian would say. If it was my fault she was looking for another job, I needed to fix it. Hadn't Josh said she still blamed herself for the mess with Bridget? I'd make sure she understood it wasn't her fault.

The pizza arrived, and we settled together in the family room to watch *Inside Out*—Lillian on one end of the sectional and me on the other. Until the boys went to bed, there wouldn't be an opportunity to talk. They might've been little, but they had big ears, and I didn't want to consider how things would escalate if they knew their mother was not only in town but was using Matty to extort money. It would be better for them to believe she was dead, even though I'd never told them that.

Or would it? How would they feel if they learned the truth about Bridget when they got older—that she was alive, but chose to break ties with them—and I'd kept it from them? I'd been honest about every other aspect but this one. A lie of omission was still a lie, right? But there was a thin line between the truth and what they could handle.

So wrapped up was I in my own thoughts, it took Lillian shutting off the television with the remote for me to come back to the land of the living.

"I'll just clear up this here mess." Lillian was efficient at stacking the plates and assigning each of the boys a task.

"I'll take the empty boxes out to the trash," I said to no one in particular. I needed a minute to pray before talking to Lillian. This was going to be too important a conversation to have without some divine guidance.

I stood outside, the sky still light enough to see by, and took a deep breath before saying a quick prayer. It was getting easier, talking to God. Drew me closer to Him and reminded me that I was never alone in my mess.

When I stepped back inside the kitchen, it was empty. Lillian must've been supervising teeth brushing, and she'd taken to having the boys kneel beside their beds to pray before climbing in. Why hadn't I thought of that? Why did it take someone like Lillian to make the simple things clear? I was so focused on *my* priorities, I'd never considered seeking out the Lord's.

I headed upstairs and entered Chase and Matty's room as they were climbing into bed. Gave them a kiss on the forehead while Lillian escaped to check on Daniel. I'd have to be quick if I was going to cut her off before she disappeared into her own bedroom as she'd been doing every night this past week. Avoiding me. I only had myself to blame.

Lillian was sitting on the side of Daniel's bed when I walked in, and Rocket was curled up at the end. We'd had a rule that he was to sleep on the floor, but it went by the wayside when we'd moved here. Daniel had needed the extra comfort then, although he seemed to be well acclimated now. But it was hard to go back once a rule had been broken.

"Now," Lillian said as she fingered a strand of hair from Daniel's forehead, "you can only read till nine. Then you turn off the light. Promise?"

He rolled his eyes. "Aww, do I have to? It's still gonna be sorta light outside."

She huffed out a soft laugh. "If the people livin' in Alaska went by that rule, no one would sleep in the summer or be outta bed in the winter."

A grin broke out. "Okay. I promise."

"That's a good boy." She gave him a peck on the cheek and stood. "Sweet dreams, Daniel."

"Sweet dreams, Lillian," he said around a big yawn. He'd never make it until nine.

When Lillian turned around, she stopped short. It would seem until that moment, she wasn't aware of my presence. Straightening her shoulders, she marched past me and out the door.

"Good night, son."

"Night, Dad."

I left the door open enough that if Rocket wanted to come out, he could nudge it with his nose and caught up with Lillian as she started to escape down the hallway to her room.

"Can we talk?" Heard the edge of desperation in my voice and cringed. Reminded me of the first fight I had with my high school girlfriend, and how desperate I was to fix things before prom.

Lillian hesitated before turning to me, worry lines between her eyebrows. "About what?"

Reasonable question. "I owe you an apology, and I could use your advice."

She glanced down the hallway like she was tempted to make a run for it. Couldn't blame her after the way I'd treated her. But then she relented with a sigh. "Okay."

Stepping aside, I waved a hand that she should precede me then followed her to the family room. She sat on one end of the sectional, and I perched on the recliner closest to her.

"I was way out of line last night, Lillian." Truer words were never spoken. "You were right accusing me of comparing you with Bridget. When Josh told me you were planning on getting another job, I jumped to conclusions. I should've just come to you and asked about it."

Shoulders hunched, her blue eyes homed in on me. "So, why didn't you?"

Wasn't expecting that, and it took me a beat to separate out excuses that would only invalidate my apology. But the truth would leave me vulnerable. Last time I left myself wide open, I became Bridget's perfect target.

"I was hurt." That wasn't so hard. "Felt like we'd become friends, if nothing else. And you tell a friend if you're looking for a new job—especially if it might affect him and his family. From where I stood, it seemed as if you were dismissing the boys' attachment to you, and that made me angry."

She chewed on the inside of her cheek for a moment, uncertainty in her eyes. "You're right, Luca. About us bein' friends and that I should've shared it with you." Her eyes welled with tears. "But you're dead wrong about me dismissin' the boys. I know they're getting attached—and so am I." She swallowed. "But with everything that's happened and the gossip spreadin' around church...it might could hurt them more if I stayed." Her sorrowful eyes caught mine. "Don't you see that?"

She had a point. Hadn't I been thinking the same thing? It's what instigated Dad's crazy idea that we should just get married. It was on the tip of my tongue to say so, but something stopped me—the Holy Spirit, maybe? Now wasn't the time.

Instead, I hedged. "I see that we have some unresolved issues ahead of us." I sounded like a politician avoiding a direct question. "One of which is my problem with Bridget." I rubbed my forehead. Had a clear idea what I should do, but confirmation would help me pull the trigger. "That's where I could use your advice."

She frowned. "I don't think I'm the best person to ask. Standin' up for myself isn't my forte." She wrung her hands. "Still, if I were you, I wouldn't give into her demands. If she decides to come after Matty, you could still fight her."

That was the same conclusion I'd come to, but hearing her say it released the tension in my shoulders.

"If you're gonna meet with her," she continued, "you really should take Josh with you. Someone to be a witness to what's said. I wouldn't put it past someone like your ex-wife to accuse you of something just to muddy the waters even more."

Lillian didn't give herself enough credit. Bridget was likely to do exactly what she'd warned me of, and I hadn't considered taking backup to our meeting.

"Thank you, Lillian." Peace washed over me as I stared at this beautiful, gentle, and intelligent woman in front of me. I'd deal with the baggage from my past, and then I'd do everything I could to convince Lillian she was my future. Dad's crazy idea suddenly didn't sound crazy after all.

CHAPTER TWENTY-FIVE

Lillian

It was funny how one short conversation could put a new spin on an old situation. With Luca's apology, the tension between us seemed to drift away like dandelion dust. And there was something in his eyes—admiration, maybe? If I was gonna be foolish enough to take a trip down Fantasy Lane, I'd even say it might could've been love. But nothing had really changed, and wishing for it didn't make it true.

My nana used to say, "If wishes were horses, then beggars would ride." Didn't understand at all what that meant until my eyes caught ahold of Luca's Saturday night. Had to keep reminding myself all day Sunday that daydreaming was for girls, not full-grown women.

Monday came soon enough, and the dread of what Luca had to face was an ugly reminder that dreams often turned into nightmares right quick. Hadn't that been the case for Billy and me? There was no such thing as happily-ever-after, and believing different was a set-up for a whole lot of disappointment.

While Luca prepared himself for his meeting with Bridget, I took the boys out back to tend to our garden. The zucchini blooms were just beginning to sprout miniature squash, and we had honest-to-goodness tomatoes growing in. They were puny and green, but they held promise.

"What if they don't turn red?" Chase touched one of the green orbs with a finger.

"They will," I assured him. "But if for some reason, we got us an entire batch of deformed vines, we'll just have to make do. Ever heard of fried green tomatoes?"

"What?" Matty wrinkled his nose and leaned his little body against mine as we squatted around the plants. "They gotta be red."

"Oh, they don't either." I ruffled his hair. "Fried green tomatoes are a South- ern delicacy. We'll just have to pick us a few early so I can show you." Two months ago, I wouldn't've had the confidence to make that promise. Been doing more than half the cooking and hadn't come close to a house fire since the first one.

Matty took ahold of my hand and his blue eyes met mine. "I love you, Miss Lillian."

Tears welled in my eyes and my throat went tight as I hugged him. "I love you too, Matty."

"Are you gonna be our mommy?" He pulled back and blinked.

Oh, Lord, how am I supposed to answer him? Swiping my eyes, I glanced at Daniel and Chase, whose gazes were every bit as intense as Matty's. "That's real sweet, and if I had my way, I'd love to be your mommy. But I'm afraid it's not so simple."

Daniel kicked at a dirt clod. "Told you, Matty." Had they been discussing this among themselves? "It's just a bunch of lies."

"What're you talkin' about?" My voice came a tad sharp as a thought took shape.

"So, you don't love Dad?" Chase's lip trembled.

"I care a whole lot about your Daddy." What else could I say? "But I just work for him. There's nothin' else between us." My gaze shot to Daniel. "Who's sayin' otherwise?"

He pinched a tomato leaf and shrugged. "Just some kid in Sunday school."

"What kid?" I could take a wild guess. "Bucky Chambers?" Elsie Chambers' grandson.

Daniel kept his head down and shrugged. "I guess," he mumbled.

It wasn't their fault people liked to talk. "Let's go sit down and have us a chat." I pointed to the patio then led the way. When we were seated at the table, I asked, "Y'all know what gossip is?"

"It's when a person lies." Daniel blew out a breath. "Like Bucky did."

"Not always." I patted his grubby hand where it rested on the table. "Sometimes it's sayin' what's true, but it's still gossip 'cause none of us should talk about another person behind their back. It's bein' ugly when we do that."

"You mean Bucky *didn't* lie?" Chase's eyes lit up with hope.

I sighed. What if I made a mess of this? "Bucky probably didn't know it was a lie, Chase. He was just repeating what he heard from someone else, but it's still gossip. There are some adults at church sayin' your daddy and I are a couple 'cause I live here with y'all. But we're not. They're spreading gossip, and when Bucky repeated it, he was spreading it, too. None of us should treat others that way."

Time to change the subject. "How 'bout y'all get your swim trunks on." Enticing them with the pool was a surefire way to take the focus off me. It'd rained cats and dogs yesterday, so for sure they'd be itching to go swimming by now.

They fussed some but trudged inside to get changed while I rummaged in the kitchen for snacks that might could cheer them up. Rocket stretched out beneath the kitchen table with a sigh, tuckered out from keeping track of us all when we were foraging in the garden.

Luca came in, raking a hand through his thick, dark hair. "I'm off to meet Josh. We're going to strategize before I face Bridget." A muscle jumped along his jawline as he reached into the fridge for a bottle of water. "Hopefully, all of this will be over by the end of the day." He had to be nervous as a cat in a roomful of rockers. There was no way of knowing how Bridget would react to him standing his ground.

My stomach did a flip. Maybe I shouldn't've advised him like I did, even though it was what he'd planned to do anyway. But if everything went south, would he hold it against me? Without giving it a second thought, I moved across the kitchen and slipped my arms around his waist. If one of the boys came in now, they'd think I was the one who'd lied. But he needed comforting, and I needed to give it. He hesitated a heartbeat, then wrapped me in his warmth. It'd been a long time since a man had hugged me, but now wasn't the time to relish in it.

I pulled away as my face heated. "I'll be prayin' for you, Luca."

He reached out and fingered a strand of hair that'd come loose from my clip while my heart pounded loud enough the angels in heaven could hear. "Appreciate that." He cupped my cheek so briefly I might've imagined it. "Hey, Lil?"

Hope had my heart racing. "Yeah?"

"Regardless of what happens, I need to tell the boys the truth about Bridget." He grimaced. "To a point. I've deflected their questions for too long now. I was hoping you'd help me with that tonight."

Disappointment had my smile wavering. "Of course." What had I expected? A vow of undying love right here in the kitchen? *Foolish girl.* Just because the boys wanted me as their mama didn't mean Luca did. Maybe the church ladies were only reading what was on my face when I looked at him. Humiliating.

After he slipped out the garage door, I put some juice boxes and peanut butter crackers on a tray and carried it out back. Took the few minutes of quiet to open my phone and check my emails. When I caught sight of MTSU's return address at the top of my inbox, I held my breath. Took my chest nearly exploding for me to let it out.

Guess if I got the job, Lord, I'll take it as a sign. Surely, Luca and I couldn't go on like we were without causing the boys to be hurt. If I stayed, the gossip would continue, and I'd be wishing it were true. Love was the last thing I'd wanted when moving in nearly two months ago. Now it was on my mind so much, it bordered some on idol worship.

Heart racing, I thumbed the email open and squinted to read the small print.

Dear Ms. Murphy, after interviewing a number of applicants for the Director of Library Technology, we would like to offer you the position. Please contact Deidre Reynolds no later than Wednesday of this week for an appointment to complete the employee packet and schedule your orientation. Fall semester begins on August 25th, and you are expected to be available for a start date of August 18th. We are excited to partner with you in this career endeavor.

I should've been ecstatic with joy. This was what I'd wanted since entering the master's program five years before, wasn't it? A position that would set me up for future advancement. It would give me some level of financial freedom and make it possible to pay off what debt I owed. Yep, I should feel downright joyful.

So, why did I wanna bawl like a baby?

Luca

Heard years ago that men's brains are like waffles while women's resembled spaghetti. It was an interesting enough idea that I felt the need to delve deeper. It turned out that particular analogy came from a marriage book a Christian couple wrote. Since Bridget and I had already been over the proverbial waterfall in our own marriage, I'd dismissed the concept. It wasn't useful in measuring productivity, and I had no desire to be shackled in the future.

But as I drove across town to Josh's office, bits and pieces of what I'd read came back to me. Men compartmentalized. It's what allowed us to set aside one matter (Lillian's possible abandonment and her unexpected hug) to tend to another—Bridget's attempt to extort money from me and using Matty as leverage. And while I wasn't eager to confront her, I was able to keep my focus where it needed to be.

Of course, it did beg the question—how did women function with emotional wires crisscrossing in their brains all the time? In their book, Bill and Pam Ferrell even claimed that men had an empty box they could slip into when needing to decompress. It allowed them the luxury to think of nothing. Women weren't blessed with the same ability. I pondered this while parking across from the courthouse. It gave me a whole new appreciation and respect for Lillian—for all women, really. They were challenged in ways most men could never comprehend.

Maybe Bridget's personality defects were a result of misfiring wires. Rather than seeing *her* as evil, I needed to have compassion for how lost and alone she was. Although pointing that out would most likely not go over well. But that wasn't necessary if it changed my approach.

Adele greeted me as I walked into Josh's office. "Mr. Cummings is waiting for you in his office." The woman was a robot. Efficient, pleasant, and as far as I could tell, unemotional. Just what I used to think would make the perfect nanny for the boys. Until Lillian.

"Thank you, Adele." I walked unattended down the hallway, rapped a knuckle on Josh's door, and entered.

"Right on time." He popped up from the chair behind his desk and came around to shake my hand. "You ready to take this on?"

"Been praying about it over the last few days, and I have a compromise in mind I'd like to discuss with you."

Frowning, he rubbed the side of his nose. "I'm not sure your ex-wife is the compromising sort. From what you've told me, it's all or nothing with her."

Hate the sin; love the sinner.

"True, but I still have to think of Matty's best interest." As he sat, I followed suit. "The only way I can assure his protection is to legally adopt him. If I can get Bridget to agree to that, it's a win."

"The process is a simple form with both your signatures. The harder part is getting her on board. How do you propose to do that?"

"Talk to her like I should've from the beginning. I don't know what motivates Bridget to act like she does, but there must be a kernel of love somewhere deep inside. Otherwise, she wouldn't have had the boys in the first place. She made it clear she wasn't happy about being pregnant, and yet she delivered three healthy babies." Especially Matty. A part of her might've wanted to rub my face in her affair, but she could've found other ways to accomplish that humiliation.

Josh was silent for a moment, possibly catching up to my way of thinking. "You're right," he finally said. "So, what are you thinkin'?"

By the time Bridget arrived for the meeting, we had a plan in place. She hadn't been thrilled when I agreed to meet only at Josh's office. It gave me a modicum of protection from false accusations if she chose to go that route. Needed everything to be professionally handled.

Adele poked her head into Josh's office. "Your ten o'clock is here. I showed her to the conference room."

Despite being prepared as possible, my gut clenched. Bridget was a wild card. I could plan every detail down to the nth degree, but there was no telling how she'd react.

"You ready?" Josh stood over me.

"Give me a minute. I don't want to go in there without praying."

He nodded. "Need to remember that for myself more often. You want me to pray with you or step outside?"

Where two or more are gathered... As awkward as it was for me to pray out loud, solidarity trumped discomfort. "Have a seat, and I'll get to it." I bowed my head and closed my eyes. "Lord, You know every crevice and corner of this situation, every heart and motivation involved. You know my prayer—to put an end to the deception and protect Matty at all costs. I haven't had a lot of sympathy for Bridget over the years, and that's where I failed both her and You. Rather than criticizing her in my heart, I should have been praying for her soul and salvation. I'm doing that now, Lord. Soften her heart to accept what's best for Matty. I know somewhere deep down she has a love for her boys. Let that be her motivation. In Jesus' name, I pray."

"Amen," Josh mumbled. He slapped his knee. "Good prayer. Now let's see what the Lord does with it."

Bridget, mask in place, sat at the far end of a table large enough to seat an entire jury. The minute she glanced at me, her eyes went hard, and she snapped a hand toward Josh. "I suppose this is your lawyer."

Josh reached across the table. "Josh Cummings, Bridget. Pleased to meet you."

She snorted but didn't reject the overture. "Sure you are. If you're here to put the fear of God in me, let me save you the trouble—it won't work."

His smile didn't slip. "That's not what I aim to do. Fact is, we're fixin' to see what we can work out here."

Nostrils flaring, she cut a look my way. "I gave you my conditions, Luca. Bringing in your fancy lawyer isn't going to change that. You have no legal right to Matthew, and if—"

"Well, Bridget," Josh cut in. "That's where you're wrong." He indicated that I should sit across from her while he took the seat at the head of the table and folded his hands. The epitome of calm. "You abandoned your children, and any court of law is gonna see that as a real problem. Luca here has provided for Matty, as well as Chase and Daniel, and you've never made an effort to see them. That right there is grounds for losing them."

My intention wasn't to bully her but help her see reason. It wouldn't mean squat coming from me, but Josh's matter-of-fact assessment of the situation might get through.

She dropped her gaze, but not before I saw the flick of her tongue. Dry lips were a sign of nervousness, weren't they? "I'm still the boys' mother," she mumbled. "That has to count for something."

It came in handy being able to compartmentalize. Shoved aside the ugliness I'd associated with her over the years and tried to see her with new eyes. Jesus's eyes. "Yes, Bridget, giving birth to those boys counts for a lot." Her widened eyes met mine. "But that's where your commitment to them ended, and I'd like to understand why."

Blinking, she looked away. "What difference does it make now? I've made my choices, and there's no going back."

"That's not true." Leaning toward her, I rested my elbows on the table. "Did you really come all this way with the express purpose of extorting money from me? You could've done that from a distance." Which had come to me while I'd prayed for guidance. The Holy Spirit showed me what I'd been too angry and jaded to see.

She swept a hand across her face, and it was as if doing so shifted the mask that kept her hidden from discerning eyes. "I wanted to see the boys." Her voice caught, and she swallowed. "I watched them for a couple days from a distance, and it became pretty clear they don't need me." She twisted her mouth. "They probably don't even know I exist."

Guilt pierced me. Hadn't I done everything in my power to eliminate all evidence of her? No pictures, no talking about her, nothing. I told myself it was for their protection, but was it really? Or was I subconsciously punishing her for not being what I'd expected? Telling them now was a case of too little too late.

Josh cleared his throat. "Seems you went to a whole lot of trouble just to get near them. Even changed your appearance."

She twisted her mouth. "All it got me was an earful of how perfect your Lillian is." She shot a glance at me. "The way they went on about her made me angry. Those are *my* boys." She slapped a hand to her chest. "I carried them and gave birth to them, not her." Her eyes went suspiciously bright. "I know I failed you as a wife, Luca. And I know I made a colossal mistake leaving those boys like I did." Was she sincere, or was this another one of her master manipulations? The Bridget I knew could cry on command.

"So, why did you? You might've been unhappy married to me, but you didn't have to walk away from them."

She fingered the tears from beneath her eyes, leaving a smear of black mascara. "I was messed up. I didn't know how much until I got some help last year. All the time we were married, I felt like a caged animal. I thought running away would help, but it didn't."

The tension eased from my shoulders, and I could breathe freely for the first time since Lillian told me about Bridget being at the house. The question now was where we'd go from here. It would take a lot of work on her part before I'd be able to trust her with the boys.

Lillian

The whole time Luca was gone, my stomach felt like a bag of kittens being carried to the river. Kept trying to picture how things were going with Bridget. Would this drama get drawn out for a month of Sundays? Would Matty eventually be carted away by his vindictive mama? Or would the good Lord provide a miracle and make it all disappear?

It wasn't only Luca's predicament that had me feeling sick. No matter what news he carried home, it didn't change what I'd need to tell him—that I was taking the library position and fixin' to move out as soon as I found me an available apartment.

I didn't rightly know if getting the job was a sign from God, but it just made a whole lot of sense anyway I looked at it. Luca could find himself someone else to help out, but I didn't need to get my heart broken all over again. Was hoping I'd gotten some wiser since the last time.

To keep from getting caught up in a runaway train of thoughts, I decided to fix a special supper. If the boys had their way, they'd eat hotdogs every night with pizza as a backup. But I wanted this meal to be something Luca might could never forget. Meghan had given me a recipe she said was easy as pie. Course with my limited culinary experience, the only pie I figured was easy to make was of the Mrs. Smith's variety—premade and frozen.

A quick trip to the store and back with three disgruntled boys was distraction enough. Dragging them from the swimming pool was on par with assigning them manual labor. I could hardly ask someone to come stay with them. Who ever heard of a nanny needing a sitter for her charges? Bribed them with a box of Popsicles, which I had to keep reminding them as we trolled the aisles for ingredients.

"What's that?" Matty pointed at the bunch of kale I was inspecting, his nose wrinkled like he'd just gotten a whiff of Rocket's pungent lawn deposit.

"It's good for you, that's what it is." Shook out a plastic bag and slipped the kale inside. "You never had kale before?"

He twisted up his face, made a gagging noise, and shook his head. Wasn't the least little bit surprised. He'd acted like green beans were poison, and broccoli, its first cousin.

"Well, I think you'll like this just fine." I collected Chase and Daniel, who were checking out all the odd-shaped produce and headed for the check-out line. So busy keeping the boys from touching things they shouldn't, I didn't realize it was Elsie Chambers standing in front of us until I caught her disapproving sniff.

"Good afternoon, Miss Elsie." Butter wouldn't melt in my mouth. "How are you doin'?" What I wanted to ask was why she couldn't tend to her own business instead of spreading lies about mine. But it wouldn't do me a lick of good, and it'd set a poor example for the boys.

"Lillian." Her gaze perused the boys. "Seems you have your hands full with this crew."

"Yes, ma'am." I removed a packet of bubblegum from Chase's grasp. "You got yourselves some popsicles, kiddo. Don't need the extra sugar." When I turned back to Elsie, she'd already moved on, which suited me just fine. A body could preach loud enough to reach the stars, and more often than not, those who needed to hear it turned a deaf ear.

When we pulled into the driveway, the garage door was open, and Luca's car was parked inside. My belly did a little flip, and my heartbeat kicked up a couple notches. "Your daddy's home, boys. We need to have us a talk, so why don't you help me get the groceries inside and take your popsicles out back?"

We carted everything through the garage and into the kitchen, but Luca wasn't there. Must've gone up to his office or maybe napping off a bad headache. I surely had one after my little set-to with Billy the other day.

Then I caught movement through the back door right before Luca came in, Rocket at his heels. He looked a sight calmer than when he'd left earlier, which must've meant things had gotten themselves resolved.

"Where've you been?" He raised a glass of sweet tea to his forehead and blew out a breath. Sweat glistened on his face and neck.

Held up a grocery sack. "Kroger's. Thought I'd make us a gourmet meal for supper tonight."

"Can we have our popsicles now?" Daniel tore open the box and handed them out before I could answer.

"As long as you take 'em outside," I said. Even if talking with Luca put me on edge, it had to get done.

As the boys headed out, hand-slapping their daddy on the way, I gathered the empty bags and tucked them all into one. "I'm almost afraid to ask how it went with Bridget. You don't look any worse for wear."

A smile tugged at his mouth. "I survived." He pulled a stool from the island and sat. "It helped that I didn't rush in ready to battle. Praying helped put things into some perspective." He grimaced. "Maybe if I'd done that years ago, things might've been different."

It was on the tip of my tongue to ask how so, but I swallowed the question. Did I really wanna know?

"Turns out she didn't come here with the express purpose of hurting us. In fact, she just wanted to see the boys. Then when she saw you and heard Matty raving about you, everything shifted. She felt slighted and angry—"

"Because of me?" I pressed a hand to my heart. "I was just doin' my job." How dare she shift the blame onto me? "She's the one who walked away from her babies." Heat filled my face and adrenaline pumped through my veins. Why did I feel threatened by what Luca said? I was fixin' to leave anyway, wasn't I?

Luca's eyes widened, and he came around the island to take hold of my shoulders. "Hey, I didn't mean to upset you. I'm not validating her excuses—not even sure I believe them. I'm just reporting what was discussed."

Stepping out of his grasp, I swiped a hand through my hair while tears burned at the back of my eyes. When he touched me, it made me all kinds of confused.

"No. I'm sorry. Don't know why I got all worked up." But I did. I was losing the lot of them, and Bridget had every right to slip back into their lives. "Guess I'm just surprised is all. Never heard you say a kind thing about her, and now with one conversation, everything's changed."

His gaze narrowed some, and he stared at me like I'd grown horns. It was no wonder. My emotions were bouncing around like a ping pong ball gone wild. "You're right, Lillian. I've been angry and bitter for years, and I suppose it's clouded my viewpoint. But really, nothing's changed, except she wants a chance to see them. And they deserve to know their mom, don't you think?"

I had to work around the fist in my throat. "Of course. It's just—"

"Who're you talking about?" Both Luca and I spun around to find Daniel standing at the entrance to the family room, straight as a pin, face red, fists clenched. "Is our mom alive?"

Luca blew out a breath. "Yes, son, she is. And she'd like to see you and your brothers."

"Well, we don't wanna see her. She left us, and I don't care if she never comes back!"

Luca glanced at me before moving around the island toward Daniel. "Let's all sit down and talk about it, son. It's complicated."

Backing away, he shook his head, tears pooling in his eyes. Mine filled as well. He was too young to get his little heart broken. "I thought maybe she was dead. You didn't say she was alive."

Luca crouched down in front of Daniel and put an arm around him. "Until she showed up here, I didn't know what happened to her." He twisted around to look at me. "Will you get Chase and Matty? Think it's time we had that talk."

Swiping the tears from my cheeks, I slipped out back where the boys were rolling around on the lawn with Rocket. They were so innocent and happy. But surely, they would've wondered what happened to their mama. Matty said just this morning that all his friends had one, as if he was talking about a shiny, new bicycle rather than one of the most important relationships he'd ever have. Made me wanna call my own mama and tell her how much I appreciated her.

"Come on in, boys," I called. "Your daddy has something he needs to talk to you about."

While they went into the family room, I slipped away. I didn't trust myself to remain unemotional, and they surely didn't need the hired help muddying the familial waters.

Chapter Twenty-Six

Lillian

It took a whole lot of praying for me to keep my emotions buttoned up when I was around Luca and the boys. Still hadn't talked to Luca about the job or how I was planning to move out soon as I could find me a place. Then Sherrie told me about a small house one of her clients had available for rent in Bell Buckle, and I knew it was time to fess up.

Sherrie and I were fixin' to go see the place Wednesday evening. Even though I wasn't expecting a house would work for me, I'd take any excuse to not be at Luca's. Bridget was coming by for the first time to see the boys, and I couldn't stomach being a part of their reunion. It just tore me up something awful to know I'd be out of their lives.

Soon as I got off work Wednesday, I rushed home and popped a casserole I'd made over the weekend into the oven. Didn't like to heat up the place when it was so hot outside, but I wasn't about to ask Luca to cook supper so I could go search out a new home—even if he was practically pushing me out the door to make room for his ex-wife. Or at least that's how it felt. In the rare moments I thought like a mature human being, I knew different.

Glancing out the back door, I saw Luca seated at the picnic table with his computer open, watching the boys as they splashed around in the pool. The minute I stepped outside, Rocket nudged my hand with his wet nose. I gave him a quick rub before making my way to Luca.

"Hey, boys," I called out with a wave before sitting across from Luca. My stomach was tied up in knots with what I had to say.

Luca glanced at his watch and blinked. "I had no idea it was so late." He started shuffling together the paperwork he had spread out on the table. "Bridget will be here in an hour, and the boys need to eat before she arrives. Guess I can grill hot dogs."

As he started to hop up, I waved him back down. "We need to talk."

He dropped onto the bench with a *thud*. "Those are never words a man likes to hear." The twinkle in his eyes and tug of his lips told me he was fooling. Little did he know.

Wringing my hands, I took a deep breath. "I've been meaning to tell you something since Monday but haven't had the chance." That wasn't the God's honest truth. If I'd wanted to tell him, I could've found a way.

A crease formed between his brows as his eyes narrowed. "Okay." He drew the word out real slow, like he was expecting bad news.

"I got that job I applied for at MTSU." His reaction wasn't near what Mama's was when I told her. Instead of whooping and gushing over me, he just stared, face hard as stone. Put me on the defensive right quick. "I think it's for the best, Luca. You got Bridget comin' back into the boys' lives, and me bein' here will just confuse them. Actually, it's already started—the confusion, I mean. They're hearing gossip at church about the two of us, and Matty just the other day asked if I would be their mama." That one had my throat going thick. "So, you can see why this is the right thing to do, can't you?"

A muscle jumped along his jaw like he was clenching his teeth. "Thought you couldn't afford to live on your own." That's all he had to say? There I was, once again, expecting poetry and flowers only to be disappointed.

"Couldn't afford it on what I was making at the library, that's for sure. But this job pays a whole lot better, and it's a big step up—career-wise." If he wanted to keep it all business, I could do the same.

"What about a first, last and security deposit?" He bulleted the words at me like they were weapons.

"Came into a little money last week, so that's not a problem at all." Wasn't about to tell him how I'd been left at the altar (with the wedding bill) last year, which was the reason right there I'd been in a pickle. Or how Billy and I had us a meet-up just last week so I could get some of that money back. A girl had her pride. Besides, my relationship with Billy wasn't his business anymore than his relationship with Bridget was mine.

"I put a casserole in the oven for supper," I said, easing from the bench. "It should be ready in less than a half hour." I turned to go back inside and just about ran into Matty who had somehow snuck up on me.

"Where're you goin', Miss Lillian?"

"I've got an appointment, kiddo." I planted a kiss on top of his wet head. "But I'll see you in the morning."

He grabbed ahold of my hand. "But if you're not home tonight, who's gonna read a book to us before bed?"

I glanced at Luca with raised brows. "I suppose your daddy's capable as I am." Or maybe Bridget would hang out long enough to play the doting mama to her boys. She had a lot of years to make up for. "It'll be fine, sweetie." I escaped before his Bambi-eyes could persuade me to stay.

Sherrie must've been keeping watch from the front window, because the moment I pulled onto their driveway, she came out the door. She should've been slap wore out from a long day at work, but instead, there was a bounce to her step that made me feel old as Methuselah.

"Good evening," she sing-songed as she slipped into the passenger seat then buckled herself in. "You excited about seein' this house?"

"Apparently not as much as you are?" I put the car in reverse and backed out of the driveway. "I thought you started work at six this morning."

"Actually, I went in at five. Had a ninth-hour court case thrown at me that I wasn't prepared for. Why?"

"Because you're practically glowing after a twelve-hour day, and—" A random thought hijacked my brain. Glowing? "Are you pregnant?"

Her eyes went wide, and laughter bubbled out of her. "How'd you know? I only found out myself this morning."

My best friend was gonna be a mama, so why did it feel like I was the one with raging hormones? "Oh, Sherrie. That's amazing news. Y'all didn't wait long, did you?"

"If I want three kids, we don't have a whole lot of time to waste." She grinned. "And I even figured out a way I can be home with the baby and still work. Don't know why I didn't think of it before. I mean everyone's doing it these days."

I laughed. "Baby brain's already kicked in, 'cause girl, your train of thought is all cattywampus. Everyone's doing *what* these days?"

She rolled her eyes. "Workin' from home. Convinced Josh I can still do a lot of my job remotely, and if that doesn't work, I'll do consulting instead. Just as long as I can be home."

Patting her on the leg, I sniffled. It seemed I had an endless supply of tears lately. Tears when I was sad, tears when I was happy.

"What's this?" Sherrie swiped at a tear on my cheek. "Don't think I've ever seen you cry before, Lillian. Not even when that no good, leather-for-brains Billy left you at the altar."

I scowled. "Just so you know, it's all your fault."

"Because I'm pregnant?" She flicked a strand of hair off her face.

"No, because you talked me into lookin' after Luca's boys. And now here I am, two months later, right back where I started."

She rubbed my shoulder. "That's not at all true. You've got yourself a great job and you stood up to Billy. I'd say that's real progress."

"All of which I could've done without getting my heart broken to boot." I shot her a quick glance as I pulled up to a stop sign. "It's not a fair trade-off at all."

"It doesn't have to be a trade-off, Lil. All you gotta do is tell Luca how you feel. Just because his ex-wife is visiting the boys for the first time in years, doesn't mean anything's changed. You can't think he's gonna take up with her again."

"Stranger things have happened. Bridget's beautiful and very smart."

"And you're not?" She nudged my arm. "You don't give yourself enough credit. Listened to your mama for too long."

"She's a different smart," I countered. "Luca says she's a manipulator. If she wants him back, she'll figure out a way to make it happen."

Sherrie made a rude noise. "And here you are, leaving the door wide open for her to just walk through. Maybe you're not so smart after all. We both know you got feelings for Luca and those sweet boys of his, so why aren't you doin' something about it?"

I could just see me pouring out my undying love and Luca staring at me like I'd grown two heads. The humiliation would slay me something fierce. "Because I have enough pride that I'm not gonna put myself on the chopping block again." Besides which, if God in His infinite wisdom decided Luca and me were supposed to be together, He'd make it happen. Whenever I took things into my own hands, it made matters worse.

Even though I struggled with the notion of leaving Luca's place, there was an itty-bitty part of me that softened when we pulled up in front of the Bell Buckle house. It was a cute little cottage—no bigger than the apartment I'd shared with Sherrie. An old cottonwood stood majestically in the front yard, filled with all sorts of birds singing their hearts out.

Could have me a houseful of cats—no, a dog. Maybe two so they could keep each other company while I was working. There was even a fenced backyard. If I couldn't have Luca and the boys, I could still be surrounded by love. The unconditional variety that didn't disappoint in the end.

Luca

If I lived to be a hundred, I'd never understand women. Spaghetti brain was just too complex for a simpleton like me to figure out. Between Lillian and Bridget, it felt as if I was walking a tight rope while juggling knives. One wrong move, one misstep, and the damage would be irreversible.

The move to Tennessee had been motivated by one thing—what was best for the boys. Somewhere along the way, the lines got blurred. My feelings for Lillian shifted from employer and friend to—I don't know what. No doubt Lillian loved the boys, but that obviously wasn't enough to keep her here. And now that Bridget was in the picture, it got even messier.

While the boys sat at the kitchen table eating Lillian's chicken-and-something casserole and fruit salad, I wandered through the house. It was still somewhat bare, even though the shelves now had a couple collections of books and family photos—none that included Bridget. No doubt she'd notice, and it would set her off. But there was nothing I could do about it. Couldn't conjure up pictures I didn't have, and it was no one's fault but hers that she wasn't around for the key events in the boys' lives.

Found myself at the end of the hallway staring at Lillian's bedroom door. I hadn't been in there since she got settled. Didn't even know if the furniture I'd bought for her was a good fit. I turned the knob, ignoring the pang of guilt that pressed its way in. I didn't have any more right to enter her bedroom than she did snooping through my office files. Could try and justify it since this was my house, but I knew better even as I entered her domain.

The bed was neatly made, colorful pillows spread across a white comforter. Never did understand a woman's need to clutter things up with pillows. They served no purpose, really. Although, it did give the room a lift. The nightstand beside the bed held a small lamp, two paperback books, and a tube of hand lotion. Was that what I smelled, or was it the scent of her shampoo lingering in the room?

Against the far wall were the two bookcases I'd ordered—crammed with books. The peach on white chair and side table were positioned to the right.

There was no artwork on the walls or photos on any surface, and it should've felt sterile as the rest of the house. But it didn't. It was as if Lillian's presence went beyond the physical. She was here, even though she wasn't.

Curious about what she read, I crossed toward the bookcases and was caught up short when I spotted a small drafting table tucked into the corner. There were pads of art paper and charcoals spread out. Reminded me of that day she sat on the patio drawing the boys and asking me about my non-existent hobbies. How dull and stuffy I must seem to her with my charts and calendars.

A clamp-on lamp hovered above the table, and I turned it on, spotlighting the sketches. She'd captured the essence of the boys and Rocket so perfectly, the drawings came to life. She was an artist. I noticed a thick folder set to the side, and I flipped it open. These charcoal drawings had added color to them with accompanying words on the opposite page. *It's a book. A children's book.*

When I turned the page, my breath caught. It was me with all three boys and Rocket splayed across the couch while I read to them. The dog's goofy grin, tongue hanging out, the concentration lines between Daniel's brows, the curiosity in Chase's eyes, and Matty's sweet innocence. It was humbling.

"Dad!" Chase's voice ricocheted down the hall over Rocket's sudden barking. "Someone's at the door."

Bridget.

Took care to put things back the way I'd found them. If she knew I was here, she'd have every right to lay into me. Closed the door behind me and took a deep breath. No telling how this would go. Daniel made it clear he was seeing Bridget under duress. Chase and Matty didn't understand why they needed a mom when they had Lillian. Yeah, this could be a colossal mess.

Rocket had Bridget backed up against the door, his teeth bared, while the boys stood around like stumps.

"Rocket!" I grabbed hold of his collar and pulled him away. "What's the matter with you boys letting Rocket get away with that?"

"He's just protecting us," Daniel said.

Scowling at him, I pointed at Rocket. "Take him out back, and while you're at it, find your manners." Bridget was going to think I raised a trio of delinquents.

She moved away from the door, patting her hair into place. "You better hope that beast doesn't bite anyone."

"Rocket's never hurt anyone in his life." Chase glared at Bridget, his little fists clenched.

"Settle down, Chase." I put a hand on both boys' backs and steered them into the family room. "Why don't we all sit down and get acquainted. Can I get you something to drink, Bridget? Sweet tea, water?"

She perched on the edge of a recliner while the boys sat at the far end of the sectional. "A glass of wine, if you have it."

"Afraid not."

"Lillian gots Kool-Aid in the fridgerator," Matty said. "It's cherry."

She shuddered. "Water's fine."

I hesitated to leave her alone with the boys. No telling what they'd say. Then Daniel came back in, and I gave him the chore while I took the other recliner.

Cleared my throat. "Boys, this is your...Miss Bridget." Almost introduced her as Mom, but that was too confusing even for me.

Bridget smoothed the wrinkles from her shirt. "We already met, sort of. Do you remember when I tagged along to the library with Meghan and her daughters?"

Daniel crossed the family room and handed Bridget a half-filled glass. Hope he got a clean one. "You said your name was Jamie." An accusation hardened his tone. I could step in, but she was going to have to be accountable for her own actions.

Her stiff smile wavered. "Yes."

Chase shook his head. "No. Miss Meghan's friend had black hair, and it was short."

"I was wearing a wig, Chase. You've heard of wigs before, haven't you?"

He wrinkled his nose. "Why?"

She squirmed but didn't answer. How did she expect the boys to respond when they found out she'd purposely tricked them?

"So, you lied to us." Daniel, eyes narrowed, folded his arms and sat next to Chase. "Dad says we're never supposed to lie."

She took a quick sip and set the glass on the coffee table with a grimace. Either the water was lukewarm from the tap, or she was reacting to Daniel's reprimand.

"You're s'posed to use a coaster," Matty said. "Miss Lillian says we're only allowed to bring drinks in here if we use a coaster."

Her mouth tightened. Bet that reminder didn't go over well.

Time to step in. "Why don't you get her one, Matty, since she doesn't know where they are?"

He lifted his shoulders to his ears and sighed. "Okay." When he handed her the coaster, he said, "Daddy says you might got polar bear order. That's why you didn't come see us."

A crease formed between her eyebrows as she looked at me for a translation.

I hid the sudden grin behind my hand until I could get control of it. "That's bi-polar disorder, Matty. Doesn't have anything to do with bears."

She scowled. "And I don't have bipolar disorder, either. I just…" She sighed. "You boys are too young to understand. Can't we just start fresh?"

This whole meeting was a bad idea. There was too much pressure on her and the boys to sit face-to-face and hash things out this way.

"I have an idea," I said. "Why don't you boys change into your swim trunks, and we'll go out back?"

They didn't need to be asked twice.

As they clambered up the stairs, I gave Bridget an apologetic smile. "It'll get easier."

She shook her head. "I don't think so. They hate me."

I barked out a laugh. "What'd you expect, Bridget? That they would fall all over themselves because you deigned to drop back into their lives? Chase and Matty have no memory of you, so it means nothing to them. Daniel's hurt that you chose to stay away."

She folded her arms and shot me a glare. "And why'd you tell them I had bipolar disorder?"

"Isn't that what you told Josh and me the other day?"

"Yeah, so?" She uncurled her arms and shot a hand my way. "They don't need to know anything about where I've been or what I've been doing."

"Well, I'm afraid that's where you're wrong. You expect these boys to ever trust you, you need to tell them the truth. Not every dirty detail, but enough for them to understand you didn't just walk out and leave them because you didn't care."

"I don't know if I can do this." She jumped up.

Before she could bolt, I took hold of her shoulders and looked her in the eyes. "You walk out of here, Bridget, and you will destroy those boys."

She shook her head. "They couldn't care less about me. They have their precious Lillian, don't they?"

Wasn't about to tell her Lillian wasn't a concern. Still hoped she'd be in their lives. "You're their mother." I shook her just enough to get her attention. "It's not going to be easy, but eventually, they'll get to know you—"

"And they'll hate me."

"Do you care at all about them?"

She nodded as tears spilled from her eyes. "But I don't know how to do this."

"One day at a time. It's what I've been doing since the day you walked out. I promise it'll get easier."

She sniffled. "Can't get much harder." Her tears failed to move me, but there was something in her eyes I'd never seen before. Fear.

"Truth is, it can and probably will." I sighed. "So, if you're going to cut and run, let me know now."

Chapter Twenty-Seven

Lillian

Luca and I agreed to wait until I got off work on Saturday afternoon to tell the boys about me leaving. I didn't know how things went with their mama, but since they hadn't said a thing about her, and Luca's response when I asked about it was dismissive, I had me a feeling it wasn't a joyful family reunion. Proved I was a sinner in need of Jesus that I felt a little smug over it. Should've been more concerned about what was best for them—not me. Except I knew in my heart that *I* was what was best for them, even if the Lord didn't seem to be leaning in that direction. Can anyone say prideful?

Was a wreck all day on Saturday just knowing what would face me when I got home afterwards. Shelved a whole cart of books in the wrong section before Carrie pointed it out. And when Kathleen wanted to go over the next week's activity calendar, I almost blurted that I'd be moving on at the end of summer just to get it over with. I had to tell her, but I needed a little more time to build up my courage. Leaving the library job was almost as hard as leaving Luca's.

I got off at two, and it didn't take but ten minutes to arrive at Luca's. Sat in the car a good long time with the air conditioning blowing on me. Wanted to pray, but I didn't have the least little idea what to pray for. No matter how

I tried, I couldn't see how the pieces could all fit—like being handed a jigsaw puzzle without a picture to give it context. Made the whole kerfuffle with Billy seem downright tame compared to what I was dealing with now.

Finally climbed out of the car to be hit with a wave of heat. Sweat was trickling down my temples and the small of my back by the time I reached the front porch. I'd never even taken the time to sit here with a glass of sweet tea and just watch the world go by. It'd be one of the first things I'd do at my new home. Stepping through the front door, I waited just a beat before Rocket made his usual appearance. All grins and wagging tail.

I dropped down onto my knees in front of him and rested my forehead on his warm, furry head. "You're a good boy, do you know that?" Tears clogged my throat. Goodness, if I couldn't keep it together with him, how would I ever tell the boys without bawling my eyes out?

"Miss Lillian!" Matty yelled from the top of the stairs before plunging down toward me. As I stood, he wriggled his way past Rocket to throw his arms around my waist.

Blinking to clear my tears, I hugged him tight and rubbed his back. "What have you and your brothers been doin' all day?" Would he hear the frog in my throat?

"We gone swimming, and Daddy says we can get a pizza tonight and watch a movie." Luca's plan to soothe broken hearts?

"Where's Daniel and Chase?" And Luca. Was he hiding up in his office fretting over what needed to be done as much as I was?

"They're outside. Daddy found a red tomato, but he says we can't pick it until you got home."

Taking his hand, I led him through the family room and out the patio doors. Sure enough, the boys and Luca were rooting around in the small garden. Looked like the vegetables would get taken care of whether I was here or not. Should be some consolation, but it was instead a reminder that their lives would go on just fine without me. If that wasn't the biggest slice of humble pie I'd ever had, I don't know what was.

"Hey, Miss Lillian's home!" Chase waved his gangly arms at me.

Forcing a bright smile, I waved back. I wanted to tuck away every enthusiastic display of affection these boys offered me. There'd come some dark moments when I might could pull them out like old photos and let the memories shine some much-needed light my way.

Luca rose from the vegetable bed, and with a hand on each of the boys' shoulders, led them around the pool enclosure. It wasn't until he drew close, I could see the tension along his jawline and in his dark eyes. Should've taken some comfort in knowing he wasn't any happier about this than I was.

I ruffled Chase and Daniel's heads. "Hey, boys. You havin' a good day?"

Chase nodded as Daniel pulled away. There was a scowl marring his features, and I had me a feeling he knew something was up. The boy was more sensitive than he let on. He'd make a fine husband and daddy when he grew up.

Luca caught my eye then cleared his throat. "Look boys, there's something Miss Lillian and I need to discuss with you."

"I knew it," Daniel mumbled, crossing his arms.

"What?" Chase's voice held a tinge of panic. "Is somethin' wrong? Are we in trouble?"

Matty tugged on my hand. "I didn't do nothing bad."

"Nobody did anything wrong." Luca steered everyone toward the patio. "And no one's in trouble. We just need to talk." He grimaced. Maybe remembering what he'd said when I told him we needed to talk earlier in the week—*Never words a man wants to hear.* The boys would learn that little fact right quick.

We sat around the table, my stomach knotting up like a mess of necklaces at the bottom of a jewelry box. Luca and I hadn't planned what to tell the boys or even how much. Just that I'd be leaving the following weekend. The Bell Buckle house was move-in ready, even if I wasn't. Didn't have a lick of furniture, other than my bedroom set, or even a pot to boil water in. Wouldn't've mattered a couple months back, but now I genuinely enjoyed cooking.

I tucked a stray strand of hair behind my ear and cleared my throat. "Y'all know how much I care about you, right?" My voice caught on the last word.

Don't you dare cry. "But I got me a new job at a big college in Murfreesboro, so I'm gonna have to move closer."

Daniel picked at a dirty fingernail. "You're just gonna leave us?" The accusation stung more than it should've. I wasn't their mama, but I sure felt like I was abandoning them every bit as much as Bridget had.

I reached across the table and touched his hand, but he pulled it away and lowered it to his lap. "It's not that simple, Daniel. If I could stay here, I would, but—"

"Why can't you?" Chase jutted out his chin.

I started to answer when the sight of tears trickling down Matty's cheeks squeezed my heart.

"Listen boys," Luca said, "Miss Lillian's new job won't allow her the time needed to help take care of you. She'll be working longer hours, and the drive from here to there is too far."

"We can move, can't we, Daddy?" Matty swiped the tears with the back of a grubby hand, leaving a streak of dirt across his cheek. "We don't gotta live here."

I swallowed the fist that sat at the base of my throat. "The thing is, Matty, I won't have enough time to help out your daddy, and that's why I moved here in the first place. It was my job to take care of y'all. If I can't do that, there's no reason for me to live with you."

"Yes, there is!" Matty's lower lip trembled. "'Cause we love you. You don't gotta take care of us. We'll be good. Promise."

My eyes filled, and my breath hitched. It didn't hurt this much being left at the altar. "You're always good, sweetheart." I placed my hand over his and squeezed. "Look at me, Matty." I waited until his water-logged eyes met mine. "You're such a good boy, and I love you, too. And I promise to help your daddy find someone else you'll love just as much."

He shook his head. "No! I don't want anyone else."

"Me, neither," Chase said.

Daniel glared at me. "It's because of what that jerk Bucky said, isn't it? That gossip thing."

Luca, elbow on the table, pinched the bridge of his nose. "I know this is hard, and there are things you boys are too young to understand. Miss Lillian doesn't have a choice. She needs to support herself. Do you know what that means?" He dropped his hand and glanced at each of the boys in turn.

"Make lots of money," Daniel mumbled.

I shook my head. As if it were that simple. "Not lots, Daniel. But I have to be able to take care of myself."

"Daddy can take care of you," Chase said. "Can't you, daddy? You gots lots of money."

Luca sighed. "It doesn't work that way, son. There is nothing we can do about this. You boys just need to accept it."

"No!" Matty yelled. "I hate you." He jumped from the table and tore into the house like the hounds of hell were after him.

Luca started to rise, but I stopped him. "Let me." My legs were pillars of cement as I pushed from the table and crossed the patio.

Rocket followed me through the house and up the stairs to Matty's bedroom, where he was shoving underwear into a small backpack, tears sliding down his cheeks. The dog jumped onto the bed and whined like he was hurting for his little master.

"What're you doing, sweetheart?"

He glared at me. "Runnin' away, that's what. If you can't be my mommy, I don't wanna live here anymore."

Heart heavy as lead, I sat on the edge of his bed. "You can't mean that. What about your daddy? If you leave him, it'll make him so sad." I thought about what he was willing to do to keep this child with him. It didn't matter they weren't connected by blood; Luca was his daddy.

"He gots Chase and Daniel. He don't need me." Matty went to his closet and came back with Oscar, his stuffed bear, and shoved him into the backpack.

"Oh, sweetheart, your daddy needs you as much as he needs air to breathe. You're his precious little boy. No one can take your place. If you leave him, you'll break his heart."

His hand stilled, and he glanced up at me then swiped at the tears. "I don't wanna break him."

"Of course, you don't." I fingered a sweaty strand of hair from his forehead. "And besides, if you run away, how will I come see you?"

His blue eyes widened. "You're gonna still see me?"

I opened my arms, and he didn't hesitate to fall into them. "Nothing's gonna keep me away." Closing my eyes, I rested my cheek on his head and breathed in his scent. It was sweeter and more precious than a bottle of Creed perfume. Classy women like Audrey Hepburn and Grace Kelly could keep their Jardin d'Amalfi—I'd take eau de sweaty boy any day.

Luca

Don't know what Lillian told Matty to soothe his pain, but when they came back out to the patio, he hugged my neck and told me he loved me. If the conversation we'd had before he took off hadn't tripped my emotional switch, that would have.

Hoped that a movie and pizza night would help soften the news of Lillian's impending departure, but it was a somber group that gathered around the television a few hours later. Even the antics of the St. Bernard, Beethoven, didn't crack their mood. So, when Josh called midway through the movie to ask if I could come over and sign a few forms before he could get Matty's adoption finalized, I was happy to comply. Lillian was still on the payroll, and it might be good if they had her to themselves for a bit.

"I won't be long," I told Lillian as I headed out the door. I hadn't bothered telling her where I was going, just that I needed to tie up some loose ends.

It was only seven, but clouds had obscured the sun, making it feel later. It smelled like rain, and a thunderstorm was predicted for later in the evening. It'd be good to get home before it started. Both Chase and Rocket would no doubt end up in my bed tonight, given their fear of loud noises.

I'd only been to Josh and Sherrie's house the one time, when I helped move the women out of their apartment. The brick and vinyl two-story house sat on four acres at the outskirts of town. Wasn't nearly as large as the monstrosity mine was, but they had plenty of room to grow a family, if that's what they wanted.

Josh met me at the door and ushered me through the modest family room toward the kitchen. Why was it most everything took place in the kitchen? The few times I'd bothered to have a get together in Wheaton, everyone conglomerated in this one room. Didn't matter that it was crowded and inconvenient.

"Have just a few forms for your signature, so I can have the judge make it official," Josh said, as if I hadn't gotten the gist over the phone.

"What about Bridget's signatures? You have anything scheduled for that?"

"Already done. She called on Thursday and said it needed to get handled sooner than later. Came in yesterday and finished up her part."

"Seriously?" I was nearly giddy with relief. Figured she'd want to hold it over my head as long as possible.

When we stepped into the kitchen, Sherrie was leaning against the sink eating ice cream from a pint-sized carton. "Hey, Luca."

"How're you doing, Sherrie?" Didn't really expect an answer—I was still disassembling Josh's news. Wasn't sure what it meant. When Bridget left the other night, things seemed unsettled. She couldn't give me a clear answer about when she'd see the boys again. I wasn't sure if she was going to jump into a relationship with them or run the other way. Only time would tell.

"Need your John Hancock on these." Josh spread three forms out on the kitchen table and handed me a pen.

Sherrie plopped down in a chair and slid the carton of ice cream aside. "Did Lillian tell you about the house we looked at Wednesday night?"

I squinted at the first page, noting where my name was typed, before signing it. "Uh, no. Not really. Just that she found a place."

"Here's the next one." Josh slid number two into view. "It's just at the bottom there." He tapped a finger on the signature line.

"Yeah," Sherrie went on as if we'd never interrupted her, "it's a cute place. Two bedrooms, fireplace, brand new appliances. Which I believe she'll get some use from, now that she's acquired a few recipes."

"And here's the last one." Josh waited until I signed it before gathering them together. "Should have this wrapped up right quick." He slapped me on the back. "Congratulations. Looks like it's official."

I grinned and shrugged. "Far as I'm concerned, it was official the minute I held that little boy in my arms. This is just a formality." I glanced at Sherrie. "We told the boys this afternoon that Lillian's going to be moving out soon." That put a damper on my excitement over Matty's adoption.

Sherrie raised her brows. "How'd that go over?"

The image of Matty taking off, tears streaming down his cheeks, had me frowning. "About like you'd expect. They're pretty broken up over it—especially Matty." But there was nothing I could do.

Sherrie pursed her lips. "It doesn't have to be this way."

Josh cleared his throat. "Can I get you anything, Luca? Sweet tea, a beer?"

Needed to get home, but Sherrie's comment had me curious. "Sweet tea would be great, Josh. Thanks." I plopped into the chair across from Sherrie. "What'd you mean about it not needing to be this way?"

She shrugged. "Seems to me things have been workin' out just fine at your place. The boys are happy, Lillian hasn't poisoned anyone with her cooking, and you appear none the worse." What was she getting at?

"You make it sound like it was my decision that Lillian leave. You forget she's the one who went out and got another job?"

"What choice did she have?" Her lips thinned. "Despite Brother Paul's sermon on gossip a couple weeks back, busybodies aren't getting the message. She doesn't want the boys to be hurt by people talking," she flung a hand toward me, "or you either, for that matter."

Josh slid an icy glass of tea across the table at me while rubbing Sherrie's upper back. "Now babe, we talked about this. It's between Luca and Lillian. We need to steer clear of it."

She tilted her head to glare at him. "No, babe, *we* didn't talk about this. You did. Lillian's closer to me than my own sister, and I'm not gonna sit by while she gets her heart broken because Luca here doesn't have the sense God gave a goose."

I barked out an incredulous laugh. "Hey, wait a minute. How'd I end up being the bad guy here?"

Sherrie threw her hands in the air and scooted her chair back, tears brimming her eyes. What did she have to cry about? "I was the one who talked Lillian into taking this position, thinking the two of you would be perfect for each other. I mean, she fell in love with those boys lickety split, didn't she?"

"Uh, yes, I suppose she did. But that doesn't have anything to do with me. I don't think she even liked me. Not at first, anyway."

Sherrie snorted. "Of course, she did. She was just protectin' her heart after Billy treated her so badly."

Felt like I was being attacked, and I didn't know why. "I'm not sure why you're so angry with me. I've been nothing but kind to Lillian. And I'll admit, I'm more than attracted to her. In fact, I thought maybe there could be something between us, but I'm not sensing that she feels the same way."

"Oh, my word." Sherrie scraped her hair back and shrieked. "Like I said, you don't have the sense God gave a goose. Y'all could use a mediator. She thinks you might could want to go back with your ex-wife, and—"

"Where in the world would she come up with that?" Of all the asinine ideas.

"Hey, children," Josh cut in, both hands raised in surrender. "I think it's time we take us a step back."

"And you can't see what's right in front of your eyes," Sherrie continued, as if Josh hadn't spoken. "Talk to her, Luca. If you have feelings for her, tell her. Otherwise, she's gonna take a job she doesn't even want to spare you and the boys when it seems to me she's exactly what y'all need."

Was Sherrie right? Had I been so completely obtuse that I missed it?

CHAPTER TWENTY-EIGHT

Luca

I drove around town for a while hoping to get my head clear. Needed to put everything into perspective without letting emotions overcome reason. But it didn't matter how I lined things up, the facts were the facts. I was in love with Lillian. Yes, it was a fickle emotion, and there were studies that showed people didn't fall in love in such a short amount of time—they fell in lust. What I felt for Lillian couldn't be narrowed down into such simple terms. Was I attracted? Absolutely.

But it wasn't just the physical. It was the connection over shared values (such as our love of the Lord) and our mutual affection for the boys. On one level, I knew her well, on another, not at all. Seeing the children's book in her room was proof of that. I could spend a lifetime unwrapping her every nuance. And it had nothing to do with lust. I hadn't even kissed Lillian, although I'd thought about it before—okay, to be completely transparent, I'd fantasized about it.

And if Sherrie was right, Lillian felt the same way about me. Stuffy, anal-retentive, type-A me.

When I finally pulled into the garage, it was after nine. So much for not being gone long. The boys would most certainly be in bed, but what about

Lillian? Would she still be up? Was I even ready to face her if she was? Our next conversation might decide our futures, and I could very well blow it. As Sherrie pointed out, I didn't have the sense God gave a goose. These Southerners did have a way with words.

The under-counter lights in the kitchen were on, bathing the room in a soft glow. Lillian had cleaned up the dishes and wiped down the counters. The only evidence that we'd had pizza for dinner...supper...was the faint aroma of tomato sauce, Italian spices, and grease.

Moving through the kitchen, I stopped in the dining nook and scowled at the over-sized calendar—an indicator of my need for control. Some of Lillian's charcoal drawings would be a lot more appealing. If I had her as my wife and partner, I wouldn't need to obsess over my schedule. It would be a shared endeavor.

Stepping into the family room, I stopped short. The floor lamp spotlighted Lillian sitting in the corner of the sectional, legs spread across two cushions. She had a hardcover book propped up on one of the decorative pillows that had found their way into our home. Until that moment, those pillows were nothing but a nuisance. But if Lillian left, they'd forever be a reminder of her too-short presence in our lives.

"Hey, Luca."

My gaze shifted to her as she was closing the book. "What're you reading?"

Her eyes darted away. "Nothing special." She tucked it between her and the couch back. Interesting.

Now I needed to know. "Come on, what is it?" I crossed the room and reached behind her to grab ahold of it. "A steamy romance?"

She snatched it from me before I could read the cover and held it to her chest. "I don't read romance novels. They're too predictable."

I started to sit, and she pulled her legs in to give me room. "Let me guess." I tapped my chin and searched my memory for classic female authors. "Something by Jane Austen?"

She shook her head, and a grin flirted at the corners of her mouth.

"Emily Brontë?"

A giggle erupted. "Not even close."

"I suppose Charlotte Brontë is out then, huh? What about Jane Eyre?" If not, I was out of guesses. I was more a Vince Flynn or Clive Cussler fan.

She blew out a sigh. "Richard White."

"Who?"

"Yes, who is the first word of the title." She flipped the cover so I could see it. "*Who Killed Jane Stanford?*"

Took the heavy book from her and squinted to catch the subtitle: *The Gilded Age Tale of Murder, Deceit, Spirits, and the Birth of a University.* "Who knew you had a dark side?"

A snort erupted from her. "Most everyone who grew up with me. Believe it or not, I tend to be a tad suspicious." She folded her arms. "Fact is, until I got to know you, I wondered if you might've done away with your ex-wife." She was kidding, right? The thrust of her chin told me no.

"Now I know why you didn't care for me."

She grinned. "Well, you'll be happy to know I got over it." I was caught up in the depth of her eyes, and her smile wavered. "What?" She swiped at her mouth. "Do I have pizza sauce on my face?"

I cleared my throat. "We need to talk."

Her eyes widened. "Uh, oh. We both know what that means." She shifted and swung her legs to the floor and set the book on the coffee table. "I know my leaving puts you in a bind, and I'm really sorry, Luca. When I told the boys I'd find a replacement, I meant it."

Blowing out a breath, I took the plunge. "What do you want, Lil?"

A crease formed between her brows. "I'm not sure what you mean. Are we talkin' right now or life in general?"

Reaching out, I took her hand in mine and watched as she sucked in a breath. Her skin was soft. Warm. I rubbed her knuckles with my thumb. "If you had a magic genie and could make any wish, what would it be?"

Eyes fixed on our hands, she seemed to be at a loss for words. After a few seconds, she looked up at me. "Anything?" The question came out in a squeak.

"Anything. Sky's the limit." I was taking a huge risk here. Should've kept it casual. Just two friends throwing out possibilities. But the moment I touched her, everything shifted.

She shrugged, slipped her hand from mine, and tucked it between her knees. Not a good sign. "Sounds like a loaded question to me." Her cheeks turned pink, and it seemed as if she'd lost the ability to look me in the eyes.

Couldn't ask her to put it all on the line if I wasn't willing to do so first. Never thought before that being in love required courage. "Okay, let me tell you what I want."

Blowing out a breath, she straightened her shoulders as if she'd received a reprieve. "Shoot."

This was it. The moment of truth. "I want you, Lil." When her head snapped back, I rushed ahead. "I know it's only been a couple of months, but I'm in love with you."

Her eyes went so wide, I could swear I saw all the way to her soul. "You are? I mean, you really want me?" She pressed a hand to her chest as if to calm her heart.

"I do. And it's not about the boys, either, although I can't imagine them having a better mom. But if you don't feel the same way—or don't think there's a possibility that you can in time, then just say so, and I'll never bring it up again."

The rest of my life hung in the balance awaiting Lillian's response. She had the power to make me or break me. Talk about letting go of control.

Lillian

When Luca had received the phone call in the middle of *Beethoven*, and said he needed to go out for a spell, it didn't take long for my imagination to run amok. I jumped to conclusions fast as ants scattering from their flooded hill. Only reason I could see to keep it a secret, was if it was Bridget calling. Once the pang of disappointment settled some, I decided there was no sense spending what time I had left under his roof longing for something that just wasn't gonna happen. Couldn't be miffed at Luca for not meeting my fantastical expectations. Especially since he didn't even know they existed.

So, when he came in an hour after I'd gotten the boys down, I played it cool as a cucumber. But the minute he took my hand in his, that ol' imagination took flight right quick. My heart fluttered, and it was near impossible to draw in a full breath. I couldn't give into that—not when I'd just an hour before declared myself immune to flights of fancy.

So, when Luca said flat out, "I want you, Lil," there was a full five seconds I'd thought maybe I'd fallen asleep on the couch and our whole conversation was a dream. Had to fight the urge to pinch myself just to be sure.

"Are you messin' with me?" The words came out more breath than substance, but I could tell he heard them, because his eyes went soft—like liquid caramel.

"I wouldn't do that." He reached up and touched my cheek whisper-soft like, and I thought I might pass out right there and then.

"When you left earlier—" Now why in the world would I remind him of his ex-wife at a time like this?

His eyes narrowed. "What were you going to say?"

"Just was wondering where you went off to is all." Curiosity and suspicion were kissing cousins—one might could kill the cat, but the other was a sure-fire way to kill a relationship.

He grinned. "Josh called me over to sign the documents to finalize Matty's adoption. He'll have a judge record it on Monday, and then it'll be official."

"Oh, my gosh." Tears sprang to my eyes, and I pressed a hand to my heart. Relief that Luca would no longer have to fear losing Matty replaced the guilt I'd felt over allowing Bridget into their home. "That's the best news ever."

"I didn't say anything because I didn't want Matty to hear. Still haven't figured out when I'm going to tell him. I think he's a little young right now. Wouldn't you agree?"

I nodded. "Things are a little unsettled at the moment, what with his mama just coming into the picture, and—" I was gonna say with me leaving, but now it was a toss-up over which of us was dealing with more questions—Matty or me.

"And?" Luca tugged lightly on my hand. "You were going to say with you moving out, right?"

I slid my hand from his again and rubbed my forehead. Felt like a tennis ball being lobbed back and forth from one emotion to the next.

"Lillian," he murmured. "You haven't said anything about my declaration of love." Looked as if he was trying to smile, make light of the whole thing, but it fell flat. "If you don't feel the same, it's okay. I'll get over it...in another ten years or so."

My lips twitched in response. "Until you said what you did, I thought you and Bridget might—" There I went again, bringing up his ex-wife. Was I *trying* to kill my chances with him?

He chuckled. "And until Sherrie lit into me tonight, I thought you might still have feelings for your ex-fiancé."

Guess it wasn't only the church ladies talking behind my back. "Sherrie has a big mouth." My face burned knowing Luca was privy to my humiliation.

"Maybe, but if it wasn't for her, I wouldn't be sitting here on pins and needles waiting for you to put me out of my misery." His face sobered. "Do you think you could return my feelings in time, or should I bow out?"

Was it possible that Luca could love me like he said? "That wish you asked me about earlier?"

He nodded.

"It's you I want, too. Have for a long time now." I'd've never had the courage to tell him if he hadn't confessed first. Still wasn't sure if I was dreaming. "Was just waiting on you to come to your senses and kiss me. See if we have ourselves some chemistry."

He smiled wide enough to reach from West to East Tennessee, making his eyes sparkle. He ran a thumb down my cheek and leaned in. My heart was racing like a runaway train as his lips touched mine. Gentle as a kitten at first, then with a moan, he deepened the kiss, and a zing of awareness shot through my limp body. I was either gonna swoon like some old Victorian lady or have myself a case of the vapors. Billy's best kiss didn't hold a candle to Luca's first.

After a couple more sweet kisses, he eased back. "Guess the chemistry's there." He tucked a strand of hair behind my ear. "So, the question is, what do we do about it?"

Wasn't sure I understood the question. "What choices do we have?" If he thought I was gonna give away the milk for free, he'd be sadly mistaken—and not the man I'd prayed for.

"Depends on you, but I say we should get married as soon as possible."

My mouth fell clear to the floor. He was proposing, literally, the opposite of what I'd expected. "We don't hardly know each other, Luca."

"We've lived together for more than two months. I know your sad past, and you know my sordid one. If you truly want that university job, we can sell this place and move closer to Murfreesboro. If you don't, we can stay put. I'll do whatever you want.

"And if you need more time before we get married, I'm not going to push it. But it wouldn't be appropriate for you to live here. People would talk more than they do now, and," he grimaced, "the temptation would just about kill me."

Billy and I had been engaged for almost two years before the almost-wedding fiasco. Long engagements were overrated, as far as I was concerned. "I don't want the university job. I like the library here just fine." In for a penny... "And I'd like to get married soon as we can arrange it."

Guess I wasn't gonna become a cat lady after all. Praise the Lord!

Chapter Twenty-Nine

Lillian

Circumstances being what they were, Luca and I decided it'd be best to have a justice of the peace marry us the next weekend and then have us a huge reception in a couple of months. It would give me time to plan my dream reception without the worry over whether the groom was gonna show up to the wedding.

Sunday morning, I was slipping a stack of chocolate chip pancakes into the oven to keep warm when Luca wandered in. His eyes were droopy enough I could see he didn't sleep any better than I had. Was he worried over telling the boys about us getting married?

"Mornin'." I closed the oven. Wasn't sure if it was the heat coming from it that had my cheeks going hot or the look Luca gave me. If he could do that with his eyes, I'd be liquid jelly when he touched me. Which is what kept me tossing and turning half the night.

"Morning."

"Thought I'd fix the boys' favorite breakfast to help celebrate." Or at least I prayed they'd see us getting married as something to celebrate.

"They'll be too excited to eat once we tell them." Luca moved up so close to me, there wasn't much space left over to breathe. His eyes held mine captive until our lips touched. Liquid jelly, just like I suspected.

"Hey!" Chase's shout had us jumping apart. "How come you guys are kissing?"

"Who's kissing?" Daniel's question floated into the kitchen seconds before he and Rocket appeared.

"We are." Luca put a little space between us but kept his hand on my waist. "You'll be happy to know Miss Lillian and I are going to be married."

Daniel spun around and shouted, "Hey Matty. Get in here."

It was only moments before all three boys were clamoring around us with a million questions—half of which I hadn't thought of before—as I got them seated at the table. But I should've been prepared for Matty's.

"Does that mean you're gonna be our mommy?"

I shot a glance at Luca for help. Even if Bridget only came around once in a while, it wasn't right for me to usurp her position. His shrug told me he wasn't any more prepared to answer Matty than I was.

I ruffled Matty's hair. "You got yourself a mama, sweetie. But you can call me Mom if you want. It could be short for My Other Mother."

Daniel snatched a couple pancakes from the platter in the middle of the table and slapped them onto his plate. "Can't we call you Mama and make Bridget be the mom?"

"Yeah," Chase chimed in.

The boys couldn't have tugged at my heartstrings anymore if they'd tried. It was near impossible to think that only a year ago, I thought my world had come crashing down around me with Billy's abandonment. Little did I know, God was working out a better plan, even when I'd been foolish enough to go my own way without so much as praying for His guidance.

The rest of the week went by in a blur of giddiness. Was expecting Mama, and even Daddy, to have something to say about me marrying a man I'd known such a short time. It turned out they'd only had two dates before Daddy proposed.

Way to bury the lead. Had no idea my parents were such romantics. Seemed to work out just fine for them, too.

Then when word spread that we were getting married, (again, thanks to Sherrie's big mouth) Brother Paul jumped in and offered to marry us the following Sunday right after church service. Next thing I knew, we had us a list of impromptu wedding guests. Mama and Daddy drove up from Florida, Luca's mama and daddy drove down from Wheaton, Sherrie and Josh, Meghan and her family, Carrie and Kathleen, and the church busybodies who needed to see for themselves that Luca was gonna make an honest woman out of me.

I expected our wedding night would be awkward, with a houseful of guests and three little boys to tend to. But Luca had other ideas. He made us reservations at the Belmont Inn, had Sherrie pack a bag for me, and left his mama and daddy in charge of the boys—all without me knowing until after we climbed into his car. Our parents, with the boys in tow, went in one direction, and we went in the other.

As we drove across Main Street, Luca reached across the console, took my hand in his, and raised it to his lips. "Well, Miss Lillian, it looks like the two of us are now official."

A zing of excitement shot through my body, turning me into a mass of nerves. "Luca, there's something I should tell you."

His gaze darted my way. Could almost read the questions in his mind. Was I fixing to tell him some deep, dark secret, maybe disappoint him the way Bridget had?

My heart thumped so hard, I was afraid I'd pass out right there. "It's kinda embarrassing. I've never...I mean, you'll be the first..." Heat moved up my neck and burned clear up to my hairline. Should've told him this *before* we got married.

Grinning, he let out a breath, and his shoulders sagged. "It's not embarrassing, babe. It's an honor." He kissed my knuckles. "And just so you know, I'm not all that experienced myself. We'll have to teach each other."

Butterflies took flight in my belly.

"Oh, hey." He squeezed my fingers. "Forgot to mention that I have a wedding gift for you." He let go of my hand so he could steer while he rooted around for something in the storage compartment of his door. Then he handed me his wallet.

"Why are you givin' me this?" I waved it in the air, and the faint scent of leather tickled my nose.

He tilted his head. "There's a business card tucked in front of my driver's license."

I flipped open the wallet, slipped out the blue and orange card, and held it up. "I don't get it."

"He's a new client of mine. Handles the children's end of the publishing company." He shot me a grin. "I have a confession of my own to make."

Had me a suspicion I knew where he was going with this. "What?"

"That night you went to look at the house in Bell Buckle?"

I nodded for him to continue.

"I snuck into your room. Thought I'd already lost you and was feeling nostalgic. Saw your children's book sitting on the drafting desk."

I snorted. "You can't seriously think a publisher of this caliber would be interested in my little book."

He slid a glance my way. "I do, and he is. You have a meeting with him a week from tomorrow." Grimacing, he shrugged. "If you're interested, that is. Totally your call. I think you're extraordinarily talented, Lillian. No reason to hide what God's gifted you with, is there?"

Warmth at his praise spread through me, even if I thought it was a tad overrated. "Good to know, since I've been working on a present for you, too." Had almost completed the charcoal piece of the boys and Rocket.

In a spurt of pure spontaneity, I unhooked my seat belt, and twisted around until I could plant a warm kiss on Luca's smooth cheek. "I love you, Luca. Can't wait to live this new life of adventure with you."

He swallowed, and I could swear there were tears hovering in his eyes. "I love you, too, Lil." His voice was husky, and he cleared his throat. "You've changed my world from black and white to full-blown color. Can't imagine living this life now without you in it."

Didn't care much for romance novels because they were just too predictable. Then again, I'd always dreamt of a happily-ever-after. This might not be it, but it was darn near close enough.

Acknowledgments

A huge shout out to Annie Hinojos for inspiring me to write *Mayhem and Moonlight*. Thank you for sharing your unconventional love story with Peter and his three young boys. Lillian can't hold a candle to you, my friend!

And though Demir and Carey Bentley don't know it, their non-fiction book *Winning the Week: How to Plan a Successful Week, Every Week,* not only inspired my career choice for Luca Giordano, but the techniques laid out in this book made me a more productive writer. Thank you.

Writing doesn't happen in a vacuum, and I am so blessed to have an amazing critique team. Thank you, Katie Shands for your editing skills and teaching me "Southern." I couldn't do it without you. And Wendy Cunningham, you have become quite the editor yourself, but you truly shine with your acting background and always knowing when my characters need a "beat." Both of you have helped me grow tremendously as a writer.

I'd also like to give a shout out to my dedicated Street Team. Y'all have been such a huge blessing to me. Thank you!

But most of all, I want to thank my Lord and Savior, who is faithful to keep bringing new stories to my heart. I am nothing without You.

Also by Jennifer Sienes

Apple Hill Series:

Surrendered

Saving Faith

Illusions

All That Glitters

Providence

Wish Upon a Star

Bedford County Series:

Night Songs

These Simple Gifts

A Sojourner's Solace

Shadow Dancing

Itty Bitty Faith

Tangles and Tinsel

Mayhem and Moonlight

A Canine Christmas

Norfolk Southern Series

Train-Wrecked Hearts

Did you enjoy *Mayhem and Moonlight*? If so, please leave a review on Amazon, BookBub, and/or Goodreads.

About the Author

J ennifer Sienes holds a bachelor's in psychology and a master's in education but discovered life-experience is the best teacher. She loves Jesus, romance and writing—and puts it all together in inspirational contemporary fiction. Her daughter's TBI and brother's suicide inspired two of her three novels. Although fiction writing is her real love, she's had several non-fiction pieces published in anthologies including four in *Chicken Soup for the Soul*. She has two grown children and one very spoiled Maltese. California born and raised, she now lives in Middle Tennessee with her real-life hero and husband.

Visit her at www.JenniferSienes.com